Florence & Giles

John Harding

W F HOWES LTD

This large print edition published in 2010 by
W F Howes Ltd
Unit 4, Rearsby Business Park, Gaddesby Lane,
Rearsby, Leicester LE7 4YH

1 3 5 7 9 10 8 6 4 2

First published in the United Kingdom in 2010
by Blue Door

A CIP catalogue record for this book is available
from the British Library

ISBN 978 1 40741 021 0

Typeset by Palimpsest Book Production Limited,
Falkirk, Stirlingshire
Printed and bound in Great Britain
by MPG Books Ltd, Bodmin, Cornwall

FSC

Mixed Sources
Product group from well-managed
forests, controlled sources and
recycled wood or fiber
SA-COC-1565
www.fsc.org
© 1996 Forest Stewardship Council

Florence & Giles

For Norah

The Swan

It was April, I remember, though my spirit
  was December,
When a broken bird was lifted from the
  darkness of the lake,
In the sun white feathers gleaming, from
  her mouth black water streaming,
While within my voice was screaming until
  I thought my heart would break;
It was I who watched her dying, drifting,
  drifting, waiting in her wake
For God her soul to take.

PART I

CHAPTER 1

It is a curious story I have to tell, one not easily absorbed and understood, so it is fortunate I have the words for the task. If I say so myself, who probably shouldn't, for a girl my age I am very well worded. Exceeding well worded, to speak plain. But because of the strict views of my uncle regarding the education of females, I have hidden my eloquence, under-a-bushelled it, and kept any but the simplest forms of expression bridewelled within my brain. Such concealment has become my habit and began on account of my fear, my very great fear, that were I to speak as I think, it would be obvious I had been at the books and the library would be banned. And, as I explained to poor Miss Whitaker (it was shortly before she tragicked upon the lake), that was a thing I did not think I could bear.

Blithe House is a great barn, a crusty stone mansion of many rooms, so immense it takes my little brother, Giles, who is as fast of limb as he is not of wit, three minutes and more to run through its length, a house uncomfortabled and shabbied by prudence, a neglect of a place, tightly pursed (my absent uncle having lost interest in it), leaked and rotted and mothed and rusted, coldly draughted, dim lit and crawled with dark corners, so that, even though I have lived here all of my life that I can remember, sometimes, especially on a winter's eve in the fadery of twilight, it shivers me quite.

Blithe is two-hearted, one warm, one cold; one bright, the other shadowy even on the sunniest of days. The kitchen, where the stove is always burny hot, is jollied by fat Meg, our cook, smiley and elbowed in flour, often to be found flirted by John, the manservant, who seeks a kiss but is happy to make do with a floury smack. Next door, with a roaring fire nine months of the year, is the house-keeper's sitting room, where you may find Mrs Grouse either armchaired and sewing or desked with a puzzlery of papers, trying, as she says, to 'make head nor tail' of things and – what seems to me contradictory – to make their ends meet. These two rooms together make one heart, the warm.

The cold heart (but not for me! Ah, not for me!) beats at the other end of the house. Unloved and unvisited, save by me, the library could not be more unlike the kitchen: unfired, cool even in the burnery of summer, freezing in winter, windows darked by never-opened thick drapes, so I have to steal candles to read there and afterward scrape their guilty drippery from the floor. From one end to the other is one hundred and four of my shoed feet, and

6

thirty-seven wide. Three men could stand one upon the other and scarce touch the ceiling. Every inch of wall, aside from the door, the draped windows and their window seats, is wooden shelving, from floor to ceiling, all fully booked.

No maid ever ventures here; the floors are left unbroomed, for unfootfalled as they are, what would be the point? The shelves go unfinger-printed, the wheeled ladders to the upper ones unmoved, the books upon them yearning for an opening, the whole place a dustery of disregard.

It has always been so (apart from the governessed times, of which more anon), leastways as far as I remember, for I first made my way here a third of my lifetime ago, when I was eight. We were then still ungovernessed, because Giles, who is some three years my junior, the one the teaching's for, was considered too young for school or indeed any kind of learning, and we were hide-and-seeking one day when I opened a strange door, one that hith-erto had always been locked – or so I had thought, probably on account of its stiffness, which my younger self could not manage – to refuge from him there, and discovered this great treasury of words. The game was straightway forgotten; I shelf-to-shelfed, extracting book after book, the opening of each a sneezery of dust. Of course I could not then read, yet that somehow wondered me even more, all these thousands – millions more like – of coded lines of undecipherable print. Many books were illustrated, woodcutted and colour-plated, a frustratory of captions beneath, every one of which taught me the miserable impotence of finger-tracery.

Later, after I had been scolded for going missing for so long that Mrs Grouse had everyone searching for me, not only all the maids but floury Meg and John too, I asked her if she would teach me to read. I instincted not to mention the library and it feared me quite when she gave me a quizzical look and said, 'Now missy, what in the world has made you think of that?'

It was one of those questions it's best not to answer, for if you keep quiet, grown-ups will always go on to something else; they lack the persistence of children. She deep-breathed in and long-sighed it out. 'The truth is, Miss Florence, that I'm not exactly sure your uncle would want that. He has made clear to me his views on the education of young women. I think he would say that this was not the time.'

'But please, Mrs Grouse, he wouldn't have to know. I wouldn't tell a soul and if he should visit unexpectedly I would hide my book behind my back and stuff it under the cushions of the chair. You could teach me in your sitting room; even the servants need not know.'

She laughed and then serioused again. She lined her brow. 'I'm sorry, Miss Florence, I wish I could, I really do, but it's more than my job's worth.' She got her mouth into a smile, something it was always ready to do. 'But I tell you what, there's a little housekeeping left this month, maybe enough for a new doll. Now, young lady, what say you to a new doll?'

I said yes to the doll; it was better to appear bought off, but her refusal to help me, far from discouraging me, opposed, and merely stubborned my resolve. Slowly, and with some difficulty, I taught myself to read. I lingered the kitchen and stole letters from John when he was reading the newspaper. I would point to an 's' or a 'b' and ask him to tell me its sound. One day in the library I fortuned upon a child's primer and from that and from here and there, I eventually broke the code.

So began the sneakery of my life. In those early days Giles and I were let wild; much of the day we could play as we liked. We had only two restrictions: one was to avoid the old well, although that was anyway covered up with planks and paving slabs too heavy for us to lift and so was just one of those things grown-ups like to worry themselves about and presented no danger to us at all; the other was to stay away from the lake, which was exceeding deep in parts, and perhaps might. How like grown-ups it is to see danger where there is none; to look for it in a lake or a well, which offer no harm in themselves without the agency of human malevolence or neglect. Yet these same cautious adults would be all unaware when the threat to us children actually came, for unlike us, for all their talk of the house being full of ghosts and ghouls, they had long ago ceased to hear unexplained footsteps in the dark.

Running apart, my brother Giles has not many talents, but one thing he is good at is keeping a secret. When I took him to the library, he little cared for the books, although he could be occupied by colour plates of birds or butterflies for an hour or two. He was happy enough scampering up and down the ladders and climbing the shelves or hiding behind the drapes, or else he would play outside; you could trust him, even at that early age, to avoid the lake, or Mrs Grouse's prying eyes.

I, meanwhile, spent hour after hour reading, and because my absences, although unremarked during the daytime, would be noticed in the evenings, my bedroom became a smugglery of books. After Giles reached the age of eight and was sent away to school, of course, my life turned into an unheedery of anyone else. I could come and go as I liked; this part of the house was largely unvisited, and I grew so bold I scarce worried about anyone seeing me enter or leave the library, or disturbing the dust that lived there. In this way I absorbed Gibbon's *Decline and Fall*, the novels of Sir Walter Scott, Jane Austen, Dickens, Trollope, George Eliot, the poetry of Longfellow, Whitman, Keats, Wordsworth and Coleridge, the stories of Edgar Allan Poe, they were all there. But one writer towered them all. Shakespeare, of course. I started with *Romeo and Juliet*, moved on to the histories, and soon made short work of the rest. I wept for King Lear, I feared Othello, and dreaded Macbeth; Hamlet

I simply adored. The sonnets weeped me. Above all, I fell in love with the iambic pentameter, a strange passion for an eleven-year-old girl.

The thing I liked most about Shakespeare was his free and easy way with words. It seemed that if there wasn't a word for what he wanted to say, he simply made one up. He barded the language. For making up words, he knocks any other writer dead. When I am grown and a writer myself, as I know I shall be, I intend to Shakespeare a few words of my own. I am already practising now.

It was always my greatest ambition to see Shakespeare on stage, but there is no theatre between here and New York City, hopelessing my wish. Last summer, not long before Giles was sent off to school, the people who have the estate next door, the Van Hoosiers, came calling; they had a son, Theodore, a couple of years older than me, an only child they wished to unbore. They lived in New York most of the year, travelling the hundred miles or so up here only in summer to escape the heat of the city, and the young man had no one to keep him amused and so he excited to find me. He sat and doe-eyed me all through tea.

Afterward Mrs Grouse suggested I show Theodore the lake. Now it misfortuned that Giles was ill in bed that day, confined by a severe headache. My brother is as sickly as I am well; he has illness enough for us both, while I have no time to be indisposed, having all the looking after and worrying to do. Giles's absence now, when

11

young Van Hoosier and I outdoorsed, gave my visitor free rein with me. He nuisanced me, obsessed as he was by my allowing him to give me a kiss. I had no fixed objection to this, being, as I was, not much younger than Juliet when she got herself romanced, but young Van Hoosier was no Romeo. He had a large head and eyes like balls that stood out from their sockets. He looked like a giant bug. Now, I am tall for my age, but Theodore was even taller, without half as much flesh; he beanpoled above me, which did not endear him to me, for I have never been one who could stand to be looked down upon.

We were side-by-siding on a stone bench beside the lake and I shifted myself to other-end from him, for I found his attentions annoying and was about ready to get up and leave, but then he let slip, no doubt at some mention of mine of Shakespeare, that he had seen *Hamlet*. I alerted and sat up straight and looked at him anew. Perhaps, after all, this boy might not be so unbooked as he succeeded so well in appearing; there were possibilities here, I sensed. I offered him a deal. I would allow him the kiss he so craved, if he would write a love poem for me.

Well, he pulled out a notebook and pencil and got right down to it there and then, and in no time at all was ripping out the page he'd written on and handing it to me, which impressed me quite, though I dare say you can guess what befell. Foolish girl, I wanted him to summer's day me,

I really thought he might. Instead, of course, he doggerelled me and, after he'd forced the kiss he claimed was his due, left me crying by the lake, not only roughly kissed but badly Longfellowed too. Here is how the Van Hoosier ode finished, so you'll understand for yourself:

> What fellow who has any sense
> Would not want to kiss Florence?

CHAPTER 2

Giles was sent away to school last fall when he was eight, which, although young, was in keeping with other boys of his class who lived in remote places such as Blithe, where there was no suitable local school. We horse-and-trapped him to the station, John and Mrs Grouse and I, to put him on the train to New York, where he was to be met by teachers from the school. We cried him there; at least Mrs Grouse and I did, while John losing-battled with a quivering lower lip. Giles himself was happy and laughing. He could not remember ever having been on a train and, in his simple, childlike way, futured no further than that. Once on board, he sat in his seat, windowing us with smiles and waves, and I bit my lip and did my best to smile him back, but it was a hard act and I was glad when at last the train began to move and he vanished in a cloud of steam.

I berefted my way home. All our lives, Giles and I had never been apart; it was as though I had lost a limb. How would he fare unprotected by me, who understood his shortcomings so well and loved him for them? Although I had no experience of boys apart from Giles and the silly Van Hoosier boy, I knew from my reading how they cruelled one another, especially at boarding schools. The idea of my little Giles being Flashmanned weeped me all over again when I had just gotten myself back under control. When we neared Blithe House and the trap turned off the road into the long drive, avenued by its mighty oaks rooked with nests, it heavied my heart; I did not know how my new, amputated life was to be borne.

Most girls my age and situation in life would long have been governessed, but I understood this was not for me. By careful quizzery of Mrs Grouse, and a hint or two dropped by John, and general eavesdroppery of servantile gossip, I piecemealed the reason why. My uncle, who had been handsome as a young man, as you could see in the picture in oils of him that hung at the turn of the main staircase, had at one time been married, or if not actually wed, then engaged to, or at least deeply in love with, a young woman, a state of affairs that lasted a number of years. The young lady was dazzlingly beautiful but not his equal in refinement and education, although at first that seemed not to matter. All futured well until she took it into her head (or rather had it put there by my uncle) that she beneathed him in intellectual and cultural things; their life together would be enriched, it was decided, if they could share not just love, but matters of the mind. The young lady duly enrolled in a number of courses at a college in New York City.

Well, you can guess what happened. She wasn't there long before she got herself booked, and musicked and poetried and theatred and philosophied and all ideaed up, and pretty soon she offrailed, and most probably started drinking and smoking and doing all sorts of other dark deeds, and the upshot of it was that she ended up considering she'd overtaken my uncle and intellectually down-nosing him, and of course then it was inevitable but that she someone-elsed. At least, I think that's what happened, although I misremember now how much of the above I eavesdropped and how much my mind just made up, as it is wont to do.

And so my uncle took against the education of women. He pretty much decultured himself too, far as I can tell. He shut up Blithe House and left the library to moulder and moved to New York, where I could not imagine he could have had so many books. I had no idea how he passed his time without books, for I had never met him, but I somehow pictured him big-armchaired, brandied and cigared, blank eyes staring out of his once handsome, but now tragically ruined, face into space and thinking about how education had done for his girl and blighted his life.

So I lonelied my way round the big house, opening doors and disturbing the dust in unslept bedrooms. Sometimes I would stretch myself out on a bed and imagine myself the person who had once slumbered there. Thus I peopled the house with their ghosts, phantomed a whole family, and, when I heard unidentified sounds in the attic above me, would not countenance the idea of mice, but saw a small girl, such as I must once have been, whom I imagined in a white frock with a pale face to match, balleting herself lightly across the bare boards.

The thought of this little girl, whom I began to believe might be real, for Blithe was a house abandoned by people and ripe for ghosts, would always eventually recall me to the games I had played with Giles. To unweep me, I would practical myself and search for new places to hide for when he should return at the end of the semester, and when that staled, which it did with increasing frequency, I libraried myself, buried me in that cold heart that more and more had become my real home.

One morning I settled myself down with – I remember it so well – *The Mysteries of Udolpho*, and after two or three hours, as I thought, I'd near ended it when I awared a sound outside the window, a man's voice calling. Now, this was an unusual occurrence at Blithe, any human voice outdoors, for there was only John who worked outside and he had not, as I have, the habit of talking with himself, and everywhere was especially quiet now with Giles gone and our sometimes noisy games interrupted, so that I ought to have been surprised and to have immediately investigated, but so

17

absorbed was I in my gothic tale, that the noise failed to curious me, but rather irritated me instead. Eventually the voice began to distant, until it died altogether or was blown away by the autumn wind that was gathering strength outside. I had relished a few more pages when I heard footsteps, more than one person's, growing louder, coming toward me, and more shouting, but this time inside, followed by a flurry of feet in the passage outside, and the voice of Mary, the maid, calling, 'Miss Florence! Miss Florence!' And then the door of the library was flung open followed by Mary again calling my name.

I froze. As luck would have it I was ensconced in a large wing-backed chair, its back to the door, invisibling me from any who stood there, providing, of course, they no-furthered into the room. My heart bounced in my chest. If I were discovered it would be my life's end. No more books.

Then Meg's voice, 'She's not here, you silly ninny. What would she be doing in here? The girl can't read. She's never been let to.'

I muttered a prayer that they wouldn't notice the many books whose spines I had fingerprinted, my footsteps on the dusty floor.

'Well, that's as maybe,' replied Mary, 'but she's got to be somewhere.'

The sound of the door closing.

The sound of Florence exhaling. I closed the book carefully and made sure to put it back in its place upon the shelf. I crept to the door, put my ear to it and listened. No sound. Quick and quiet as a mouse, I opened the door, outed, closed it behind me, and sped along the passage to put as much distance as possible between me and my sanctum before I was found. As I made my way to the kitchen I wondered what all the to-do was about. Obviously something had happened that required me at once.

I could hear voices in the drawing room as I tiptoed past and went into the kitchen, where I interrupted Meg and young Mary, who were having an animated chat. At the sound of the door they stopped talking and looked up at me in a mixture of surprise and relief.

'Oh, thank goodness, there you are, Miss Florence,' said Meg, deflouring her arm with a swishery of kitchen cloth. 'Have you any idea what the time is, young lady?' She nodded her head at the big clock that hangs on the wall opposite the stove and my eyes followed hers to gaze at its face. It claimed the hour as five after three.

'B-but that's impossible,' I muttered. 'The clock must be wrong. It cannot have gotten so late.'

'There's nothing wrong with the clock, missy,' snapped Meg. 'Begging your pardon, miss, it's you that's wrong. You're surely going to catch it from Mrs Grouse, you've had the whole household worried sick. Where on earth were you?'

Before I could answer I heard footsteps behind me and turned and face-to-faced with Mrs Grouse.

'M-Mrs Grouse, I – I'm sorry . . .' I stammered,

and then stopped. Her face, rosy-cheeked with its Mississippi delta of broken veins and their tributaries, was arranged in a big smile.

'Never mind that, now, my dear,' she said kindly. 'You have a visitor.'

She turned and went into the passage. I rooted to the spot. A visitor! Who could it possibly be? I didn't know anyone. Except, of course, my uncle! I had never met him and knew little about him except that, according to his portrait, he was very handsome, the which would be endorsed by Miss Whitaker when she arrived.

Mrs Grouse paused in the passageway and turned back to me. 'Well, come along, miss, you mustn't keep him waiting.'

Him! So it was my uncle! Now perhaps I could ask him all the things I wanted to ask. About my parents, of whom Mrs Grouse claimed to know nothing, for she and all the servants had come to Blithe only after they had died. About my education. Perhaps when he saw me in the flesh, a real, living young lady rather than a name in a letter, he would relent and allow me a governess, or at least books. Perhaps I could charm him and make him see I wasn't at all like her, the woman who had been cultured away.

Mrs Grouse stopped at the entrance to the drawing room and waved me ahead of her. I heard a cough from within. It made me want to cough myself. I entered nervously and stopped dead.

'Theo Van Hoosier! What are you doing here? Shouldn't you be at school?'

'Asthma,' he said, apologetically. Then triumphantly, 'I have asthma!'

'I – I don't understand.'

He walked over to me and smiled. 'I have asthma. I've been sent home from school. My mother has brought me up here to recuperate. She thinks I'll be better off here in the country, with the clean air.'

Mrs Grouse bustled into the room. 'Isn't that just grand, Miss Florence. I knew you'd be pleased.' She dropped a nod to Theo. 'Not that you have asthma, of course, Mr Van Hoosier, but that you'll be able to visit us. Miss Florence has been so miserable since Master Giles went off to school, moping around the house on her own. You'll be company for one another.'

'I can call on you every day,' said Theo. 'If you'll permit me, of course.'

'I – I'm not sure about that,' I mumbled. 'I may be . . . busy.'

'Busy, Miss Florence,' said Mrs Grouse. 'Why, whatever have you to be busy with? You don't even know how to sew.'

'So does that mean I may, then?' said Theo. He puppied me a smile. 'May I call on you, please?' He stood holding his hat in his hand, fiddling with the brim. I wanted to spit in his eye but that was out of the question.

I nodded. 'I guess, but only after luncheon.'

'That's dandy!' he said and immediately got himself into a coughing fit, which went on for some time until he pulled from his jacket pocket a little metal bottle with a rubber bulb attached, like a perfume spray. He pointed the top of the bottle at his face and squeezed the bulb, jetting a fine mist into his open mouth, which seemed to quieten the cough.

I curioused a glance at him and then at the bottle.

'Tulsi and ma huang,' he said. 'It's an invention of your Dr Bradley here.'

I puzzled him one.

'The former is extracted from the leaves of the Holy Basil plant, the latter a Chinese herb long used to treat asthma. It is Dr Bradley's great idea to put them together in liquid form and to spray them into the throat for quick absorption. He is experimenting with it and I am his first subject. It appears to work.'

There followed an awkward silence as Theo slowly absorbed that the subject had not the interest for me that it had for him. Then, in re-pocketing the bottle, he managed to drop his hat and as he and Mrs Grouse both went to pick it up they banged heads and that started him off coughing and wheezing all over again. Finally, when he had stopped coughing and had his hat to fiddle with once more, he gave me a weak smile and said, 'May I visit with you now, then? After all, it is after luncheon.'

'It may be after yours,' I said, 'but it ain't after mine. I haven't had my luncheon today.' And I turned and swept from the room with as much poise as I could muster, hoping that in getting rid of Theo, I hadn't jumped it back into Mrs Grouse's mind about me going missing earlier on.

CHAPTER 3

Suddenly my existence was uncosied. I was seriously problemed. First I had to make sure I didn't fail to show up for a meal again, lest next time they went looking for me they find me, with all the repercussions that would involve. But the question was easier posed than solved. I had no timepiece. Then over a late luncheon, when Mrs Grouse was so full of Theo Van Hoosier she didn't think to interrogate me as to my whereabouts earlier, I pictured me something about the library that might undifficulty me regarding my problem and, as soon as I'd finished eating, slipped off and made my way there.

Sure enough, tucked away in a dark corner, mute and unnoticed, was a grandfather clock. It was big, taller than I, though not nearly so tall as Theo Van Hoosier, the prospect of whose daily visits almost unthrilled me of the finding of the clock. Gingerly I opened the case, as I had seen John do with other clocks in the house, and felt about for the key. At first I thought I was to be unfortuned, but then as I empty-handed from the case there was a tinkle as my little finger touched something hanging from a tiny hook and there was the key. I inserted it in the hole in the face and began winding, being careful to stop when I met resistance, for John had warned me that overwinding had been the death of many a timepiece.

I had noted the time when leaving the kitchen and to be safe added fifteen minutes on to that to allow for my getting to the library and for the finding of the key. The clock had a satisfyingly loud tick and I thought how at last I would no longer feel alone here. There would be me, my books and something akin to another heartbeat, if only in its regularity. Something, moreover, that wasn't Theo Van Hoosier.

Of course, no sooner did the starting of the clock end one problem than it began another. For if anyone should venture into the library its ticking was so loud they could not fail to notice it and so be set to wondering who had started it and kept it wound and then on to working out who had been here. I shrugged the threat away. So be it. I had to know the time during my sojourns here or I would be discovered anyway. Besides, no one else had ever been in here in all my librarying years, so it unlikelied anyone would now. Too bad if they did; it was a risk I had to take.

That afternoon it colded and our first snow of the fall fell. I watched it gleefully, hoping it would mean that Theo Van Hoosier would not be able to visit. Surely if his asthma was enough to keep

25

him from school he should not be trudging through snow with it? I kept my fingers crossed and imagined him asthmaed up at home, consoling himself with a bad verse or two.

With this promise of salvation, though, the snow difficulted me in another way. Or rather the drop in temperature did. I had never wintered much in the library, because it had no fire and colded there, and because before I always had Giles to keep me amused elsewhere. Although I tried gamely, determined reader that I am, to carry on there, my fingers were so cold I could scarce hold my book or turn its pages, let alone keep my numbed mind on it. I slipped out of the room and by means of the back staircase made my way to the floor above. There I found a bedroom whose stripped bed was quilted only in dust, but footing it was an oak linen chest in which were three thick blankets. Of course, there was riskery in transporting these to the library, because if I encountered anyone en route I would be completely unexplained. And unlike a book, I could not simply slip a bulky blanket inside my dress.

Nevertheless, without the blankets I would not be able to read anyway, so it had to be done. I resolved to take all three at once since one would be just as hard to conceal as three and the fewer blanketed trips I made, the lower the risk. They were a heavy and awkward burden, the three together piled so high I could scarce see over them, but I outed the room and pulled the door shut after me with a skill of foot-flickery. I had halfwayed down the back stairs and was about to make the turn in them when I heard the unmistakable creak of a foot on the bottom step of the flight below. I near dropped my load. It was no good turning and running, one way or another I would be caught. There was nothing for it but to stand and await my fate. I held my breath, listening for another step below. It never came. Instead I heard Mary's voice, talking to herself (ah, I thought, so I am not the only one who does that!). 'Now where did I put the darned thing? I made sure it was in my pocket. Damnation, I shall have to go back for it.'

I heard a slight grateful groan as the stair released her foot and then angry footsteps hurrying along the corridor below. I waited a moment after their sound had faded away, then scurried down, tore along the passage and ducked through the library door.

There I pushed together two of the big leather wing-backed armchairs, toe to toe, and nested me in them with two of the blankets for a bed and the third stretched over the tops of the chair backs to make a canopy. I thought of it as my own four-poster, though of course it had nary a single one. When I left the room I pushed apart the chairs again, folded the blankets and hid them behind a chaise longue. It might offchance that someone entering the room would just not notice the clock, or attach the correct significance to it if they did,

27

clocks being an ever present in many rooms and an often unnoticed background kind of thing. But they could not fail to see my nest and so it had to be constructed every day anew.

Thus began a new pattern to my days. The mornings I tick-tocked away in my nest, contenting me over my books until the clock struck the quarter hour before one, when I denested, slipped from the room and hurried to lunch. But soon as Theo Van Hoosier began to call, the afternoons problemed me anew. I had no way of knowing what time he might arrive and despite my best efforts to schedule him he proved as unreliable as he was tall. Sometimes he appeared directly after lunch; others he turned up as late as half past four. He excused himself on the grounds that he had a tutor and was dependent upon the whimmery of same.

Now, suppose I went to the library and young Van Hoosier came while I was there, it would be as bad as the time I missed lunch. They would search for me and either my secret would be discovered or later they would question it out of me. On the other hand, if I hung around in the drawing room or the kitchen waiting for Theo and he arrived late, I could waste hours of precious reading time.

That is what I was forced to do, the first few Van Hoosier days. I sat in a twiddlery of thumbs looking out the window at the snow or playing solitaire. The worst thing was my idleness attentioned me to Mrs Grouse and set her to wondering why she had not noticed it before; she didn't guess how I had always out-of-sighted-out-of-minded me, and it started her talking about me doing something useful, such as learning to sew. She even sat me down one day and began to mystify me with stitchery. I thought I would lose my mind.

I have read somewhere that boredom mothers great ideas and so it was with me. Where I was going wrong was in my association of reading with the library, whereas in fact all I needed was somewhere I could private myself and from where I could keep an eye on the front drive to see the approach of Theo Van Hoosier. No sooner had I thought of this than I solutioned it. Blithe House had two towers, one at the end of either wing. They were mock gothic, all crenellations, like ancient fortresses, and neither was at all used any more. I suspect they were never made much of, since each had its own separate staircase, its upper floors reachable only from the ground, so that to go from the room on the second floor to one on the same floor in the neighbouring part of the house, you first had to descend the tower stairs to the first floor, go to one of the staircases leading to the rest of the house and then ascend again. But what the towers promised to offer was a commanding view of the drive. From the uppermost room, of either, I guessed, I would be able to see all its curvy length. The function of the towers had always been decorative rather than practical, and the one on the west wing had been out-of-bounded to Giles and me because it was in need of repair, which naturally, with my uncle's tight pursery, never came. Therefore I could be sure that no one would ever go there. If I could get to it unobserved, I would be able to read whilst looking up from time to time to observe the drive. Moreover, the west tower had another great convenience: it was only a short corridor and a staircase away from the library, a necessary proximity, because I would have to carry books up there.

Consequently, the following afternoon, armed with a couple of books in readiness for an afternoon of reading and Van Hoosier spotting, I duly set off for the west tower, only to be met by the most awful hope-dashery at the foot of its stairs. In all my plotting there was something I had quite forgot. Placed across the bottom of the stairs, nailed to the newel post, were several thick boards, floorboards no less, completely blocking any ascent, put there, like the planks and stone slabs over the well, to prevent Giles and me from dreadful accidenting. I set down my books and tried to move the planks, but they were firmly fixed, so I only splintered a finger for my trouble; no budgery was to be had. I was in a weepery of frustration. I tried putting my feet on one board to clamber over, but there was no foothold for it, access was totally denied. Besides, I realised, even if I had been able to climb over, any entry so arduous and difficult would be so slow I'd be laying myself open to redhandery should anyone chance that way.

I picked up my books and had started to walk away, utterly disconsolate at the loss of my afternoons just when I thought to have recovered them, when I brained an idea. I dashed back, went around the side of the staircase, pushed my books through one of the gaps between the banisters, then hoisted myself up and found I could climb the stairs from the outside, by putting my feet in the gaps. In this way I was able to ascend past the barricade and then, thanks to my leg-lengthery, haul myself over the banister rail and onto the staircase. I stood and looked down with satisfaction at the barrier below and felt how safe and secure I would be in my new domain. I certained no one else would be able to follow me. I couldn't imagine Mary or fat Meg or plump Mrs Grouse stretching a leg over the banister rail, even if they had been witted enough to think of it.

I made my way up to the second floor, then to the third and finally through a trapdoor to the fourth, the uppermost, from which I could look down upon not only the driveway but also the roof of the main building. The top of the tower consisted of a single room, windowed on all sides. I stood there now, mistress of all I surveyed, fairy-taled in my tower, Rapunzelled above all my known world. I looked around my new kingdom. It was sparsely furnished and appeared to have been at one time a study. There was a chaise and a heavy leather-topped keyhole desk, the leather itself tooled with a fine layer of mould, and before the desk, a revolving captain's chair. It was heads or tails whether the library or this room contained more dust and I would not have liked to wager upon it. The windows were leaded lights and a few of the small panes were missing, so a fine draught blew through the room and there were bird droppings on the dusty floor, showing that the wind was not the only thing that entered this way.

Still, it was all a wonder to me. The windows had drapes at the four corners but these were all tied back and I realised I would have to be careful and keep my head low so as not to be visible from below. No matter, if I sat at the desk, I could Van Hoosier the drive and so long as I did not move about excessively no one was likely to see me.

The ventilation of the missing panes meant the room would always be cold and my first task was to secure more blanketry. I set down my books and duly went scavenging. It tedioused having to go right down to the first floor and then up again to the second for my purloinery but there was no other way. I had emptied my old chest of blankets for the library and I did not fortune upon another such. However, I did find a couple of guest bedrooms that were kept in readiness should we ever have another guest and I to-the-winded my caution, stripped them of their quilts, stole two of the three blankets beneath and then replaced the quilts. I surveyed what I had done. I had skinnied the beds but I couldn't imagine anyone would notice, and should a maid remake the bed she probably wouldn't suspect. After all, who at Blithe – other than a shivering ghost – would steal a blanket?

I made sure the coast was clear and sped down the staircase to the first floor, along the main corridor, and threw the blankets over the barrier at the bottom of the tower stairs. I had just hauled myself up onto the outside of the stairs when the door to the main corridor opened. No time to wait! I hurled myself head over toe over banister rail and onto the stairs, where I crouched behind the barricade, hoping for unseenery through the gaps.

'Oh my goodness, what was that!' It was Mary's voice.

'Ghosts most likely,' said a voice I recognised as belonging to Meg. 'They say Blithe is full of ghosts.'

'Tch! You don't believe in that nonsense, do you?' Mary's voice betrayed a certain lack of confidence in the words it uttered.

I spyholed them through the barricade. Meg raised an eyebrow. 'I reckon I've worked here five years and seen many things. When you've been here as long as I have, you'll know, you'll know.' And she opened the door to the main corridor again, picking up a dustpan into which she'd evidently just swept something. She disappeared inside; before Mary followed her, she pulled a face at the older woman's retreating back.

So here I was, princessed in my tower, blanketed at my desk, shivering some when the wind blew, but alone and able to read, at least until it twilighted, because I could have no giveaway candles here. I suddened a twinge, thinking – I knew not why just then – of Giles, away at his school, in turn thinking perhaps of me, and I wondered if he was happy. It brought to mind how I had once torn in two a playing card – the queen of spades it was – straight across the middle, thinking to make two queens from one, the picture at the top and its mirror image below, but found instead I did not even have one, the separate parts useless on their own, and it struck me this was me without Giles, who was a part of my own person. How I longed for his holidays to begin so I could show him our new kingdom. This was all I lacked for happiness, for Giles to be here to share it with me.

It was not to be. And so I started off on my new life. I morninged in the library and afternooned in my tower. I reasoned early on that it would be foolish to keep returning books to the library after finishing my day in the tower; carrying them about increased the likelihood of being caught. This meant that if I were reading something in the morning, I could not continue with the same book in the afternoon. I resolved therefore to make a smugglery of books in the tower (where there was little chance of detection anyway), which would remain there until they were finished, and for my reading day to be of two separate parts. I libraried the mornings away on solid books, philosophy, history and the like; I also began to teach myself languages and to work up a passable knowledge of French, Italian, Latin and Greek, although I would not vouch for my accent in the two former, never having heard either of them spoke; the afternoons were my fantasy time, appropriate for my tower. I indulged myself in Mrs Radcliffe, ancient myths and Edgar Allan Poe. The only fly in my ointment here, though, was that I must never let my concentration lapse, must never surrender myself too much to the words that swam before my eyes and in my head and distract myself to my doom.

On the day after I first occupied my tower, I morninged out up the drive, measuring how long it would take Theo Van Hoosier to walk its length, from the moment he first visibled from the tower, to the moment when he vanished from view under the front porch of the house. How did I work out the time, I who had no timepiece? I counted it out, second by second, and to make sure my seconds were all the right length I figured them thus: one Shakespeare, two Shakespeare, three Shakespeare. In this way I reckoned that young Van Hoosier would be in view for four and a half minutes. Thus, when I set out for the tower room after lunch I would first sneak into the drawing room, which has a direct view of the drive, and make sure Van Hoosier was not in view. If he was not, then I had four and a half minutes to get to the tower, otherwise, if I took any longer and he should appear unviewed at the precise moment my back was turned when I set off, he could have reached the front door and be out of view again before I was at my post and so occasion all the dangerous calling and searching for me. Let me tell you, it was a stretch to make it to the tower in that time. If I happened to meet John or Mary or Meg or Mrs Grouse and they delayed me for even a few seconds it impossibled my journey in the allotted time and so meant I had to go back and check the drive and start once more from the beginning. Not only that, all the while I had to be one-Shakespearing-two-Shakespearing and if someone should speak to me and I should lose my number, then it was back to the drawing board – that is the drawing room – all over again.

By the time I reached the bottom of the tower staircase I was usually up to two hundred-Shakespeare and it was touch and go whether I could climb the outside of the staircase, haul myself over the banisters, take off my shoes (for fear of my running feet booming out on the un-carpeted treads) and get to the tower room in time. On one occasion I just made it, peeped through the window and saw Van Hoosier's hat disappearing under the front porch, so that I had to tear back down the staircase, haul myself back over the banisters, climb down the outside bit and get myself into the main corridor all over again before they started hollering for me. But then, no one had ever told me having a secret life was going to be easy.

CHAPTER 4

That first day when it snowed I figured myself likely weatherproofed against the Van Hoosier boy, but I had made the very mistake that all too many people made with me (who would have thought I had two book nests? who would have thought I Frenched and Shakespeared?), namely I judged him by appearances. I figured him a spineless sort of tall weed, who would buckle in two without his starched shirt to hold him upright. So I grudged an admiration for him that day when I upglanced the drive from the drawing room (I had not then found my tower refuge, of course) and saw him Wenceslasing his way through the drifted snow. A dogged and doglike devotion to me, I realised, worth so much more than his doggerel could ever be.

Mrs Grouse told me to wait in the drawing room. I heard her open the front door and invite him to shake the snow from his boots, followed by an interval of quite prodigious stamping. Shortly afterward, the door to the drawing room opened and Mrs Grouse said, 'Young Mr Van Hoosier to see you, miss,' as though we didn't both know I was sitting in there waiting for him and as if, too, I were much used to visitory. In this, and in adjectiving our guest as young, Mrs Grouse showed that she herself didn't know how to behave, that she was a housekeeper and childminder, not a hostess. When she shut the door behind him, I noticed she had even neglected to relieve Van Hoosier of his hat.

I invited him to sit down. I had positioned myself in an armchair so as to preclude any possibility of him nexting me and he couched himself opposite, folding himself as though he were hinged at the knees and hips. We sat and smiled politely at one another. I did not know what to do with him and he did not know what to do with his hat. He sat and Gargeried it, twisting it this way and that, rotating it with one hand through the thumb and forefinger of the other, flipping it over and over. Finally, after he'd dropped it for the third time, I upped and overed to him. I irritabled out a hand. 'Please, may I take that?'

He gratefulled it to me. I outed to the hall and hung it with his coat. But when we were seated again I realised I might have removed the hat but I had not removed the problem. Indeed I had exacerbated it, for now he had nothing to fiddle with. He was forced to fall back on cracking his knuckles, or crossing and uncrossing his legs, this way and that. I hard-stared his shins and he caught my gaze and, uncrossing his legs, put both feet firmly on the floor. He looked scolded and in that moment his face so Gilesed I twinged guilt.

39

'Well,' he said at last, 'here we are.'

'It would appear so,' I frosted back.

'It is very cold outside. The snow is deep.'

'And crisp and even,' I said.

'What?' He knew he was being made fun of, but could not quite figure out how.

We sat in silence some moments more. Then he said, 'Oh yes, I almost forgot,' and began patting the different pockets of his jacket and pants in an unconvincery of unknowing the whereabouts of something. Finally he pulled out a folded paper and began to unfold it. 'I wrote you another poem.'

The look I gave him was several degrees colder than the snow and like enough to have sent him scuttling back out into it. 'Oh no, it's OK; you don't have to entertain a kiss this time. There's no question of any kissing being involved.'

I thawed my face and settled back in my chair. 'Well, in that case, Mr Van Hoosier, fire away.'

Well, the least said about the second Van Hoosier verse, the better. The best you could say was that it was nowhere near as bad as the first, especially as it didn't carry the threat of a kiss, although, then again, I wasn't too impressed by the final rhyme of 'immense' and 'Florence'; fortunately the reference was to the supposed number of my admirers, not my size.

When he'd finished reading it, Theo looked up from the paper and saw my expression. 'Still not the thing, huh?'

40

'Not quite,' I said.

He crumpled the paper into a ball and thrust it into his pocket. 'Darn it,' he said good-naturedly, 'but I'll keep going at it till I crack it, you see if I don't. I'm not one for giving up.'

In this last he proved as good as his word, not just in the versifying but in the snow trudgery too. It didn't matter if it blizzarded, or galed or howled like the end of the world outside, he Blithed it every afternoon for the next couple of weeks. After he'd visited with me a few times I began to see that, like his verse, his lanky body rhymed awkwardly and scanned badly. His long limbs didn't fit too easily into a drawing room, where it seemed one or other of them was always flailing out of its own accord, tipping a little side table here or tripping a rug there; he was like a huge epileptic heron. It impossibled to comfortable him indoors, so on the fourth or fifth visit, when he suggested we take ourselves outside, I was somewhat relieved, for if we stayed in it was only a matter of time before china got broke; not that I minded that, for there was nothing of value at Blithe and no one to care about it anyhow, but I could imagine how distraught he would be. It was only as we put on our coats that I second-thoughted. Was it really safe to have him clumsying about on snow and ice? Would not his parents blame me if it were one of his arms or legs, rather than china, that got broke? God knows, there was enough of them to damage.

'Is this wise?' I said, as he mufflered himself up.

'What do you mean?'

'Well, your asthma and all. Taking it out into the cold.'

'Not at all. It's the best thing for it, a nice bright frosty day like today when the air is dry and clear. It's the damp dreary days that get on my chest and set me to coughing.'

So out we went and, to my surprise, my very great surprise, we funned it for a couple of hours. It was not that Theo lost his awkwardness in this new element, but rather that this element was so bare and empty of obstacles that he had nothing to do but fall over on the ice, which he did time and time again. When he went you had to stand clear as his great arms windmilled fit to knock your head off if you should happen to put it in the way of them and his legs jerked up like a marionette's and then everything collapsed like a deckchair and left a dead spidery bundle on the ground. It was so comical that the first time I burst out laughing before I could help myself and then, when the pile of his bones didn't move, rushed to him, fearfulling what I would find. But he always pulled himself up with a smile and so after a while we got to making snowballs and throwing them at one another, at which he took a terrible pasting because his own throws were so bad he was as like to hit himself as put one on me. And then he suggested we make a snowman, and we started but we had only got halfway through fashioning a sizeable head when it reminded me of the winter before, how I'd done this with Giles, and it guilted me. I thought of him classroomed somewhere while I was still here enjoying myself and not thinking of him for a single moment for two whole hours together, and all at once I was chilled to my core and couldn't unchatter my teeth, so that Theo, seeing this, insisted we repair indoors.

As if my thoughts had either been stirred by those of Giles himself or themselves stirred him, next day there was a letter from him. He was not a great correspondent, lacking as he did my facility with the written word, although I had done my best to teach him to read and write. Mrs Grouse, who totally ignoranted this, of course, thought it a marvel how quickly the school had taught him to write, although his letters were so badly formed it took me a great while to figure out even this short epistle. Before I had the letter to myself, though, I had to listen to Mrs Grouse's guesses as to what Giles's mangled hieroglyphics might mean, for, of course, I was not supposed to be able to read them for myself. The poor woman, who was, I suspected, as literate, or rather illiterate, as my brother himself, could make a fair fist of only three-quarters of it and more or less guessed the rest. But when I had it to myself, I managed by long study, and knowledge of Giles, to pretty much figure it out.

Dear Flo,

I am to write home every other Sunday. We have a time for it and all the boys must do it. I hope you are well. I hope Mrs Grouse is well. I hope Meg and Mary and John are all well. I am very well thank you. I am not homesick. I am very slow with my lessons but I don't mind. The other boys laugh at me for this, but I don't mind the laughing so much. I will close now.
Your loving brother
Giles

What did it mean, 'I don't mind the laughing so much'? So much as what? Were there other things that he minded more, physical intimidation perhaps, some kind of pinching or hitting or hair-tugging or fire-roasting? Or was it merely a figure of speech, a way of saying he wasn't greatly bothered by it? And why did he talk about not being homesick? Why mention it at all, unless perhaps he was and had been instructed not to worry those at home by writing them about it. The letter weeped me and that night in bed I puzzled over it again, then pillowed it, wanting thereby to feel close to poor Giles.

CHAPTER 5

You should not deduce from that afternoon in the snow with Theo Van Hoosier that I was all joy unalloyed at his visits. There was plenty to alloy my joy, but nothing more so than the disturbance to my reading. It was not simply the long and often untimely interruptions the visits occasioned. It was also all the moments when he unappeared. You will recall that whenever I was towered I had to check the drive once every four and a half minutes. To leave margin for error this meant once every four minutes. But, of course, I was untimepieced and I didn't see myself hauling no grandfather clock over the banisters and up the stairs. The only way I could judge the time, therefore, was by the turn of my pages, the pace at which I read. So before taking each book from the library I timed myself reading a few pages by the grandfather clock, to determine exactly how far four minutes would take me. If it were three and a half pages, then up in the tower room I would have to look out the window at every such interval. I cannot begin to tell you how annoying this was. It was like trying not to drop off to sleep;

45

all the time, as the book drew me in, as its author surrounded me with a whole new world, some part of me was fighting the delicious surrender to such absorption and saying, *three and a half, three and a half, three and a half.* Sometimes I'd sudden I'd forgotten, that seven or eight pages, or even ten or fourteen, had passed with no looking up. When that occurred I had no way of knowing whether Van Hoosier had all unseen upped the drive during my relapse, and so there was nothing for it but to down book and clamber all the way down the stairs, and run along the corridor to check out the hall and drawing room and then, if they were unHoosiered, upglance the drive, and if that were likewise Theo-free, make the mad dash up to the tower again. On a good book such as *Jane Eyre* I might be up-and-downstairsing four or five times in an afternoon.

One day in the tower, I lifted my eyes from my book, resenting this crazy, jerky four-minute way of reading and, through the window, saw a rook pecking at something in the snow. The scene was the perfect picture of a new state of mind I realised I had reached. The perfect white snow, the black rook a nasty stain upon a newly laundered sheet; for the first time I understood that there was nothing wholly good and nothing wholly bad, that every page has some blot, and, by the same token, I hoped, every dark night some distant tiny shining light. This hoped me some. The rook on my landscape was Giles, and all the suffering he might be going through, and all the suffering I endured from the great hole inside of me where he should have been. But the rook was one small black dot and the rest was all white. Did that not offer the prospect that most of my brother's school life might be happy and carefree, with perhaps one or two small things he did not like? And yet, why had he mentioned not being homesick, except to reassure me? What could it mean but that he was?

Anyway, there were the Christmas holidays to look forward to when Giles would be home and I would be able to worm the truth from him, although what good that would do me I couldn't be sure. Meanwhile I read all the mornings and some of the afternoons and then Van Hoosiered my way through the rest. Because of his restless and wayward limbs and the need to keep them from fine china, Theo was always up for getting out in the snow. One day I looked out my tower window and saw a bent figure trudging up the drive and almost went back to my book, for I thought it must be some delivery man and could not be he. This fellow appeared to be a hunchback with a great lump on his spine, but it fortuned me to watch him a bit longer and then the hump moved, leapt off his back and dangled from one of his hands and the rest of the shape organised itself into the unmistakable gangle of Theo and I was off, leaping the banisters and racing the corridor.

In the hall Theo opened the leather bag he was

carrying with a flourish like a magician dehatting a rabbit. 'What . . .?' I cried.

'Skates. Well, you have a lake out back, don't you?'

Mrs Grouse was all concern. Suppose the ice crust was too thin and broke and we fell through it and drowned? What would she say to Theo's mother then? I thought that seeking to concern us about her social difficulty rather than our own deaths was the wrong way to go with this argument, but I held my peace. Of course, nobody was worried about what to tell *my* mother. And significantly Mrs Grouse hadn't mentioned any possible embarrassment with my uncle, for we both knew he would mourn such an event as a disencumbrance.

John fortuned at this point to be passing through the hallway on some errand and to overhear and intervene. He assured Mrs Grouse that he had skated on lakes in these parts every winter as a boy and that at this time of year the ice was at least a foot thick. He undertook to accompany us out there and, at Mrs Grouse's insistence, check the lake's surface very carefully 'lest there be any cracks', which caused John to roll his eyes and smile behind her back.

To my great surprise, especially after his previous slipping and sliding on the snow around the house, Theo proved to be an accomplished skater. Once he had those skates on he was transformed. From an early age, he'd had plenty of practice every year in Central Park, and was able to zoom around the lake at great speed, to turn and spin and glide, every movement smooth and graceful. He minded me of a swan, which is ungainly as a walker, waddling from side to side, and awkward as a flier, struggling to get off the ground and into the air, and then making a great difficulty of staying up there, but which on the water serenes and glides. I guess it was a great relief to Theo to be out on the frozen lake with nothing to collide with, no delicate side tables and fine china out to get him, no rug-trippery to untranquil his progress.

By contrast I hopelessed the task. My legs were determined to set off in opposite directions, my head had an affinity with the ice and wanted to keep a nodding acquaintance with it, my backside had sedentary intentions. But Theo kinded me and helped me; he was a different person, taking control, instructing me, commanding me as I commanded him on unvarnished land. And gradually, over a period of a couple of weeks, I began to improve, so that soon I was going a whole ten minutes without butting or buttocking the ice.

So it was that each afternoon I found myself looking up every page or so, instead of four-minuting, for I longed to see Theo upping the drive. And then, one day, he didn't come at all. I was reading *The Monk*, making the hairs on my neck stand on end, shivering myself in the dead silence of the tower, when I looked up anxiousing for Theo and realised I could scarce see the drive, as the light was fading fast; I was still able to read,

49

for my tower, being the highest and westernmost point of Blithe, is where the sun lingers longest. I put down my book and downstairsed. What could have happened to Theo? Why had he not come? True, it had snowed mightily that morning, but that had never put him off before. Had his tutor forbidden his visits? Had he perhaps some new work schedule that disafternooned him?

I found Mrs Grouse in the kitchen. 'Where have you been?' she demanded crossly, adding before I could answer, 'A note has come for you,' and she produced an envelope that she opened, taking out the single sheet inside and unfolding it. She put on her spectacles and peered at it. 'It's from young Mr Van Hoosier,' she said, and then began to read.

Dear Florence,
   I am sorry I cannot come today. Asthma is my companion this afternoon. Doctor called, strenuous exercise forbidden. Please continue to skate and do a circuit or two for me.

The note ended with a poem:

To Florence I would make a trip
But asthma
Hasma
In its grip

I liked that. It wasn't exactly Walt Whitman. But it was better, much better.

As she folded the note and handed it to me (although what she thought I, whom she supposed unable to read, could do with it, I do not know) Mrs Grouse said, 'You must pay a visit to the Van Hoosiers, to ask after him. It's what they would expect. It's what a young lady should do.'

'But . . .' I was about to say I never visited anywhere, for I never had. Giles and I had never played with other children, for we knew none. This was one reason why I so concerned for him at school. But Giles leaving home and all the Theoing I'd had had changed all that. I saw that now.

'Very well, I'll go in the morning.'

And Mrs Grouse smiled and I could feel her eyes on my back as I walked off to the kitchen to ask Meg what sweet pastries she might have for me to take to Theo.

CHAPTER 6

I don't know when the nightwalks started, for I had had them as long as I remembered, and of course, of the walks themselves I recalled nothing, except the waking-up afterward in strange places, for example the conservatory, and once in Mary's room up in the attic, and several times in the kitchen. I knew, though, how the walks always began; it was with a dream, and the dream was every time the same.

In it I was in bed, just as I actually was, except that it was always the old nursery bedroom which was now Giles's alone but which I used to share with him, until Mrs Grouse said I was getting to be quite the young lady and ought not to be in a room with my brother any longer. I would wake and moonlight would be streaming through the window – often-times, though far from always, the walks happened around the time of the full moon – and I would look up and see a shape bending over Giles's bed. At first that was all it was, a shape, but gradually I realised it was a person, a woman, dressed all in black, a black travelling dress with a matching cloak and a hood.

As I watched she put her arms around Giles and – he was always quite small in the dream – lifted him from the bed. Then the hood of her cloak always fell back and I would catch a glimpse of her face. She gazed at my brother's sleeping face – for he never ever woke – and said, always the same words, 'Ah, my dear, I could eat you!' and indeed, her eyes had a hungry glint. At this moment in the dream I wanted to cry out but I never could. Something restricted my throat; it was as though an icy hand had its grip around it and I could scarce get my breath. Then the woman would gather her cloak around Giles and, as she did so, turn abruptly and seem to see me for the first time. She would quickly pull her hood back over her head and steal swiftly and silently from the room, taking my infant brother with her.

I would make to follow but it was as though I were bound to the bed. My body was leaded and it was only with a superhuman effort that I was finally able to lift my arms and legs. I would sit up and try to scream, to wake the household, but nothing would come, save for the merest sparrow squawk that died as soon as it touched my lips. I would put my feet to the floor, steady myself and walk slowly – my limbs would still not function as I wished them to, in spite of the urgency of the situation – to the doorway. There I would look in either direction along the corridor but have no clue which way the woman had gone. It was no good trying to reason things, she was as likely to have gone left as right and I was wasting valuable time prevaricating. And so I would choose right, it was always right, and begin to walk, urging my weighted legs to move. And then . . . and then . . . I would wake up, sitting on the piano stool in the drawing room, perhaps, or in Meg's chair in the kitchen, sometimes alone but like as not surrounded by the servants, who would be watching me, making sure I did not have some accident and harm myself, or somehow get outside and drown myself in the lake. When I woke, my first words were always the same: 'Giles, Giles, I have to save Giles.' And Mrs Grouse or John or Meg or Mary, whoever was there, would always say, 'It's all right, Miss Florence, it was only a dream. Master Giles is safe and sound asleep.'

Because I remembered virtually nothing of the walking part of the dream what I knew of my nightwalking came from the observations of other people. Often I liked to nightwalk in the long gallery, a windowed corridor on the second floor that stretched along the central part of the front of the house. John told me how, when he first came to work at Blithe, he had been to the tavern in the village one Saturday night and was returning home up the drive somewhat the worse for wear when he looked up at the house and saw a pale figure, all in white, moving slowly along the long corridor, now visible through one window, then disappearing to reappear a moment later in the next. At the time he knew nothing of my nocturnal habits. 'I don't mind telling you, miss,' he told me many a time, 'I ain't no Catholic but I crossed myself there and then. Knowing as I do the reputation Blithe has for ghosts, how it has always attracted and pulled them in, I convinced myself it was some evil spectre I was seeing. I was sure I'd come in and find the whole household murdered in their beds.'

Mrs Grouse told me that I always walked slowly, not as sleepwalkers are usually depicted in books, with their arms outstretched in front of them as if they were blind and feared a collision, but with my arms hanging limply at my sides. My posture was always very erect and I seemed to glide, with none of the jerkiness of normal walking, but smoothly, as if, as she put it, 'you were on wheels.'

It was true what John said about Blithe and ghosts. Mrs Grouse reckoned it all stuff and nonsense but Meg once told me the local people thought it a place ghouls loved, a favourite haunt, as it were, to which any restless spirit was attracted like iron filings to a magnet. And now, even though it was only I, Florence, sleepwalking, I seemed somehow to have added to this superstition.

Meg told me that when I woke from my walks it uselessed to speak to me for several minutes, that I seemed not to hear. Often, before I was myself, at the moment when I seemed to have emerged from the dream but had not yet returned to real life, I began to weep and was quite distraught, and if any should try to comfort me I pushed them away and said, 'No, no, don't worry yourself about me! It's Giles who needs help. We must find him, we must!' Or something like.

After I had nightwalked three or four times and it began to be a pattern, they called in Dr Bradley, the local doctor, who came and gave me a good going-over, shining lights in my eyes and poking about in my ears and listening to my heart and so on. He pronounced me fit and well and told them it was likely the manifestation of some anxiety disorder, which was only natural considering my orphan status and the upheavals of my early life. This was confirmed, he said, by my fears focusing upon Giles, who was, after all, the only consistent presence in my life. I read all this in a report I found on Mrs Grouse's desk one day, when she had gone into town on some errand. I curioused over the words 'upheavals of my early life'. I could not remember anything of my parents – my mother died in childbirth and my father some four years later with my stepmother, Giles's mother, in a boating accident. I recalled nothing of any of them, and as the servants were only engaged after they were all dead, they could tell me nothing either. As far as my early life went, it was all a blank, a white field of snow, without even the mark of a rook.

CHAPTER 7

Before I set out to visit the Van Hoosiers next morning, John came back from town with a letter, a rare enough occurrence at Blithe, where Mrs Grouse received correspondence from my uncle maybe two or three times a year and little else. It was for me, and I reflected that from being completely unlettered but a few weeks ago I was now the most epistolatoried person for miles around. The letter was, of course, from Giles and I heart-in-mouthed as Mrs Grouse commenced to read it, after she had first sniffed and said, 'Humpf, seems folks think I've nothing better to do all day than read letters to you.'

> Dear Flo,
> Thank you for your letter. I have read it ever so many times and it is tearing from so much folding and unfolding. I like the sound of your ice skating and cannot wait for the holidays. Do you think Theo Van Hoosier will be able to find any skates to fit me? Will the ice bear the weight of three of us? Or will we take turns? I am very slow

57

at my lessons, but I don't mind when the others laugh at me. It is better than being hit or pinched. But you are not to worry about it because it does not happen often. Not so very often, anyway. I hope you are well. I hope Mrs Grouse and John are well. I hope Meg and Mary are well.

Your loving brother

Giles

The letter from me Giles referred to was, of course, written by Mrs Grouse and so contained none of the things I would have liked to tell him, about the tower room, for instance (although I had not yet decided whether or no to let him in on that), and none of the anxious inquiries about himself I longed to make. His references to pinching and hitting shivered me quite, although it uncleared whether he had actually suffered phys-ical abuse or if 'you are not to worry about it because it does not happen often' merely referred to the teasing, but I had no time to reflect upon it now. I was all done up ready to go visiting, so I took the letter from Mrs Grouse and slipped it into my overcoat pocket, where it heavied my spirit as if it had been a convict's leg iron or a hunk of stolen bread down a schoolboy's pants. I had wanted to walk to the Van Hoosier place but Mrs Grouse would have none of it. It was more than a mile and although the roads were clear of snow today, if it blizzarded again I might be stranded halfway, not to mention that even if that didn't happen I would death-of-cold me. She never-minded that I had been out in the cold on the ice every afternoon anyway. So John was to horse-and-trap me there, which was fine by me, for once we out-of-sighted Blithe and Mrs Grouse's prying eyes he handed me the reins and let me drive, as he often did when the housekeeper wasn't around. The old horse we used on the trap, Bluebird, was so docile and knew all the local routes so well that in truth there was not much driving to be done, and even should it snow, it little dangered the horse leaving the road and wandering into a ditch.

I had never seen the Van Hoosier place; it was approached by a long driveway, and set in wood-land so far back from the main road as to invisible all but its chimneys when we drove past. So I was surprised to find it smaller than Blithe, although in every other respect much grander. You could tell that from the moment you turned off the road and through the entrance gates, which were newly painted, in contrast to our own peeling and chipped portals. The edges of the drive were neatly mani-cured and the lawns either side trimmed to within an inch of their lives. The house itself sparkled and gleamed in the winter sun; it did not absorb the light like dull old Blithe. John dropped me at the front door. 'I'll drive the trap around the back and make myself comfortable in the servants' kitchen, Miss Florence,' he said as he handed me down.

'Just have them send for me when you're ready to leave.'

I anxioused as I reached for the bell pull. I was all best-frocked today and did not feel in my own skin. The door was opened (soundlessly, it did not creak like nearly all the doors at Blithe) by a uniformed footman. 'Yes, ma'am,' he said, questioning an eyebrow.

'I – I came to inquire after the health of Mr Van Hoosier,' I mumbled. 'That is, I mean, well, young Mr Van Hoosier.'

'And you would be . . .?'

'Florence, from Blithe House.'

He held open the door and bowed me in. I found myself in a grand hallway with a great sweeping staircase, chandeliered and crystalled to the nines, mirrors everywhere, so that I was surrounded by what seemed dozens of pale, gawky girls, staring at me from all directions. 'If you'll just wait one moment, miss, I'll tell Mrs Van Hoosier you're here.'

He went off, heels clicking the tiled floor. I gazed at myself in the mirrors some more then decided to concentrate on looking down at my boots, which I found far more comfortable. After what seemed an age – I figured he had a mighty long way to walk – the man clicked his way back and invited me to follow him. He led me down a long corridor, opened a door and insinuated me into a small sitting room, where Mrs Van Hoosier was seated at a walnut writing desk, evidently in the middle of penning a letter. She looked up and sugared me a smile. 'Come in, my dear, come in and make yourself comfy. You must be frozen after your journey over here.'

She stood up, walked round the desk and shook my hand. I handed her the paper bag of pastries I had brought. 'For Theo,' I explained.

She opened the bag and peered at its contents and then, without comment, placed it on the desk and indicated a chair by the fire. 'Melville, bring us some coffee and cake, would you?' I heard the door close behind me. I sat down. I had met Mrs Van Hoosier but the once, the time they called at Blithe to introduce us to Theo. I had little attentioned her on that occasion, being much more taken with Theo and wondering how long it would be before he broke something. Observing her now, what struck me most was what a huge battleship of a woman she was. She was tall, and you could see that was where Theo got his height from, but she was also filled out, solid, not bendy like her boy. She was mantelpieced by a large bosom that cantilevered out in front of her; you could have stood things on it, a vase of flowers and a bust of Beethoven, and a family photograph or two, maybe. Her hair was all piled up on her head and that probably added another few inches. When I sat down she gianted over me, which didn't help my nervousness.

She put one hand on the mantelpiece over the fire and leaned against it.

'I – I came to inquire after Theo, I mean Mr Van Hoosier,' I muttered. 'I was hoping perhaps to visit with him and maybe cheer him up.'

She insincered me a smile. It felt like a grimace. 'Ah yes, how kind of you, but I'm afraid that won't be possible. He's much too sick. The doctor has forbidden him any excitement.'

I smiled at the thought that I might constitute excitement.

'You find that amusing?'

'Oh, no, ma'am, not at all. It was just, well . . .' My words died away.

The door opened and Melville reappeared with a tray. Mrs Van Hoosier sat down on the opposite side of the fireplace from me. Melville moved a side table next to her and set the tray on it. He placed another table beside me. 'That's all right, Melville, you can go.'

She poured the coffee and added milk and handed me a cup. 'You have enjoyed Theo's company, it seems.'

I nodded. 'Oh, yes . . .'

'Well, of course. He's a fascinating boy.'

It wasn't the word I'd have used for Theo.

'And I thought it would be good for him to have some companionship here.' I nervoused a sip of coffee. She raised her cup to her lips but then paused and lowered it slightly. 'Though I wonder now, in the light of what's happened, whether that wasn't a mistake.'

'A mistake?'

She proffered a plate of tiny tea cakes but I declined. She took one herself and popped it whole into her mouth and masticated slowly for a moment or two. The clock on the mantelpiece began to tick louder. She swallowed. 'Yes, a mistake. All that skating and running around in the cold. I fear it has done his chest no favours.'

'But, Mrs Van Hoosier, if I may make so bold –'

'You may not.' She inserted another cake into her mouth and chewed it so angrily I all but felt sorry for it. When it was finally dead she turned and fixed me a look, as though she were a scientist and I some kind of bug she was microscoping. 'The problem is, Florence, that you have been left to run wild. I think your uncle should have kept a closer eye on you. There is more to being a guardian than providing a home and food.'

I eagered a question. 'Do you know my uncle?'

'No, I'm afraid I never had that pleasure, never even heard of the man until we bought this place, although I did meet your stepmother once.'

'What was she like?'

She screwed up her eyes, as if shutting out the present and gazing at the long-distant past. Finally she opened them and picked up a bell from the table beside her. 'Do you know, it was years ago, when she wasn't much more than a girl. She was pretty, though not at all sophisticated, but other than that I don't rightly remember her at all. Then I heard she'd married someone from these parts.' She rang the bell.

'That would be my father,' I said.

'So it would seem,' she said.

'And they died, in a boating accident, I believe.'

'How tragic,' said Mrs Van Hoosier as if it wasn't at all. Melville appeared in the doorway. 'Anyhow,' she continued, 'I think perhaps it would be a good idea if Theo were to visit you a little less. He has his lessons to learn and, what with his illness, his tutor fears he's getting behind . . .'

'Y-you're stopping his visits?' I shocked how this suddened to matter to me. I would not have thought to have cared.

'No, my dear, I wouldn't want to deprive my son of all amusement. I'm just reining back on them a little, is all. I think too much excitement is not good for him. Melville, ask for the young lady's carriage to be brought round, would you?'

CHAPTER 8

That night was all toss-and-turn and longing for dawn; I was too mindfilled to sleep. From being a girl who had too much time on her hands, I now found myself fully occupied by all the things that were happening in my life. First there was poor Giles, and what I between-the-linesed from his letters. Other than that ambiguous phrase about the pinching and hitting, there was nothing I could actually put my finger on, no direct complaint, although I certained he would make one if he were really in trouble or upset. Then, at one of my many wakings, it came to me, wondering me why I hadn't thought of it before. Of course, his letters would be censored; a teacher would read them before they were allowed to be sent home. Any bald statement of bullying would certainly be excised; the school would not want bad impressions being conveyed that might anxious parents; that would not do at all. As you may imagine, the thought did not comfort me one bit.

Next I was thinking about Theo Van Hoosier. Not just how I would miss his visits, odd fellow though he was, but also how Mrs Van Hoosier had in-betweened me with her ruling that he could still visit, but much less often. It would have been better if she had banned him altogether. As things stood, I would not be able to take to the library in the afternoons, but would still have to keep watch for Theo from the tower. Only now there would be a great deal more three-and-a-halfing, for there would be many more afternoons when Theo didn't show at all, and the frustatory of it was that I would never know when he was coming and when not, so would have to do it for longer and, most of the time, for no reason at all. I cursed Theo that he had ever come into my life and inconvenienced me so, and at the same time I found myself missing him and wishing him here. It was the rook and the virgin snow all over again.

But by far the most wakery thing that night was not what Mrs Van Hoosier had said about her son, but the remarks she had carelessed about my uncle and my stepmother. Even when I was thinking about Theo, or worrying over Giles, whatever my thoughts, that undertowed them all.

Of course, I had not gotten myself so far through life without wondering about my parents. I had tried asking Mrs Grouse about them but she always stonewalled me. 'I only know what I have been told. Your mother went out of the world as you came into it and your father died in a boating accident, along with Master Giles's mother, when he was still a baby,' was all she would say.

I attempted going at it another way, by questioning her about my lineage, putting it to her that since Giles and I bore the same surname as our uncle, then our father must have been his brother. 'I have met your uncle only once, Miss Florence,' she said, in the manner of someone ducking a question not because they subterfuged but rather to discount any possibility of making a mistake, 'and that was in New York when he engaged me to come here and run the house and look after Master Giles and you. You were four years old then and that's all I know. We didn't discuss your family tree.'

Now I thought how I could maybe find out more if I wrote my uncle and simply asked him straight out to tell me who I was and all about my parents, but then of course it was not so simple. My uncle had given strict orders to illiterate me; he wouldn't be best pleased to find my penmanship turning up in his morning mail.

It obvioused me it was no use putting the thing to Mrs Grouse again. She was a simple soul who transparented her feelings; she was like George Washington, she couldn't tell a lie. If she'd been hiding anything, I would have guessed straightway. She told me nothing, not because she would not, but simply because she didn't know. Asking her again about my mother and father would bring no information but simply alert her to my curiosity and any other action I might take.

Quite what that action would be conundrummed

me quite. I spent a whole afternoon in the tower not reading but thinking about it, and dozing, of course, having sleeplessed the night. Every time I felt my head nodding and jerked back to waking, I had to make the mad dash down to the front door in case I'd missed Theo, even though in my heart of hearts I knew he wouldn't be coming that day; I couldn't take the risk. I wished he were there and, back in the tower after fruitlessing yet another front-dooring, I pretended he was and imagined us face-to-facing, me on the chaise, he on the captain's chair, discussing my problem.

'So that's it,' I told him, having nutshelled the whole thing for him. 'What can I do?'

He stroked his chin and got up and paced about in a most businesslike way, purposefulling long strides, hands behind his back. Finally he stopped and looked down at me, cracking open a smile. 'Documents,' he said.

'What do you mean?' I asked.

He came over to me and bent down on one knee, seizing my upper arms in his big bony hands. 'Don't you see, there must be documents relating to you. Everyone has documents. And likely they're somewhere in Blithe House.' He released me and stood looking at me, awaiting a reaction.

I eagered forward in my chair and then slumped back. 'Unless my uncle took them with him to New York when he cleared out.'

My imaginary Theo shrugged, which had the

look of a praying mantis trying to slough its skin. 'Perhaps. But maybe he didn't. It's worth a try.'

I could have hugged him, except of course he wasn't there, and because even if he had have been, it might have brought on another poem. Instead, I windowed the empty drive, void of his gangling figure, and in that way thanked him by missing him more.

Theo was right. Although my upbringing had unworldlied me, I knew from my reading that nobody goes through this life or even a part of it without something of them being somewhere written down. I must be documented like anybody else; all I had to do was a paper chase. Blithe was a big house, but there were not many places where papers would be kept.

I started next morning in the library since there was plenty of paper there. I was looking for anything that wasn't an out-and-out book, a ledger perhaps, or some kind of file. You would think that in four years' free run of the place I would have happened across such if it were there, but you have to remember that not only was this room immense (it rhymes with Florence), but also that until now it had been only books that interested me.

Well, I fruitlessed a whole week of library mornings. I upsidedowned the place, deshelving what seemed like every book, opening them and giving them a good shake to release any hidden document they might contain; there was none. I up-and-downed the ladders until I made myself dizzy; my nose stung and my head ached from an overdose of dust, but nothing did I find.

The afternoons I glummed away in my tower, too distracted to read, blinding myself by gazing out at the snow, as if hoping to see some clue writ there as to where the papers I sought might lie. At last it began to obvious me that although my uncle might not have had any use for books when he quit Blithe, he had certainly taken all his documents with him. I hopelessed finding any here.

Then, that afternoon, when I had all but given up on my quest and did not even think of it, chance threw a possible answer my way. I had torn my stocking on a nail on one of the library ladders and as it was my last pair, thought it might be a good excuse for a trip into town; we children hardly ever went there, perhaps only three or four times a year, but I thought Mrs Grouse might let John drive me. It would distraction me from the desperation of my lonely days.

So I knocked upon the door of her sitting room and, gaining no reply, and seeing the door not fastened but slightly ajar, pushed it open. The room was empty. She must be in the kitchen on some errand, or perhaps outside, in the barn, giving John some instruction or other. I idled about the room, glancing at the ornaments upon her mantel and the half-done embroidery basking upon her armchair. Eventually I came to her desk and, for want of anything better to do, found myself straightening her blotter, which was lying any which way on the desk top, and lining it up neatly with the inkwell and her pen. And then, feeling impish, I plumped myself down in her desk chair, thinking to experience what it might be like to be her. 'Florence, where have you been?' I sterned aloud to my imaginary self, contriting the other side of the desk, hands behind back, head hung low. 'I have told you a hundred ti—' but then I was interrupted, for before me I saw what I should have thought of when I first began my search.

The desk had two drawers, side by side. I upglanced the door to certain Mrs Grouse wasn't about to return, and having coast-cleared, grabbed the brass handle of the right-hand drawer and slid it open. Inside lay Mrs Grouse's fat account book, which I had seen upon her desk a thousand times. Having upglanced again, I lifted it out to see what other treasure the drawer might contain. It was full of pieces of paper, separated into little piles, all neatly clipped together with hairgrips. I picked them up one after another and disappointed straightway. They were nothing but bills, this pile from the grocer, that from the livery stable, that from the draper. There was nothing more. I replaced them and the account book and closed the drawer.

At that moment I heard voices outside in the passage. Mrs Grouse and Meg. She would be in the room any moment. There was no time to examine the second drawer without being red-handed, I had to get out of her chair fast and distance myself from the desk or face the consequences, but . . . well, I could not help myself, I had to see what that drawer contained. I heart-in-mouthed as I reached for the handle, for I could hear the approach of footsteps outside, Mrs Grouse about to enter. Nevertheless, I grasped the handle and tugged and . . . nothing happened. The drawer stuck fast, it was locked.

At that moment the door of the room began to open and I near cried out in alarm at being so caught when I heard again Meg's voice from afar, the other end of the corridor, and Mrs Grouse – for it was she at the door – pause to answer. I upped the chair and skiptoed fast to the other side of the room and stood innocenting out the window when behind me the housekeeper entered the room.

'Oh, there you are, Florence. Was there something you wanted?'

I told her about the stocking, which led to a discussion that I was growing fast and needed new clothes. 'Let me have a look at the account book and see what we can manage,' she said and I heart-in-mouthed again as she slid open the drawer, terrified she might notice some disarrangement of its contents. She did not, and, satisfied that Blithe could afford it, sanctioned a trip for the morrow, herself and I, into town.

The trip to our little town distracted me, though not in the welcome way of one who is bored, but rather by diverting me from my urgent task.

The next few days I mooned around the house, unlibrarying in the morning, untowering the afternoons, for I could think of nothing but that locked drawer and how I might obtain the key.

I almost salivated every time Mrs Grouse passed me by, the jingle-jangle of her household keys upon the great iron ring she wore on her belt sounding as a dinner bell to a starving man. It impossibled I should steal them, for she would miss them the moment they were gone, even suppose I could magick the ring from around her belt, which, all my wishes notwithstanding, I could not.

My opportunity came one day as it darked and I saw her through the drawing-room window, outside, talking animatedly to John. Their discussion appeared somewhat heated, on her part, that is, for John never lost his temper. It evidented she was reprimanding him; no doubt he had wasted some little bit of something somewhere, for she was tasked by my uncle to keep all spending at Blithe on a tight rein. This was my chance. I dashed from the house and breathlessed up to her.

'Mrs Grouse, Mrs Grouse!' I shouted as I approached.

She annoyed me a look at the interruption. 'Whatever is it now, child?'

'Please, Mrs Grouse, I have dropped my needle on the floor of my bedroom and cannot look for it, for I haven't a candle. Would you fetch me a new one, please?'

She exasperated a sigh. She had been full-flowing her complaint and did not want to be cut off. In a trice she unclipped the key ring from her belt and held it out to me by a particular key. 'Here, Florence, unlock the large armoire in the storeroom and take one out – only one, mind – then lock the cupboard and bring the keys straight back here to me.'

I skipped off. Now, normally this would have been a rare chance to purloin an extra library candle or two, but I unheeded that. I straighted to the house-keeper's sitting room and her desk. Then began an anxiety of trying keys. There must have been some thirty keys on that great jangling hoop and I knew I had but a minute or two at most to find the one I wanted. It obvioused that most were too big, great door keys that they were, so I concentrated on the dozen or so small keys that doubtlessed for cupboards and drawers. I lucked it the fourth one I tried. It slipped gratefully into the lock like a child into a warm bed on a cold night. It turned with a satisfying click.

I was tempted to open the drawer and it was all I could do to stop myself, but I knew that if I did and found something I would be powerless not to look at it and so would end up redhanding me. I left the drawer unlocked, which all along had been my strategy, and hastened back outside. There was no time now to visit the storeroom for the candle and so I had to hope that Mrs Grouse would not think of it or, if she did, assume it was in my pocket and not ask to see it.

As it was, it fortuned she was still so busy complaining John she simply took the keys from me without a word or even a glance and I awayed fast before she turned her attention to me. I made my way up to my room and from under my bed pulled out the box of old dolls and other such childish things that were long unplayed these days. This was where I kept my secrecy of bedtime books, for no one but me ever looked in it. It was also the hidery for my purloinery of candles, which I needed for the library and for reading in bed at night; I filched one whenever I could. For instance, whenever I aloned in the drawing room I would remove a candle from its holder, break off the bottom half, secrete it in my pocket and replace the top part; nobody ever noticed the candles were growing shorter. In the double candelabra I operated on both candles this way, to keep the appearance of them burning at the same rate.

Tonight I intended to open the drawer I had unlocked and inspect the contents, if any, and for that I would need my own candle. I could not risk lighting Mrs Grouse's sitting-room candles. She might notice next day that they had mysteriously burned down overnight; and in the event of anyone hearing me and coming into the room, even if I heard them approach and managed to snuff the candles first, they might see them smoking or spot that the wax was warm and soft. My own candle I could snuff and then push under the rug next to Mrs Grouse's desk, for retrieval in the morning.

My intention was to pretend to nightwalk, which I had often done before when I sleeplessed and wanted to library during the night. My nightwalks had been described often enough to me to know just how I should walk, as regards posture, pace, facial expression and so on, but there was an extra difficulty this time: because my nightgown was unpocketed, I could not carry candle and matches with me, for if caught it would obvious my trip was planned and not a nightwalk at all. So I took my candle and matches downstairs and hid them in the top of a plant pot in the hall. The plant was some bushy thing with leaves like a jungle, under which my lighting equipment would not be seen.

That night I lated awake in my bed listening to the sounds of the old house as it settled itself down for the night, the creakings and groanings as it relaxed after a hard day of containing all we people and all our hopes and fears and secrets. Now and then I heard the little girl in the attic above me, pirouetting across the boards. At last, somewhere a clock struck midnight and, satisfied that all human sounds had ceased, I slipped from my bed.

I downstairsed quick as I could in the dark, which was not fast, for having to careful not to bump into things and wake the house. I eventuallied the hall and felt about for the plant pot and, finding it, plunged my hands into its spidery leaves. I felt about on the soil, this way and that, and did not touch the candle or the matches. From somewhere above came the groan of a sleeper restlessing and turning over. My heart was a poundery of panic now. I alarmed that someone had found the candle and matches, perhaps Mary when she tended to the plants, the which meant that not only was my mission defeated but that tomorrow I would be exposed.

The picture of Mary watering the plants suddened me an inspiration. Of course, there was more than one plant! I was at the wrong pot. I blindmanned my hands before me and felt about and came upon another pot, the twin of my first encounter, and sure enough, there were my candle and matches. I paused and put my hand to my brow, which was slick with sweat, even though the night was cold and my feet frozen on the bare boards.

I struck a match and lit the candle, found the door to Mrs Grouse's sitting room and swifted inside, closing the door quietly behind me. I stood and lofted the candle, surveying the room, to check it was empty, for my mind half expected to find Mrs Grouse sitting there, waiting and watching to catch me out, canny old fowl that she was. There was no one.

I overed to the desk, set my candle down carefully on top of it and sat in its owner's chair. The brass handle of the left drawer was cold and forbidding to my touch. My big fear was that Mrs Grouse would have discovered its unlockery and locked it again. For I had no idea what she stored in there or how often she opened it. Why did she keep it locked in the first place? Perhaps because the household money was kept there. And if so, what if she had needed some today to pay a tradesman or the servants? I deep-breathed and pulled. The drawer yielded, although very stiff and unwilling. I slid it out slowly, gritting my teeth at its complaining rasp, feeling sure the whole household must be woken by it. But I could not wait to listen, for inside I saw a single object, a large, leather-bound book, its layer of dust testifying to its long undisturbery.

I swallowed and gingerlied it out, as if it were some holy relic, some saint's bones that, roughly handled, might turn to dust. I placed the book on the desk and opened it and saw at once what it was, an album of photographs, such as the one Mary had once showed me, of all her family, going back years.

The first page held but one picture, a man in a business suit standing in front of Blithe House. I instanted who it was, for it was the same face as the painting on the turn of the stairs: my uncle. He had the same bold stare, the same slight play of amusement about his lips. I turned the page. Here he was again, but this time pictured in some photographer's studio, next to a potted plant. Beside him stood a woman in a white dress, a beautiful woman, her arm linked in his, smiling too, but with a free and easy happiness, not at all like the man, who, looking again, I saw was pleased with himself, like an angler prouding it alongside some big fish he has landed.

I turned the page and found another picture of my uncle, again with a woman, but whether or not it was the same woman, I could not tell, for the photograph had been cut, a ragged square hole where the woman's head should have been. This shivered me in the silent night and I over-my-shouldered, suddening a feeling of a man standing there with a knife as if to do to me what had been done to the woman in the picture. There was no one there, though already I began to see shapes in the shadowy corners of the room. I looked again at the photograph, at the decapitated woman, and calmed me a little, telling myself it was quite understandable, that someone had removed her head to place it in a locket or some such. It did not sinister in the least. Then I turned back to the first photograph and then once more to the second. The women were not the same person, for the first woman was taller, much taller than this one, which I could see despite the absence of the second's head. She must have been shorter by half a foot.

I turned the page again. Once again my uncle and the second woman, and again she had no head. Then a third picture, this time with the woman holding a baby, a small baby by the look of it, swaddled and swamped in a long white shawl. Again the woman's face had been cruelly cut. I turned the next page and there was another picture, the same as the last, except that now a small child, a girl, had joined the others. She stood beside them, tight-lipped and staring fiercely out at the photographer, as though ready to fly at anyone who took a step closer, and the look of her shivered me quite and I thought how I would not like to meet such a child, especially not now, in the dead of night. And then something familiared about her, about those defiant eyes, and it pennydropped: this scary child was me.

I turned the page and there were no more pictures. I franticked back. The family group. If the girl was I, then the baby must be Giles, and the woman without a face his mother, my step-mother, the woman who had drowned. But if so, then why were they with my uncle? It did not make sense.

I stared at the man for some time. From the pose, from their easy standing against one another, it certained he was the woman's husband and the father of this family. But how could that be? How could my uncle also be my father? I peered at him closer. Perhaps, after all, he was not the man in the oil painting at the turn of the stairs. He was like, very like, but maybe not the same. And then it perfect-sensed me. It was not my uncle after all, but his brother, who family-resemblanced him. They were almost as alike as twins, it was so good a match. Having digested this, another thought came to me and I franticked back to the first page. The man was definitely the same one as in the other pictures, it doubtlessed that. And if so, then this other woman, this woman so happy and proud, must be my mother, who died before she could ever know her little girl.

I stared and stared and the more I looked, the more the woman's features blurred, for my eyes had misted over, and I had to close the book for fear of drippery. I shut my eyes and deep-breathed. I opened the drawer, put back the book and reluctanted it closed. I picked up my candle and matches and made for the door. I had half-outed it when I suddened a decision. I turned and quicked back to the desk, tugged open the drawer, took out the book, opened it at the first page and snatched my mother's picture. I replaced the album, closed the drawer and left the room, and upstairsed fast with my candle lighting the way. Taking the photograph was a rash act, for if I was caught with it I would be redhanded and could not pretend nightwalking. So I figured I might as well be sheeped as lambed and keep the candle to light my way too. But I uneventfulled my way back to my room and, after I know not how long spent gazing at my mother's picture, at some point fell asleep.

CHAPTER 9

Next day I took my precious photograph up to my tower, where I could gaze at it and talk to it without fear of discovery. And that was what I was doing a couple of days later when, purely by chance, I upglanced and familiared a lanky figure struggling through the snowdrifts along the drive. I overjoyed, for it had been a fortnight since I'd last seen him and I longed to tell him my great news.

But no sooner did I meet him at the front door than I hopedashed. He could but brief me a visit, he had not even time to skate, indeed had come to collect his skates, for he would need them in New York. 'They're shipping me back,' he announced. 'The doc says I'm better now and they're putting me back in school for the last week before the holidays.'

I fetched my coat and his skates and we awkwarded down the drive together. I packed a rueful snowball and threw it at him, catching him in the face, causing him to cry out, and I gladded to have hurt him. 'I am so lonely,' I said. 'You have no idea what it is like. And you rush off so blithely, you have not even time to hear my news and see what I have to show you.'

'I'll be back next year when the family come for the summer again. The time will soon pass. And Giles will be back for the Christmas holidays any day now.'

He reached into his pocket, pulled out a piece of paper and thrust it into my hand. Then, without another word, he turned and trudged off through the snow. I watched him until the last moment, when he made the turn into the main road and disappeared. Then I unfolded the paper he had given me and read:

> I cannot speak, I cannot talk
> For I am sent back to New York
> But all of me will not go hence
> My heart remains here with Florence

It was such a terrible poem that as I folded up the paper again I could not help but stifle a sob.

Theo had been right that at least I had the return of Giles to look forward to and I lonelied away the days, scarce able to read, my whole being an impatience of waiting. And at last the day came when John harnessed Bluebird to the trap and we set off to the railroad station, he and Mrs Grouse and I, to meet my darling brother. We stood by the track as the great iron dragon clanged and screeched to a halt beside us and belched out a cloud of steam that enveloped both it and us and then the fog of it began to clear and before us, on the platform, stood Giles, peering through the mist. We came together in a flingery of arms and a great huggery of kisses. My brother could not keep still but jumped up and down and danced from one foot to the other and gabbled an incomprehensible of nonsense. It was only when we were in the trap, leaving the town, in silence save for Bluebird's steady clip-clop, that I understood what Giles was so excited about.

'I'm not to go back, Flo, I'm not to go back!'

Mrs Grouse doubtfulled me one from behind his back. 'Well, no, not for a while, Master Giles. Not until after Christmas, anyway.'

He rounded on her. 'No, Mrs Grouse, you don't understand. Not ever!'

It was true. When we reached Blithe, Giles opened his trunk and produced a letter. Of course, as I was not able to read, Mrs Grouse did not show it to me, nor did she read it aloud, except for one or two phrases, 'a too timid and fragile disposition for the hurly-burly of a lively boys' school', 'not sufficiently mature or academically advanced', 'one or two incidents which, although trivial in themselves, give cause for concern, given his somewhat vulnerable nature', 'suggest tutoring at home would be more appropriate for the time being, possibly with the gentler nature of a female instructor'. I had no need to see the whole thing, but gisted it from this. It obvioused that Giles's simple nature had led to him being bullied. It was easier to remove him than deal with the bullies, and that was what the school had done.

Mrs Grouse all-concerned as she folded the letter and tucked it into her pocket. I slipped my hand into Giles's and gave it a squeeze. I near cheered aloud. It was such wonderful news. My little brother was safe and sound and I would not lonely any more. All would be as it had always been.

Mrs Grouse bit her lip. 'I shall have to write your uncle about this. He will have to engage someone, a governess, I guess.' She looked up and seeing us smiling at her, beamed one herself. 'But not now. I won't write yet. It will need a lot of careful thought, a letter to your uncle, for I have strict instructions not to bother him, and I have not time this side of Christmas. Let's get Christmas out of the way and I'll write him then.'

Well, as you may imagine, we had a fine old time. I had asked Mrs Grouse to buy skates for Giles as his present and on Christmas morning we took to the ice and had a jollity of falling over and pulling one another over and generally returning to a time when we were small. As I watched Giles so happy and carefree upon the lake, so sweet that he laughed even when he was hurt, I thought how I would never again let him into the world where he would be evilled and tortured, but would utmost me to keep him always here by my side at Blithe, where I could protect him from all the bad things beyond.

I thought to show him the photograph of my mother, but then I knew that it would not do, eagering to though I was, because then I would have to explain about his own mother. The shocking vandalism that had been carried out on her image must never come to his attention. What would anyway be the use of showing him pictures of his mother without her face? What would he feel but that the desecration of her was a cruel attack upon himself? So I tonguebit and own-counselled. I would let nothing spoil our new happiness.

But, of course, something did. Or rather someone. A month later Miss Whitaker arrived.

Now, the least said about Whitaker, the better, at least in her first incarnation. She was a silly young woman who stood and besotted before the portrait of my uncle on the stairs and twittered about how handsome he was and how when he interviewed her he had seemed quite taken with her and had all but given her the post of Giles's governess before she had spoke a word. I saw through this straightway; it obvioused our uncle, who had no time for us at all, could not be bothered to question the stupid woman, but wanted to not-more-ado the matter. It doubtlessed she was the only person he saw for the post, for anyone else must have been preferred.

Suffice it to say, I did not see the icy heart of this creature then or things might have worked out different. All I awared was that she neglected Giles, in whom she had less interest than in

brushing her hair and mirroring her looks; I inno-
cented her true nature and when she tragicked
upon the lake I near drowned myself in a lake of
my own tears, it so upset me. I thought her merely
foolish and I guilted I had so despised her almost
as much as I guilted that I did not save her, even
though it impossibled me to do so, and kept
thinking 'if only I had this' and 'if only I had that',
even though all these things would nothing have
availed. I reproached me, too, for the bad thoughts
that were in my head when she went to her watery
grave, for it was the very day after she unlibraried
me and I had spoke the words over and over in
my heart, 'I wish she would die, I wish she would
die', but never meant them, and when my wish
was granted I near died of grief myself that I could
no way call them back.

PART II

CHAPTER 10

We were history-repeating-itselfing in front of the house, the three of us, Mrs Grouse, Giles and I, lined up to welcome the new governess just as we'd been for poor Miss Whitaker what seemed a lifetime ago (as indeed it was, her lifetime). Because our uncle was travelling in Europe and it difficulted to contact him, Giles and I had halcyoned it for four whole months, the time from when Miss Whitaker misfortuned until now, the day of the arrival of her replacement. It had been like the old pre-Whitaker, pre-school days, only better, because having twice lost our former life of just Giles and me feralling throughout the house and grounds, first for one reason, him awaying to school, then the other, Whitaker, I now precioused it all the more. I had forgotten how busy life with Giles could be, how he could December a July day, making it fly past so that dusk always seemed to come early. And when the Van Hoosiers arrived for the summer vacation, Theo had joined us in our games nearly every day and the three of us had run wild as if there was no tomorrow. But of course there was and it was here. School would be starting and Theo was returning to New York. And Miss Whitaker's replacement would be here any moment.

All we had left of our golden summer was the time it took John to horse-and-trap the new woman from the railroad station in town, and that little was taken up by Mrs Grouse inspecting us for general cleanliness and tidiness. Giles was school-suited and I best-frocked, with a shining white pinafore thrown in for good measure. Satisfied that we were presentable, or at least as presentable as we were ever going to be, Mrs Grouse spent the last few minutes good-mannering us and attempting once again to teach me how to drop a curtsey (I had so half-hearted it with Miss Whitaker when she arrived as to make it unnoticeable). For some reason, although I was more than willing to courtesy the governess with a curtsey, my limbs reluctanted until finally Mrs Grouse exasperated. She regarded me critically and forlorned a sigh. 'Well, it will have to do, I guess. At least Miss Taylor will be able to see the intention is there, even if the execution is somewhat lacking.'

So there we stood, in front of the house where the horse and cart would pull up, a little guard of honour, the three of us on parade. At last you could hear Bluebird's hooves on the metalled main road and then the horse and trap hove into sight at the top of the drive and we all eagered to make out the person seated behind John.

Moments later she stood before us. She was much older than poor Miss Whitaker, her appearance hovering on the brink before middle age. Her skeletal figure was dressed all in black and I thought how strange that was, for Miss Whitaker had told me governesses always wore grey, but I noticed how well it matched the rooks which were even now circling above us, as though they too had turned out specially to welcome her. She was a handsome woman, with strong features, and dark eyes and black hair. As John handed her down from the trap her eye caught mine and there was something in her look, not familiarity exactly, but some kind of recognition of who I was, that all at once anxioused me, as though she could see clear through the me I pretended to be. This glance discomfited me and evidently her too, for no sooner did our eyes connect than she turned away and gifted Mrs Grouse a smile.

'You must be Miss Taylor,' unnecessaried Mrs Grouse; the new arrival unlikelied to be anyone else.

'And you must be Mrs Grouse,' returned Miss Taylor, with not quite enough mockery for Mrs Grouse to know it was there. She turned to Giles and me and – her eyes ready now and revealing nothing – larged us a smile. 'And you of course are Florence and little Giles.' I dropped her the curtsey when she cued my name, though it wasn't a great success. 'Pleased to meet you, ma'am,' I muttered, trying to sound as if I meant it, but it somehow

93

came out like Sunday-morninging the Lord's Prayer.

'Well, Giles,' said Miss Taylor, 'have you nothing to say to me?'

My brother nervoused and bit his lip.

'Come now, Giles,' urged Mrs Grouse, 'don't be rude, speak up.'

'Well,' said Giles, screwing his face up with genuine interest, 'would you rather be boiled in oil and eaten by cannibals, or bayoneted by a Confederate soldier and watch him pull your guts out before your very own eyes?'

Miss Taylor stared at him a moment, then eyebrowed Mrs Grouse. 'I fancy we have a little work to do here,' she light-hearted in a manner that somehow managed to critical too.

Inside she didn't look around much or say anything about the house; it was as though it weren't any different from what she'd expected. It wasn't exactly something you could have put your finger on, but it seemed as if she had no curiosity or interest in it, the way most people have in a new place. She turned to Mrs Grouse and brusqued, 'Now, if you would have your manservant take my bags up to my room, I would like to freshen up and lie down after my journey. What time is dinner served?'

'Well, we generally eat at six o'clock.'

'Very well, I shall be down then.' And so saying she followed John up the stairs. Behind her she left the scent of some flower, but try as it might,

my mind could not clutch what it was. Mrs Grouse
stood watching her until she disappeared, and
then weaked a smile at Giles and me. She wasn't
used to being spoken to like that. And nobody
had ever before used the word 'servant' about
John.

It was at supper, or rather before it even got
started, that the first difficulty asserted itself. Miss
Taylor appeared just before the appointed time
and Mrs Grouse showed her into the small breakfast room off the kitchen where we always ate.
Miss Taylor stopped in the doorway and stared at
the table.

'Is there something wrong?' anxioused Mrs
Grouse, forced into a squeezery between the
governess and the door to get into the room.

'Why, yes. There are four places.' She swung round
to face Mrs Grouse, who coloured. Miss Taylor
tigered her a smile. 'Is there perhaps another child
I don't know about? Come, Giles, how is your math?
You, Florence and me, how many does that make?'

'The fourth place is for me,' said Mrs Grouse.
'I've always eaten with the children. You see, it
was only we three for years and years until Master
Giles went off to school, and when Miss Whitaker
came she just joined in with the rest of us.'

'That's as maybe, but you see it's not appropriate.
You are the housekeeper and I am the governess.
We must maintain the proprieties. For the sake of
the children's education, you understand.'

Mrs Grouse bridled. She was not one to be

walked over. 'Miss Whitaker was quite happy with the arrangement.'

Miss Taylor raised an eyebrow. 'Ah yes, but I am not Miss Whitaker.'

Mrs Grouse left the room. The three of us sat down. A moment later a very red-faced Mary came in and began removing the crockery and cutlery from the fourth place. Miss Taylor smiled up at her. 'You may serve the food now,' she said.

That night I couldn't sleep. Outside, the wind howled like a wild beast stalking round the house looking for a way in. And within me, too, there was a howling, one that I couldn't block out by pillowing my ears. It feared me to sleep that I would dream again of poor Miss Whitaker and the day she died, but my waking anxiety was a shadowy thing I couldn't quite see or put a name to, and all the worse for that. In the end I decided to do what I often did at such times, to sneak down to the library and read there for a couple of hours until I should be tired enough for sleep, though there was an increased risk that I would be caught now that Miss Taylor was here, of course. Although the wind huffed and puffed without, within the house was quiet as the grave, save for the ticking of the clocks and the occasional creaking of the joists as Blithe settled itself down for the night. But then, if I were caught, all I had to do was pretend to be on one of my nightwalks. It much more difficulted to reach the library in this fashion than it had to sneak down to Mrs Grouse's sitting room. The library far-ended the house, whereas the housekeeper's room bottomed the stairs, being almost directly below mine. My main problem, as always, lay in not being able to have a candle to light my way, for that I never had on my night-walks. In the darkness I had to careful not to stumble against some piece of furniture, some random occasional table, for example, and so wake the whole household; also I must map in my mind where I was. It would be all too easy to wrong-turn and so end up wandering the whole night until dawn showed me the way.

Still, as this was not a nightwalk, I was able at least to blindman my arms and so feel ahead of me for any obstruction. In this manner, slowly I reached the long corridor. There was no light coming in through the windows there because the night was unmooned, a fact which unlikelied, but not impossibled, a nightwalk, although I wasn't concerned about that. It was when I penetrated a little further and was not far from the staircase that would take me down to the first floor that I heard something. I stood still and listened, all my senses alert. At first I took it for the wind blowing a tree branch against some part of the house, for it was exactly the sibilant sound of leaves brushing against something. But then I realised the noise was not fixed but in motion and that, moreover, it was coming toward me. A moment later I recog-nised it for what it was, the swishing of skirts against floorboards. Whoever it was was, like me, uncandled, but nevertheless able to move at a considerable pace, so that she – it could only be a woman, that noise – must soon be on top of me. It wondered me any normal woman could move so fast in this pitch black. What kind of creature could it be, other than a cat? She could be no more than ten feet away from me, and rushing toward me, so that we must at any moment collide. I instincted to flatten my back against the wall and, as luck would have it, found space behind me, a shallow alcove let into the wall. I pressed myself into it and held my breath. The woman was right on top of me now and, suddenly, the swishing stopped, and it was as if whatever creature this was had sensed my presence, or scented me, as a cat will a mouse or a dog a rat. All was quiet, even the wind seemed to have died down as though in league with this other nightwalker to enable her to better hear. I heard a small sound, a sharp intake of breath, followed by a lengthy pause as the breath was held while the breather listened, followed by a long, slow exhale. I sensed she was turning this way and that, sniffing the air like a predator seeking its prey. My lungs were near bursting from my own long breath-holdery but I dared not let it out, not only because of the noise but because my fellow nightwalker would then feel it on her face as I felt hers upon mine.

At last, just when I thought the game was up and I should have to breathe now or never would again, there abrupted a swish as if the woman had turned sharply and then the swishing resumed in the same direction as it had been headed in the first place, but now, thankfully, growing quieter and quieter until finally it whispered away. I gasped out my breath and sucked in air like a swimmer surfacing after a long dive. I had but one thought, namely to put as much distance as possible between me and this woman, if woman it were and not ghost, and so I felt my way along the corridor and down to the first floor and thence to the library. There I lit my candle and built my nest and curled up in it, although I was too disturbed now to have any hope of sleep and so fretted my way through the rest of the night until light began to finger its way around the edges of the drapes and I was able to fast my way back to my room.

I lay in my bed exhausted and troubled. Who had the woman been? The obvious answer was Miss Taylor, for I had encountered nothing like what had occurred last night ever before and it too much coincidented that she had just arrived in the house. As I recalled the incident now it seemed to me there had been something of her scent in the air, that scent I had noticed about her when we first met, and I all-at-onced what it was, the smell of lilies, which I remembered so well from Miss Whitaker's funeral, their ugly beauty upon her coffin. But perhaps all this was simply now my imagination, that love of embroidery I have, the makery-up of my mind. Then again, if what had passed me in the passage last night was not the new governess, what was it? Could it have been a ghost or some other supernatural thing? For what woman, especially a stranger so newly arrived, could so swift the house in the dark? And if it were not of this world, if it were one of the Blithe ghosts, what was it seeking here? Ghosts I knew were often troubled spirits unable to make their way in the next world because of the manner in which they had left this one. I understood all too well then who such a being might be. For had not poor Miss Whitaker tragicked a sudden and early death with no opportunity to make her peace with her maker? Might she not be tossing and turning beneath the earth in the local cemetery because of the fashion in which she passed away? I so frighted myself with these thoughts that I worried for Giles and had to rise from my bed, exhausted though I was, and sneak the corridor to his room, where I found him blissfully, ignorantly asleep. I stretched myself out beside him, folded one arm over him, and fell straightway into a deep and heavy slumber.

CHAPTER 11

In the morning, when Giles and I arrived downstairs for breakfast, the table in the breakfast room was once again set for three. As I sat down, I saw, through the open door to the kitchen, Mrs Grouse seated at the table there, over breakfast with Meg and Mary and John. When she heard me she wistfulled me such a look that I was near too guilty to eat. For all her faults, Mrs Grouse was at heart a kindly soul and also easy for a little finger twistery. Some part of me already knew Miss Taylor would not be at all like that.

Speaking of that devil (for such she was, as you shall see), at that moment she arrived. She good morninged Giles and me and walked to the kitchen door and good morninged all the servants and Mrs Grouse too. Meg and Mary flummoxed about, scraping their chairs to rise from their own meal and hithering and thithering to supply us with oatmeal and eggs and waffles and syrup. I wondered at this, for Miss Whitaker had been treated somewhat as a kind of servant, albeit on another level, along with Mrs Grouse. Miss Taylor occupied the same position and yet, already, by some force of will, had everyone behaving toward her as if she were royalty. How had that happened?

As we nervoused our food we did not speak and carefulled not to let a fork tinkle against a plate, and in the silent setting down of our milk glasses upon the table, for both Giles and I feared to draw attention to ourselves as if, by our very existence, we might somehow offend. It would have been a good time for pin droppery if you happened to have one you were having difficulty holding on to, because you would surely have heard it loud and clear. It was Miss Taylor who broke the silence. 'Giles,' she said, then took a swig of her coffee and set the cup back down, 'Giles, we do not eat in that manner.'

Giles gulped. 'What manner would that be, Miss Wh—, I mean, Miss Taylor?'

'Why, taking all those bites without recourse to chewing or swallowing. One swallow doesn't make a summer, after all.' She beamed at me and I weaked her one back; it wasn't a very good joke.

Giles got stuck into his waffle again, whereupon Miss Taylor's hand shot out like a whipcrack and knocked it from his hand. 'I told you,' she hissed. 'Not like that.'

Giles's eyes started to tear up. 'I – I'm sorry, miss, but I don't understand. Like what?'

'Why, like this!' She snatched up the waffle and began a frenetic biting of it, like some demented bird pecking at it, one bite after another, without pause to chew or swallow, until the whole thing had disappeared. There was a long silence while Giles and I open-mouthed her, for her cheeks were packed out like a hamster's, and then she finally gulped the whole lot down and said, 'That's how you don't eat, my boy. Now do you see?'

Giles's cheeks glistened and he brushed away the tears with the back of his hand. I had rarely seen Giles cry and yet this wiping of the tears was such an unconscious and therefore, I presumed, familiar action I wondered how much crying had occurred while he was away at school. We silenced our way through the rest of our breakfast.

After it was over, when we left the dining room, Giles and I turned toward the stairs to go up to the schoolroom and I heartsank at the thought of spending my day over some pointless needlepoint when I yearned to be in the library, but before we could begin to ascend, Miss Taylor called out to us. 'Not that way, children. Look, the sun is shining. I suggest that as it's such a lovely day and my first one here too, why don't you show me the grounds?'

Giles, suddenly unbound from Latin and history, as hateful to him as embroidery was to me, broke into a smile that instanted her forgiveness for the slapping of the waffle from his hand. And I, I too, thought that maybe this wasn't so bad, that perhaps this was a woman with a sharp temper, but nevertheless good-willed beneath. I little knew.

In the grounds, Giles and I ran before her, dodging

behind bushes and leaping out upon one another. At first we cautioned, for we had no idea what restrictions we might be under, but as she did nothing but smile fondly at our actions and nod approval of them at us, we bolded and all but became our old selves as though no new governess had come at all.

Miss Taylor surveyed the shrubbery where we hide-and-seeked most because it was so overgrown it offered the best concealment, and shook her head. 'It is all sadly neglected and unkempt,' she murmured. 'Why have they let it get into such a state?'

I paused in my play, not realising she was talking to herself, and answered, 'Well, you see, miss, there is only John to look after everything and he has all the jobs about the house, and the feeding and rubbing down and exercising of the horses, as well as all the grounds, and it is too much for one man, especially one who is not getting any younger.'

She shot me a look.

'I mean, that's what he says, miss, about not getting any younger.'

She distanced a smile and surveyed the shrubbery again and shook her head in a weary way. She walked on and we followed, tagging one another in her wake. Eventually we reached the lake.

'Ah, the lake,' she obvioused.

'Yes, miss,' I polited back.

She began to walk around it and we followed

her, past the old wooden jetty and the boathouse, and we were about halfway round when she stopped, and stared out over the water. It shivered me that she should pick out this particular spot. Just at that moment I happened to look down at the water's edge and saw the lilies were in bloom and all at once I remembered their scent on the unseen woman who had passed me in the night, their icy whiteness on Miss Whitaker's coffin. And I thought now, as I had on the day of the funeral, of Shakespeare's line, of how 'lilies that fester smell far worse than weeds', and it spinetingled me quite.

Before I had gotten hold of myself again I realised someone was speaking to me and then that it was Miss Taylor. 'Pray tell me, where did it happen?'

I knew what she meant immediately. This after all was the very place. But I couldn't say that. 'What do you mean?'

'The accident, of course. Weren't you in the boat with her? I understood that you were.' She stared at Giles, who wriggled around as though his collar was suddenly too tight.

'I – I –' he stammered.

'Not Giles,' I said. 'Just me. He was in the schoolroom.'

Giles nodded. 'Yes, I was in the schoolroom.'

'Miss Whitaker had set him some Latin sentences to write out. It was only she and I in the boat.'

'And what exactly happened?'

I turned my back on her. 'I would rather not talk about it, if you don't mind. I don't like to think about that day.'

She didn't reply, and when I decided it safed to face her again I found her not looking at me at all, even though I had felt sure of the weight of her eyes upon my back, but gazing out over the lake, at the very spot where the boat had been when poor Miss Whitaker was tragicked away.

Miss Taylor turned and shot me a knowing smile and then walked past me, back the way we had come, and at that moment a breeze got up and stirred the flimsy material of her blouse and there it was again, the death smell of lilies, but I did not know if it was from the actual lilies growing by the lake or the scent the new governess wore.

Afterward we wandered the grounds and rambled the woods and she would ask me questions about the place but not really listen to my replies, as if she already knew the answers or had no interest in them. It was only when we were in the woods and I explained that the footpath we were on led all the way to the Van Hoosier house, and that it was the way my special friend Theo took except when there was snow about, that her interest perked up and she questioned me some about him. I explained that with the summer nearly over he'd soon be going back to New York and school, at which she said, 'Ah,' as though that was all right, although then I added, 'But with a bit of luck he'll get ill again soon,' which made her face a puzzle, so that I laughed and explained how Theo always came here when he had asthma and so I kind of hoped he'd have another bout before too long.

'It'll start turning cold and damp in a few weeks,' I enthused, 'and that's really bad for his chest.'

It was past noon when we got back to the house, but she told us to wait outside and went into the house, where she asked Meg to set us up a picnic and Mary came and spread a big rug out on the lawn in back of the house and she and Meg brought our food out there, and afterward Miss Taylor sat with her back against a tree trunk and seemed to be dozing while Giles and I played tag, but whenever I looked at her it seemed she was watching us, her eyes strangely hooded, like a reptile's, so I had this feeling she had swallowed a snake or a lizard, and that it was trapped inside her and had taken over her body and now gazed greedily out through her eyes.

CHAPTER 12

That night I thought about pretending another nightwalk, but then I remembered that figure brushing against me in the dark, the scent of death lilies in my nostrils and most of all, Miss Taylor sitting watching us by the lake, with those hooded snake eyes, and I decided the risk of doing it a second night running was too great. Staying in bed, though, I samed as before: I restlessed and could not sleep. At one point, I'm sure it was long after midnight, I must have dropped off, for I began to have the dream, my nightwalking dream, but then it was interrupted and I awoke to find myself still in bed. I alarmed at the dream and anxioused about Giles. Who, after all, was this woman? How had she been employed? What did any of us know about her? She'd given nothing away.

The way our bedrooms were arranged, which had been carried out by Miss Whitaker, was that Giles and I each had our own room, betweened by the schoolroom, though that could only be reached from the corridor, not from our rooms. On the other side of Giles's room was where Miss

Whitaker, and now of course Miss Taylor, bedded, though in her case with not only a door onto the corridor, but also another into Giles's room.

I realised that some sound alonged the corridor from that direction, a queer sound, almost like singing, but not quite, as if the woman – for it was a female voice, no doubt about that – could not make up her mind whether she was singing or something else, keening perhaps, for someone who had died. Now, if you had asked me before what sort of noise a ghost would make, I could not have answered because I had never given any thought to them having a sound, other perhaps than a clanking of chains or outright wailing or something of that sort, but I recognised now that if the spirits of the dead did indeed walk and were able to give voice to their unquiet feelings, this is how they would sound.

I instincted to over-my-head the blankets to hide myself away from whatever it should be that walked the night and to block out the noise it made, but then, how could I think of myself when Giles all-aloned and – even if the thing meant no harm – would be in mortal terror at that awful sound? I slipped from my bed, felt for my robe and drew it about me, as much for comfort as anything else, as it was a warm late summer night and there was no one, no one living, at least, to see me in my nightgown. I barefooted it to the door, listened at it awhile but heard only the vague whistling of the night wind and comforted myself that it must have been that I had heard all along. Be that as it might, I still had to proceed, for I knew I could never rest until I had satisfied myself my precious little brother was safe. I slowed open the door, checking myself for a moment when it creaked, and then, there being no change, slipped into the passage outside.

I had scarce one footed in front of the other when I caught it again, that low keening noise, sounding like nothing so much as the wind itself, but as though it had somehow learned music and was howling in tune. I found myself almost enchanted by it, so it was a few seconds before I realised whence the noise came. It was worse than I had thought, for it, the thing making the noise, whatever it was, was in Giles's room. I pitter-pattered along the bare boards, unheeding the sound I made, indeed thinking by louding my approach to perhaps scare the thing off. But when I reached Giles's door I knew that my presence was unnoticed for the singing still persisted as before, low and eerie like a funeral dirge. I gingerlied my hand upon the handle of the door and turned it slowly, fearing once again to make any noise. I pushed open the door and what I saw near took my breath away. I shook my head in disbelief, trying to clear it of the vision before me, then somehow had the presence of mind to pinch my arm, as I have heard tell a body should to ascertain whether she dreams or not. The scene before me did not vanish, nor did I wake up.

It was almost exactly as in my dream of all those years; the same woman was bent over Giles's bed, singing softly, except now, instead of the black of my dream, she was dressed all in white, a lacy nightgown and robe. She reached out her hand toward my brother and stroked the hair from his eyes and then she said, 'Ah, my dear, I could eat you!'

The woman was Miss Taylor. I dizzied and reached out a hand to grab hold of the doorpost to save myself, but too late. The last thing I think I heard, although I felt it not, was the thud of my body hitting the floor.

I awoke in my own bed with sunlight streaming through the gaps in the drapes. So after all it had merely been my dream again. But had I simply had the dream, or had I nightwalked as well? There was something queer about all of this and for a minute or two my groggy head could not figure it out. I sensed something different from the way things always were, but what? Then it came to me. Always, I began with the dream, that was how it started. I saw the woman hovering over Giles's bed, and then I walked. But last night I had walked first, and then I had seen her. I had begun the dream, that's true, but then I'd awoken, risen from my bed and walked fully conscious. Or at least it seemed to me now that that was how it had been. Normally when I nightwalked I had afterward no recollection of having walked at all. Gradually, I began to remember more and more, the strange ghostly singing that had led me from my bed in the first place, which was not like anything in my dream.

There was a knock at the door, followed by Mary coming in bearing a tray. 'Good morning, Miss Florence, are you all right now? I'm glad to see you awake, you gave us quite a fright last night, but then your walks always do. Now sit yourself up, there's a good girl, miss, and I'll set your breakfast down in front of you.'

I obeyed her. 'S-so it happened then, I had one of my nightwalks?'

She set down the tray on my lap, opened the drapes so sunlight flooded the room, and busied herself pouring me some tea and lifting the little cosy from a boiled egg. 'Oh yes, miss, though you didn't get far. Only to Master Giles's room, where you fell down in a faint on the floor. Would you believe Master Giles slept right through the whole thing? Lucky for you Miss Taylor heard you hit the floor or you'd have been on it all night and you'd be waking up now stiff as a board.'

'Miss Taylor heard, you say? But wasn't she already there?'

Mary stared at me and chuckled. 'Good gracious no, miss. It was one o'clock in the morning. What would she be doing there at that time? No, she heard you and she was quite put out as she'd not been told of your night pursuits. She woke the whole household and in the end we had John pick

112

you up and put you back in your bed. Now, that's enough talking for you, miss.' (Though it was she who'd done all the talking.) 'You get your breakfast down you and then snuggle down and get back to sleep. You know you're always tired after one of your nocturnal adventures. Miss Taylor said you're not to think of coming down before noon.'

After Mary had gone I ate my breakfast, for I hungered terribly, but as for the snuggling down and going back to sleep, I could not, for my mind was a beehive of thoughts. On the one hand, all seemed simple enough. I had had the dream and one of my walks. In the past it had often happened that I had collapsed somewhere and been carried back to my bed unconscious. But what troubled me here was the order of things. Always the dream started with me in the same room as Giles, as we had been when we were small, not in the separate rooms we had now. And I had always sensed that the walking began after the dream, not before.

And it hadn't felt like the dream. For one thing there was the singing. There had never been any such sound in my dream before. In fact, there was normally no sound at all until the woman bending over the bed said, 'Ah, my dear, I could eat you!' Also I realised now that I was still wearing my robe; they had evidently picked me up in it and straighted me to bed, probably not wishing to wake me by trying to take it off me. But last night

113

I had gone to bed nightgowned only. I certained I had not got into bed with my robe on, and when I nightwalked I always did so in what I was wearing in bed; just as I never stopped for a candle, I never put on my robe. The whole thing did not make sense but that it had been exactly as I first remembered. I had begun the dream, but had then been woken by the noise the woman – Miss Taylor – had been making and, anxiousing for Giles, had risen, slipped on my robe, gone to my brother's room and had there been so shocked by the sight of my dream now come true before my very eyes that I fell into a faint.

If all that trued, and I certained of it, then so did something else, namely that Miss Taylor had lied when she said she heard me fall and had got up from her bed to investigate. And of course she would lie, because she wouldn't want anyone to know she had middle-of-the-nighted in Giles's room. And when they told her of my nightwalks, she had reckoned to fool me into accepting her version of the truth.

Even though I sat in bed, too terrified to move a muscle, indeed, unable to, like the man in 'The Premature Burial' by Edgar Allan Poe, my heart was racing as though I had just been running. What did it all signify? Only that the new governess meant to do us harm. Or if not us, perhaps, then certainly Giles.

In the course of a troubled morning more thoughts came to me. Principal among them was my dream. My dream had come true! Exactly as it had always happened, I had now seen it in real life. I realised at last why from the beginning there had been this feeling of familiarity with Miss Taylor, for since my early childhood I had seen her a score of times in the dream. It was not that she resembled Miss Whitaker after all, indeed she didn't look anything like her, although, strangely, when I thought about that, there was something of her that was the first governess, a look, an expression, a something in the falseness of her smile.

But how could it be that I had dreamed her before I'd even met her? How could that happen? I arounded and arounded this in my mind and could come up with no rational explanation. Eventually my frustration got the better of my fear and I got up and paced the room. And the more I paced and thought, the more there seemed but one explanation, although the thing itself impossibled, except by supernatural means, and it was this: that I had premonitioned what was to come. I had forewarned me in my dream of this woman who would one day enter our lives, and my dream had purpose: to save my brother from whatever evil she had planned. I made no mistake that it was evil, from the way she enthused those words, 'Ah, my dear, I could eat you!'; and from the way she looked at Giles I doubtlessed he was the object of her attentions, the reason for her being here. She meant to do him harm.

★　★　★

At noon I made my way down to the breakfast room, but Miss Taylor and Giles were not yet there so I casualled into Mrs Grouse's sitting room, where I found her alone.

'Ah, there you are, Miss Florence,' she beamed me. 'Feeling better, I hope?'

'Yes, thank you. Quite well.' I had thought to tell her all about the supposed nightwalk and how it had never been and of what I had seen, but, seeing her face now, dismissed the thought; she would never believe me. Oh, she would not think me to be untruthing, merely mistaken. For what person who suddenly awakes somewhere inappropriate for sleep, perhaps in a carriage or the theatre, does not insist he or she has not been asleep at all? I decided to try a different tack.

'Mrs Grouse,' I said, fiddling idly with the blotter upon her desk as though what I was saying had no significance at all for me, 'Mrs Grouse, what do you know of Miss Taylor?'

'Why, no more than you, miss, only what she has told us all.' She drew herself up huffily and sniffed. 'I am sure I receive no special confidences from her. She is the governess and I am merely the housekeeper, the person who keeps all this' – she spread her arms out to indicate everything around her, meaning Blithe and the household – 'running smoothly.'

'Did not my uncle write you about her and tell you of her history? Would he not have had references from her, you know, of her family and previous employment?'

'Your uncle had nothing to do with it.' Mrs Grouse gave another sniff, always a sign of disapproval in her. It was the nearest she ever came to criticising my uncle, although I sured she considered him neglectful of us children, ignoring us and wanting to be as little troubled over us as possible. 'He said he had only just had the inconvenience of interviewing Miss Whitaker and could not be bothered with having to interview one governess after another. Besides, he was abroad, so he appointed an educational agency to take care of the matter. The people there will have checked out her qualifications, you may be sure of that. You may depend she comes thoroughly recommended.'

I fiddled with the blotter some more, not knowing what to say. It seemed I had dead-ended. There was not another question I could think to ask. I looked up. Mrs Grouse was staring at me thoughtfully. 'But why do you ask, miss? Is there something that bothers you about Miss Taylor?' I didn't answer. 'Is it, well, is it perhaps, that you don't like her?'

This last was spoken in a wheedling tone and I knew that, nose outjointed as she was by the new governess, Mrs Grouse wished to make me her ally. I circumspected, sensing this was a dangerous course to follow. For if I shared confidences with Mrs Grouse I would be vulnerable should relations between her and Miss Taylor take a turn for the better. I had not forgotten how she had confederated Miss Whitaker. I shook my head. 'No, I like her fine. I was just curious, is all.'

We awkwarded a moment or so and then I heard the voices of Giles and Miss Taylor and excused myself and went off to eat.

Miss Taylor was all smiles. 'I hope you are recovered from your *adventure* last night?'

I stalled at that word and the way she emphasised it. In one way she was acknowledging what we both knew, that I had not nightwalked but had been conscious and had seen what she was up to, and yet, at the same time, her smiles, her dismissal by her jocular tone of what had happened as not the manifestation of some deeper disturbance but a light thing of no account, signalled that there was to be some kind of truce between us in which the truth was let slumber.

'Yes, miss. Thank you, miss.' I concentrated hard on cutting up my chop.

'And I slept through the whole thing,' said Giles gaily.

'Yes, my dear, you slept through the whole thing.' Miss Taylor reached out and ruffled his hair. I wanted to protest, for no one else had ever so familiared with either of us, but how could I when Giles fond-puppied a look up at her? I near expected him to lick her hand. Had he already forgotten the incident at breakfast yesterday? But then, that was Giles all over. I well imagined how he had responded to those bullies at his school, not with resentment, but

118

with gratitude when, during those intervals when they did not tease or hurt him, they showed him any little act of kindness, no matter how trivial or even unconscious on their part.

Miss Taylor turned to me. 'I have some understanding of sleepwalking. I believe it to be the result of an idle brain, an imagination that has not enough to occupy it and so looks for things that are not there.' This sounded like a warning of some kind. She paused and took a sip of her coffee, swilling it around her mouth awhile before swallowing and continuing. 'You have been let run wild with nothing to keep you busy. It has done you no favours. I am going to rectify that.'

'Miss Whitaker had me sewing, though I confess I wasn't much use at it.'

'Pah! Sewing.' She looked angry, but then softened somewhat. 'Well, of course there are things a young lady is expected to learn, but this is 1891. The days when ladies merely played the piano and painted a little – and badly – and embroidered useless things are on their way out. I am of the opinion that all women, and you're no different, need a little more stimulation than that.'

She wiped her lips with her napkin and stood up. She expectanted us a look and Giles and I understood that this meant breakfast was over. We leapt to our feet too and she straightway marched off with us in her wake.

'Where are we going?' I called out as we hurried after her.

She flung her reply over her shoulder, words I had thought never to hear. 'Why, where else? To the library!'

CHAPTER 13

That night there was no wind howlery; nevertheless I restlessed in bed, not so much because I anxioused, although there was some of that – how could there not be after I had seen Miss Taylor greeding over Giles in his bed? – but rather for the reason that I could not help turning over and over the events of the day. Such a lot had happened; leastways for a girl who had spent most of her life mausoleumed in Blithe. There was something good and something bad, and though the bad thing was a rook in a snowdrift, the good thing was very good – our visit to the library. Giles and I had trailed behind Miss Taylor as she marched her way there, too out-breathed by her purposeful pace to speak but wide-eyeing one another as we struggled to keep up. What did it mean, that she was taking us to the library? Did Mrs Grouse know? Did my uncle? I surely didn't think he could or he would not have allowed it after forbidding it for so many years.

Our new governess stopped outside the library and let us catch up. Then she flung open the door and stepped aside and with a gentle shove at our backs ushered us into the room. We stood in the doorway, open-mouthing what met us, disbelieving our own eyes. The drapes had been pulled back and sunlight rushed into the room, filling the vacuum where it had been denied for so long. The accumulation of dust from many years had been swept from the floor, and Mary was even now at the windows, rubbing away at the glass with her cloth. A couple of the windows were open, although that regretted me somewhat, because, for all the late-summer freshness breezing in, I lacked the usual comforting fusty smell of ancient books.

'All right, Mary, you can finish that later, if you please,' brusqued Miss Taylor, and Mary at once straightened up, picked up her bucket of water, said 'Yes, ma'am' in such a way as to seem to make a curtsey of it, although she didn't so much as bend a knee, and fled from the room.

As the door closed behind her Miss Taylor turned to us. Giles anxioused a few glances from her to me and I knew he was merely obviousing my own thought. What were we to do now? Should we butter-wouldn't-melt it and act as if we had never seen the place before? Or should we assume she had figured it out and therefore just come clean?

Giles, as usual, so nervoused he blundered the whole thing. 'Gee,' he said, gazing around in a very theatrical way, 'so many books. Who would have thought it?'

Miss Taylor watched him with just the twitch of

a smile, but not without fondness; it seemed as if she couldn't look at Giles without licking her lips, and I understood as I saw that smile that she knew all about my visits to the library. Still, I wasn't about to come right out and admit it, so I turned away and strolled slowly around the room, spine-fingering a book or two here, touching the side of a bookshelf there. In this roundabout fashion, I made my way to the back of the room, toward the chaise longue behind which I secreted my blankets and candle. As I rounded the chaise, casual as you please, or at least so I hoped, Miss Taylor's voice floated across the room to me, much as the motes of dust, stirred up by Mary no doubt, drifted in the beams of sunlight shafting through the long windows. 'It's not there, your little linen cupboard. I had it all taken away.'

I turned to brazen her. 'I'm sure I don't know what you mean.'

She was across the room like a whiplash; her hand shot out faster than a cobra strike and gripped my wrist. She put her face close to mine and I got it then, a powerful blast of dead lilies. 'Don't play the clever one with me, young lady. Don't you dare!'

She released me, and the hand that had held me went up to her head, tidying her hair, as though she regretted her action. I gulped. 'I – I'm sorry.' It was out before I could help it and I wished immediately I could call the words back. I would not kowtow to her. But as things turned out it was the right thing to say, for she seemed to soften, not with liking, but because I had done that which I hadn't wished to, namely acknowledged her as the one who held the upper hand.

She swivelled and sphinxed Giles. 'And you, I suppose you've never been here either?'

Giles squirmed. 'Well, I – that is, Miss Wh—, I mean, Miss Taylor, I –' He looked to me for rescue.

I went and stood beside him and slipped an arm around his waist.

Miss Taylor's face suddenly relaxed, and she smiled, not unkindly. 'They tell me you cannot read.'

I defied her a look back.

'Well, you and I both know that is nonsense, don't we?' Seeing me bewildering an answer, she went on, 'I know your uncle has forbidden it, but that shows how ridiculously out of touch the man is. You might as well order the sun not to shine, or the tide not to come in.'

'Like King Canute!' exclaimed Giles, attempting to please her.

She condescended him a smile. 'Yes, like King Canute.' She turned and paced about the room a little, this way and that. Giles and I rooted to the spot. Finally she came back to where she'd started, standing before us. She addressed herself to me. 'Now, listen carefully. This is what I propose. I cannot openly go against your uncle's restrictions, ludicrous though they may be. But I see no sense in you sneaking about the place after books as you have been doing these many years, I've no doubt.

Nor do I intend to waste my time trying to stop you. I suggest that when I bring Giles here with me to study, you accompany us with some piece of embroidery on which you are engaged. I suggest something quite large, bigger, say, than the average open book.'

I struggled to straight-face. I could not believe this. 'If we are interrupted by one of the servants, you need simply to make sure the embroidery conceals anything – any object, you understand, I do not name what that object may be – that happens to be in your lap. You may also –' she paused, 'suggest books that you think Giles might like to look at later in the schoolroom and I will take them there. Perhaps I should point out that neither Mrs Grouse nor the servants are able to distinguish which books are appropriate for a boy of Giles's age and which are beyond him. So they won't question the presence of any book there. Well, what do you say?'

'Yes, miss, thank you, miss.'

She turned toward the window and stared out at the sunlit lawns, as if lost in thought. I meantime gazed around the room. I had never before seen the books all at once and in all their glory. It near fainted me with overwhelming.

Miss Taylor turned abruptly. 'There is just one thing.' She looked at Giles. 'You, I know, have kept your stepsister's secret for many years and kept it well. You must continue to do so, for there will be difficulty for us all if you do not. And you, young lady, will have to learn not to be so interested in the affairs of others. You will not inquire about them, nor will you spy upon them by day *or by night*, or else I may begin to look what lies beneath your needlework. Is that clear.'

'Yes, miss. Quite clear, miss.'

So there we were that afternoon, in the schoolroom, I at one end and Miss Taylor the other with Giles, teaching him his French verbs, all of which I, of course, already knew, although I silenced in both that tongue and my native English, not wishing to do anything that might spoil a good thing. Opened on my lap I had the first volume of Wilkie Collins's *The Woman in White*. On the little occasional table at my elbow rested my embroidery, a cushion cover which I trusted would be like Penelope's, that is, never finished but always there to help me in my quest to read every book in the library. How easily does the mind selfish! How readily do we put aside the prospect of future disaster for present pleasure! I ostriched for the sake of books. I put my little brother's life at risk for my own guilty enjoyment, I do freely admit it now.

I halfwayed through the book's second chapter when there was a knock at the door. I slammed the book shut and hastened the embroidery frame over it just as the door opened and Mrs Grouse walked in. She caught sight of me first and a smile lit up her face like a match a bonfire. 'Why, Miss

Florence, what a pleasure it is to see you so busily engaged upon your needlework. This is just what your uncle would want.' She then evidently recalled what she had come for and the smile faded as she turned her attention to Miss Taylor, as though she recanted the compliment she had paid me because it complimented even more the teacher who had achieved the change. 'Begging your pardon, Miss Taylor' – she said this with a hint of mockery so understated and subtle that you could not openly have found offence in it without embarrassing yourself – 'but we have visitors.'

Miss Taylor looked up, her face somewhat troubled. I took it at the time that she was annoyed at being disturbed in the middle of her work, but later realised that might not be the reason. 'Oh, really?'

'Yes, Mrs Van Hoosier and young master Theo. Come to pay their respects before they shut up the house and return to New York.'

Our new governess seemed discomforted for a moment. She fumbled the book she was holding and it fell to the floor and she bent hastily and picked it up. By this time she was almost her usual brusque self. 'Well, now, children, we must not keep our visitors waiting, we must go and bid them farewell – or in my case hello and farewell – right away.' She stood waiting for us and Giles gratefulled his book closed and stood up too. I waited a moment until Mrs Grouse's back was turned so that I could slip *The Woman in White* from my lap and onto the side table, and then made to follow the housekeeper. Miss Taylor ushered us out the door after Mrs Grouse, and we had just stepped through it when there was a groan from behind us. We all three at once turned to see Miss Taylor leaning against the door jamb, one hand raised to her forehead as though in some kind of faint. 'Oh!' she said. 'Oh, dear!'

Mrs Grouse instanted and caught her. She turned to us and hissed, 'Go on, children. Run along to the drawing room and see Theo and his mama, while I attend to Miss Taylor.'

We did as we were told, glancing back to see Mrs Grouse supporting the governess with one arm around her waist and corridoring her in the direction of Miss Taylor's room. Giles and I looked at one another and shrugged, but then, excited at the prospect of seeing Theo, even if only for the maudlin business of saying goodbye for who knew how many weeks, at least until his next asthma attack, we made our way downstairs.

At first it was hard to see Theo, for Mrs Van Hoosier took up most of the drawing room. We sidled into it and good-afternoon-ma'amed her. Giles, who hadn't met her before, couldn't avert his eyes from her bosom but stared at it as you might a famous landmark, like one of the pyramids, maybe, or perhaps more aptly in this case, a pair of them.

Mrs Van Hoosier put her spectacles, which she

wore on a cord around her neck, up to her eyes and inspected my brother. 'What's the matter with you, boy?' she inquired. 'Never seen a lady before?'

'Please, ma'am,' burst out Giles, now completely overwhelmed by a combination of bust and bombast, 'please, ma'am, would you prefer to be pegged down on the ground naked and covered with honey and left to killer ants to sting to death, slowly of course, or put in a barrel and sent over Niagara Falls and smashed to pieces quickly on the rocks below? Which do you think?'

Mrs Van Hoosier shifted her head back near enough a foot to signal her surprise at this manner of greeting but then broke into a smile. She turned to me. 'Why, isn't that just like a boy, to be preoccupied with things like that? I well remember when Theo was that age' – at this she swivelled her head this way and that – 'Theo, where are you, boy?'

Theo emerged from behind her, smiling his eyes. 'Hello, Florence,' he said. 'Hello, Giles.'

Mrs Van Hoosier sank into an armchair. 'I explained to that housekeeper person that we can't stay long. We have to be on the six-fifteen to New York. We've just come to say goodbye and to take a look at your new governess.'

'I – I don't think that will be possible, ma'am,' I said. 'She was on the way here with us when she suddenly felt ill. Mrs Grouse is tending to her.'

'How unfortunate that she should pick just this moment to be ill. Nothing catching, I hope?'

She waved a dismissive hand at us. 'Anyhow, if you young people want to go outside for a bit I have no objection, but half an hour, Theo, no longer, and no running about; I don't want you to bring on another asthma attack just as we're going away. Oh, and Florence, be so kind as to have them send me some tea. I will have to take it alone if the wretched woman is unwell.'

Outside, Giles begged us to hide-and-seek and he ran off and hid, but Theo and I half-hearted the game. We went and sat on the stone wall behind the house so we could talk, although every five minutes or so Theo had to get up and find Giles just to keep him interested in the game and out of our hair.

'So, Theo,' I said, soon as we sat down the first time, 'you'll be going back to school.'

He looked down at his hands, those long bony fingers that seemed to have no flesh on them. He beetrooted. 'That's just what I came to tell you,' he said. He raised his head and pained me a look. 'I should have told you before. I've been putting it off because I couldn't bear to. I'm not return- ing to school, leastways not yet awhile. We're going away.'

My heart hopelessed a bird-in-a-cage flutter. 'Away? What do you mean, away?'

He was still interested in his hands, which were interlocking and freeing themselves as though he had no control over them, like two strange

130

beasts wrestling. 'We're all going to Europe, to make a tour of the place, mother, father and I. We sail on Friday week.'

'Europe,' I faltered. 'For how long?'

He looked up at me plaintively. 'Six months.'

I made no reply. Just then Giles called out so I said, 'You better go seek him. He's behind the rhododendron.'

'I know it!' said Theo and gangled away.

I tried to take in what he'd just told me. The news could not have come at a worse time. For what other ally but Theo did I have against Miss Taylor? Who else would there be to help me protect my little brother when she tried to steal him away, or worse, if such her intention was? Who else but Theo could I turn to in time of need?

Giles having been found and then told to get lost again, Theo returned and sadly plonked himself down next to me. He sat glumly contemplating the loveliness of the day. Eventually he spoke. 'Florence, I was wondering . . .'

'Yes?'

'Well, I was wondering, seeing as I'm going away and all and won't be seeing you for half a year, if I might, well, you know, kiss you, perhaps? If you're agreeable this time, that is.' He anxioused a look at me.

I stared back at him. He had those great ball eyes and a girl just couldn't romantic him. He was simply too lantern-jawed and long and bony everywhere. He would be a sharp and uncomfortable person to get into a hug with. Nevertheless, I was not inclined to send him away with a refusal.

'Does it involve a poem?' I said.

'Why, I'm afraid not. Darn it, would you believe I haven't got one today? I'm real sorry about that, truly I am.'

'Well in that case, the answer is yes.' And I inclined my head away from him, proffering him a cheek, but he ducked his head and snuck around the front and pinged me one on the lips.

'Why, Theo,' I said, 'that was a sneaky thing to do to a girl.'

'I know it,' he said, somehow both bashful and boastful at once. We sat and contemplated the day some more. It didn't seem right to feel so miserable on such a good day. A tear watermarked my cheek.

Theo reached up one of his oversized digits and gentled it away. 'Why, Florence, it ain't so bad. It's only six months. It'll soon pass.'

'No, Theo, you don't understand.' And then I blurted him the whole thing, about Miss Taylor and how I had found her walking the house in the night without any light, something no human being but only a ghost or some such could manage, and how she had stood over the sleeping body of my little brother licking her chops and how I feared that at the very least she meant to steal him away from me.

'Promise me, Theo, promise me that if you return from Europe and anything bad has happened to

Giles or me, you won't rest until that woman has been made to pay. Promise me that.'

'Why, Florence, don't talk so, it cannot be so bad as all that. I mean, ghosts! Come now, aren't you imagining a bit strong here?'

'Promise me, Theo.'

He shrugged and then, seeing how earnest I was, seized both my hands in his, making a little nest for them, and looked into my eyes and said, 'I promise, Florence, I surely do.'

CHAPTER 14

The Van Hoosier carriage couldn't have been more than halfway down the drive when Miss Taylor was behind us at the front door, from where Giles and I were watching Theo and his mother disappear from our lives for at least six months, and perhaps, I reflected bitterly, perhaps, for ever.

'Oh! Have I missed them?' she said in a way that made me think she ought to be in the same theatre company as Giles when he pretended never to have been in the library before, it so unconvinced. 'Well, perhaps they will call again soon.'

Giles's wave died in mid-air as the carriage finally turned into the main road and disappeared from view. 'Oh, no, miss, not for a long time. Not for months and months.'

'Oh, how so?'

She casualled as though uninterested, but did I detect just a hint of triumph on her lips, the ghost of a smile?

Giles looked up at her as she closed the door, drawing us back inside. 'Theo is going to Italy and France and all those sorts of places. It's the other side of the Atlantic, you know.'

'Really?'

'Oh, yes, miss, you see those places are in Europe on one side of the ocean and we're here in the Americas on the other side and it's three thousand miles between.'

Our new governess let go Giles's misunderstanding. 'What a shame,' she said, meaningfulling me a glance. 'We shall just be on our own, then, shan't we?' She turned and started off toward the stairs and we followed her.

'Are you feeling better, miss?' puppied Giles, catching her up.

'Oh, yes, thank you, Giles, I'm much better now.'

And the way she louded that last word, flinging it back over her shoulder, I knew it was meant just for me.

Afterward, lying in my bed, I thought of Theo and how I would miss him and how his enforced abandonment of me left me wholly in the clutches of this fiend, for such I believed her to be, and that led me on to considering the morning's visit and how Miss Taylor had suddened her faint. Her quick recovery obvioused it to me that she had not been ill at all, but had feigned the whole thing, and there could be but one reason for that, namely that she had wished to avoid meeting Theo and his mother.

I puzzled me awhile over that. Why would she wish to avoid them? What could it mean? I tossed and turned, which was beginning to be my normal bedtime routine these nights, ever since she came.

I eventuallied several thoughts. What was it about Mrs Van Hoosier that made Miss Taylor shun her presence? The answer had to be that Mrs Van Hoosier was not a servant but gentlefolk, and therefore not under the same constraints as Mrs Grouse and Meg and Mary and the like. She would be at liberty to make inquiries to Miss Taylor, to question her about her birth and family and where else she had governessed before. A woman like Mrs Van Hoosier struck me as someone who would worm the secrets out of a stone – though, of course, Miss Taylor couldn't know that. But no matter what Theo's mother's character might have been, it obvioused that our new governess wished to avoid any investigation into her past.

Other things struck me too. Mrs Grouse and Meg and John and Mary were simple folk who did not look beyond the obvious. Someone of a superior class likelied to be that much more observant. What if in future the police – my old friend the captain, perhaps – should be involved? What if Miss Taylor seized my brother and vanished, or – I hated even to think the word – murdered him and then disappeared? A woman of Mrs Van Hoosier's station would be more likely to provide an accurate description of her, to be able to place

136

her accent, identify her clothing and provide other clues that might lead to her eventual detection and arrest. All this Miss Taylor had sought to avoid.

If I were right (and what other motives could Miss Taylor have had for avoiding the Van Hoosiers?), then something else must also be true. That what Miss Taylor was planning was expected to be executed before the Van Hoosiers returned, or she would not have been so pleased by the news of their temporary absence. Whatever it was, it was going to happen in less than six months, it was going to happen soon.

Only one thing did not make sense to me. If her object was to harm Giles, then why not do it now? Unless, of course, she wanted to fake some accident to him so that she was not held responsible and was waiting only until she precised the means. If that were so then it might be at any time. Chance might sudden it and she advantage the opportunity on the spur of the moment. I would have to watch her like a hawk.

But if she meant simply to take Giles, and her seeming fondness for him seemed to suggest this, then why not simply act now? What on earth was she waiting for? At first this bothered me because it did not make sense, until I began to think about what might happen after she had taken him. Suppose it was for a ransom, then she would have to steal him away and keep him hidden and perhaps for some considerable time before the ransom was paid. To even take Giles away she would need his cooperation and before she could guarantee that she would have to gain his confidence, something not to be done in a minute. And if it were not for a ransom, if she intended to keep Giles for ever, then she would need first to gain a secure place in his affection.

That was it! That was surely it! She was merely waiting until Giles was sufficiently attached to her to swallow some story she would tell him about why he must steal away with her, and subsequently remain with her, and then she would be gone. It so obvioused I kicked myself that I hadn't seen it before. And she had libraried me to keep me out of her hair while she practised her wiles on Giles, every day inching him further and further away from me. Why, already he had forgotten the incident at breakfast, her sudden terrifying outburst of anger, and fawned about her as though she were the most wonderful person who ever lived. I resolved to speak to Giles about it, to warn him of the danger he was running.

Next day, though, it far from easied to find a time when I could alone him. Miss Taylor fetched him from his room first thing and took him down to breakfast with her and from then on they togethered almost always. It was only now when I sought to speak to him that I realised how much she had already sequestered him from me, how rarely the two of us ever aloned together any more. Eventually we were let out to play in the gardens as a relief from lessons for Giles, and to fresh-air us both. Even then, Miss Taylor accompanied us outside and seated herself on a recliner on the terrace, from which she watchful-eyed us. At one point, when I moved close to Giles and began to whisper that I needed to talk to him urgently, I looked up to see her already outseated and heading toward us. I instanted away from him and shouted out, 'Can't catch me, can't catch me!' and took off into the shrubbery, Giles tumbling after me.

As you will remember, the shrubbery was neglected and overgrown. I sped through it, following a path that Giles and I knew well but a newcomer would have difficulty in discerning, my brother at my heels. Somewhere I could hear Miss Taylor threshing around in the uncontrolled jungle, blundering after us. I hid myself in a rhododendron bush and listened for Giles's footsteps. As he passed by, I reached out an arm, grabbed him by the shoulder and pulled him into the bush, my other hand clamping his mouth before he had a chance to cry out. I silent-fingered him to keep quiet and we lay like that, hardly breathing, until we heard Miss Taylor go crashing past. When I was quite sure she was gone, I whispered to him, 'Giles, I have to talk to you.'

He squirmed under my grip. 'I don't want to talk. We can talk any time. This isn't the time for talking, it's the time for play.'

'You don't understand,' I hissed. 'We don't ever have time to talk like we used to. We're never alone

139

any more. I can't talk to you without Miss Taylor hearing everything. Have you not noticed?'

'Well, yes, I suppose. But then, what does it matter if she hears? Why should we care?'

'Because I am sure she is not who she pretends to be. I think she has come here for some evil purpose of her own. I am half convinced she isn't human, that she is some kind of being from the spirit world, some sort of ghost.'

Giles excited at this, although I could see he was more than a little afraid, too. 'A ghost? But why should she come here if she has no connection to Blithe? Whose ghost could she be?'

I bit my lip. 'I don't know, I haven't figured that bit out yet.'

He thought too, a process that never lasted very long with Giles, wrinkling his brow. After perhaps half a minute his face suddened alight. 'I know! It's obvious, Flo, truly it is. She must be the ghost of Miss Whitaker, come back to the place where she met her untimely death . . .'

'Oh Giles,' I despaired, 'don't be silly. She's nothing like Miss Whitaker. They don't even have the same kind of hair.'

'You can't know that, Flo. Who says ghosts keep the same appearance as they had when they were alive? Maybe they disguise themselves to fool the people who are still living.'

Giles was building this up into a great game, a big pretend that he no more believed than I did, which was not at all serving my purpose. 'Giles, you have to listen to me. You have to take care. You must not let her steal her way into your affections. She wants to gain your trust so that she can trick you into going away with her.'

Giles stared at me, amazed. Then he chuckled. 'But why should she do that, Flo?' He looked at me as though at a stranger. 'Flo, you do say the oddest things.' His brow wrinkled again. 'Anyway, if she is Miss Whitaker, why should she want to harm me, or you, come to that? Perhaps she just wants to haunt the last place she knew when she was alive. Perhaps she liked being our governess and wanted to do it again. Perhaps –'

At that moment there was a rustling nearby and before I could say another word to my brother, the leaves of the rhododendron parted, revealing in the gap Miss Taylor's face. 'Ah, there you are,' she said, falsing a smile, 'my two lost chickens. Come now, children, you've had long enough for play. It's time to get back to our books.'

CHAPTER 15

The following day we took a picnic down to the lake. Again Miss Taylor walked around it until she came to the spot on the shore nearest the place where Miss Whitaker had tragicked. On the way she hadn't spoken, but pulled ahead of us; it seemed she couldn't wait to get there, as if tugged by some invisible force. We spread out our food and Giles and I ate heartily, our appetites stimulated by the fresh air, but Miss Taylor so picked at her food that it made me watch her in a way I never had before at a meal and notice that she made no attempt to eat anything. The day was hot and after we had finished, Giles, who had brought his fishing pole, settled himself down on the bank to fish. Miss Taylor outed a book from her reticule and began to read.

I suddenly felt exhausted. The intensity of the sun, the oppressiveness of the air, its closeness presaging a thunderstorm, difficulted it to breathe. I tireded and headached; my limbs heavied and I lay back on the picnic rug and, no matter how I tried to fight it, could not prevent my eyelids from drooping and then shutting. I thought that if I closed them for only one minute, that's all, a single paltry minute, I should recover my senses.

I know not how long I slept. At some point I heard the drone of a bee, the whine of mosquitoes, the gentle disturbance of the lake's surface as a fish stirred, and then such a silence, such a stillness in the air, that something icy fingered my spine and tickled my neck. I instanted something was wrong and bolt-uprighted and eye-opened all in one movement.

I frighted naturally for Giles; he was my first thought, but there he was, down by the shore, sitting over his pole just as he had been before I slept, so that I did not know whether I had unconscioused for a mere minute or for an hour or even longer; there was no way of telling. I looked around for Miss Taylor but could see no sign of her. Her book lay open and face down upon the picnic rug, but she was nowhere to be found. Then something in that stillness, something in the icy tiptoe up and down my spine, said to me to look at the lake, not down at the shore where Giles sat, but at the lake itself, across to the middle, at the spot I never wanted to look at, the place where Miss Whitaker had misfortuned, and there I saw her, Miss Taylor, out upon the water, the most amazing sight, so that I thought I dreamed or hallucinated, except that it was all so real. She was on the surface of the water, but without any boat. She was standing there, in the very centre of the lake, the water lapping about her shoes, although, as I had good reason to know, there was nothing there to stand upon, no submerged jetty, no little island or sand bar. She was gazing down at the water with a melancholy expression, or rather something of that in her posture, for I could not discern her features from so great a distance, and then, sensing my eyes upon her, she looked up and stared right at me and, it felt, through me, so that I imagined her eyes glazed over, blank like those of a sculpted figure, and I couldn't tell whether or no she saw me at all. Suddenly she began to walk across the water, sending up little splashes every time her feet struck its surface, striding fast and purposefully toward me, so that I had but one thought, namely to run, to run away from this terrible vision.

'Giles!' I called, for always I feared me most for my little brother. 'Giles! Look up!' I rose from the ground and began to downhill to him. He showed no sign of having heard me nor of having seen the . . . the thing upon the water. 'Giles!' I essayed again. I was nearly upon him now and the figure on the water was driving for us still.

This time he heard me. He looked up at me, bemused. 'What, Flo? What's the matter? You shouldn't go shouting like that, you'll scare the fish.'

'Look out upon the lake,' I gasped, reaching him and putting my arm about his shoulders, to steer his gaze. 'Look!'

He looked instead at me, eyes alarmed, evidently

frightened by my agitation, but after a moment did as I injuncted and looked out across the water. I watched his face, awaiting his reaction. He screwed up his eyes, puzzled, then turned to me.

'What? What am I meant to be looking at, Flo?'

I shook him somewhat. 'Do you not see? Do you not see her?'

'Who, Flo? Who?'

'Why, Miss Taylor, of course, walking across the lake!'

He stared me hard. 'Don't be silly, Flo, how could she do that?'

I shook him roughly. 'You must see! You must!' I turned him to face the lake once more. 'Tell me you do not see the witch, striding over the water!'

Giles rubbed his eyes with one hand. 'I – I think I do. I – I, yes, Flo, I see her! I really can, you know.'

I followed his gaze across the water. There was no one there. She was gone.

I released my grip upon him. It obvioused he was lying to appease me and had seen nothing at all untoward. He looked up at me, muting an appeal. 'I think I saw her, Flo.'

I stared at him a moment, then looked once more at the lake, which nothinged still. I looked upon the empty water, watching the breeze wrinkle its surface, wondering me if it had happened at all. There was a rustle behind me, the sound of leaves in the wind, and, even before she spoke, I knew she was there.

'Well, children,' she said, 'I think that is enough relaxation for one day, don't you? We must be getting back to our work.' I turned and looked her in the eye. It was the snake's eye that gazed back at me, sure of itself, and I certained she knew I had seen her out on the lake, and what was worse, much worse, that she didn't in the least bit care.

CHAPTER 16

At supper that evening I resolved to observe Miss Taylor. I had thought of telling Mrs Grouse about the incident at the lake but in the end decided not to, for I knew I would not be believed. 'It's just one of your imaginings, my dear,' she would say. For was I not this strange child who nightwalked and before the days of governesses spent hours (as she thought, she didn't know, of course, about my librarying or towering) wandering the house and grounds alone, daydreaming? Moreover, if I told her and she disbelieved, she would doubtless mention the matter to Miss Taylor and all would be out in the open; our new governess would know that I had appealed for help – and failed – and that I was her enemy, if indeed she unsuspected that already. Instead I would own-counsel, speak only when spoken to during the meal, and so allow her free rein to talk and laugh with Giles while I kept watch upon her without obviousing to do so.

The meal confirmed what I had first awared of during our picnic. Miss Taylor cut up her meat, laid down her knife, took her fork in her right hand, speared a piece of meat, raised it to her lips, but then thought of some new thing to say to my brother and laid down the fork again. This happened time and again. At one point she complained that Giles had not eaten enough greens. There were none left in the serving bowl, so she took his fork from him, speared several pieces of broccoli on her own plate and transferred them to his. It was all neatly done, sleight-of-handed slick as a magician, and, were I not watching carefully, I would never have known. But I saw how clever she had been. The meat having been cut up and dispersed around her plate, it in no way seemed to amount to the single chop with which she had begun; some of the broccoli that had been on her plate having been switched to Giles's, there was no way of telling how much she herself had actually eaten. Except that I knew. I who had been hawking her all the while, I saw that not a morsel of food had passed her lips; in short, she had eaten nothing at all. And when I thought about it I was sure that, other than that mad moment when she seized the waffle from Giles and pecked at it like some demented bird of prey, I had never seen her consume a single thing.

When the meal was over I unobserved into the kitchen, where I found Meg emptying the plates into the bin John kept for the pigs. I hung around a little until she finally agreed to notice me and paused in her task. 'Well, missy, and what might you be wanting in here?'

'I don't want anything.'

She eyebrowed me. 'Oh, come now, missy, I know your ways, which are the ways of all children especially them that's growing fast. You came in here hoping for some titbit, now didn't you?'

I so morselled out a smile as to look like I was trying to hold it back and nodded. I figured that letting her think this was my motive would stop her fathoming the real one.

She looked toward the door to make sure neither Miss Taylor nor Mrs Grouse was around, then opened one of the cupboards, took down a tin, extracted a cookie and handed it to me. She went to recupboard the tin, but as she reached it up, second-thoughted, redelidded it, took out another cookie, which she betweened her teeth to free-hand herself to put lid back on tin and tin back in cupboard, then took the cookie in her hand and began to nibble it. Meg is not what you would call a slim-figured person.

'My, what a lot of food gets wasted,' I said, as she resumed her task of scraping the plates into the bin and instantly regretted that I too had joined the Giles school of theatricals, but Meg was intent on her task and seemed not to notice.

'Why yes,' she said, 'and it gets worse all the time.' She looked up at me. 'You really should eat your supper at your age, Miss Florence, then you'd have no need to come in here begging for cookies.'

'But I ate all my supper,' I said. 'And Giles ate

149

lots. Haven't you noticed the leftovers have increased since Miss Taylor came?'

Meg thought about this. 'Well, now you mention it, miss, perhaps I have.' She pondered a moment, then shrugged and scraped the last plate noisily into the bin, the knife rasping against the china, so setting my teeth on edge that it was all I could do not to cover my ears with my hands. 'Well, the lady must be eating like a bird then, Miss Florence, for if it's as you say and that plate was hers, then she has left the whole of her pork chop, no matter it's in pieces. She evidently gets her fun out of cutting rather than eating.'

I shivered at this. *Ah, my dear, I could eat you!* sprang into my mind, the memory of her greeding over Giles in the night, as if she could scarce resist the temptation to sink her teeth into his tender flesh.

'Still,' said Meg, 'some of these highfalutin' ladies, the sort of folk who give themselves airs and graces, are like that. Obsessed with their figures. I count myself fortunate that I'm not one of them. I have better things to do than go around all day worrying about my waist.'

As if to confirm this, having finished clearing the plates, she went back to the cupboard, took out the cookie tin again and we both had another go at it.

CHAPTER 17

What was I to do now? Here I was, a twelve-year-old girl, orphaned, all alone in the world save for a few fond but stupid servants and, of course, my little brother who, far from being able to aid me, rather required of me protection for himself. I thought to write my uncle but then thought more and realised I could hope for no succour from that quarter. For one thing, I was not supposed to be able to write at all and from what I knew of him a letter from me was likely to bring not assistance but some form of retribution for having so disobeyed him as to literate myself. That aside, he hated having any interference upon his time from us at Blithe and indeed had kicked up a mighty stink in his letters at the time of the Miss Whitaker incident, especially at the publicity of the inquest, when he found his business matters suddenly so pressing that he could not even spare the time to attend the proceedings.

It never but amazes me how clever is the human mind, or my own mind, at least. For here I had no sooner begun hopelessing my position and dismissing any idea of help from one quarter, my uncle, than my mind, continuing to work on its own, without any aid from me, leapt from that to the inquest and then to something else that possibly solutioned the whole thing. Captain Hadleigh. Here was someone who was intelligent and well educated but with nothing of that air of superiority grown-ups habituate toward children, a man who was prepared to listen to what you might want to tell him.

Now it trued that Captain Hadleigh was by no means my friend. I well remembered our first interview, when he sat behind his desk with his fingers steepled before his face, the tips pressed to his nose, and listened to what he referred to as my 'version of events'.

I told him what I had already told the police officer who had questioned me immediately after the 'event', pausing frequently in my story to dab my eyes with my handkerchief, for I could not unflow my tears, or to draw a deep breath before plunging in on the next bit. He listened uncommenting to the whole thing and then sat for a moment in silence, his eyes peering at me from above his fingertips as though I were a dead animal or a bird that he was about to dissect.

'Did Miss Whitaker fall straight into the water?' he asked at last.

'Why, yes, leastways, I think so.' I paused a moment, trying to remember. 'Yes, I'm pretty sure she did. Like I said, she got up to take the oars from me and the boat kind of rocked and then she stumbled and I think maybe tripped upon the hem of her gown and over the side she went.'

He sat and thought some more. 'And that's all that happened?'

'Yes sir. Far as I remember. Of course, it all happened so fast.'

'And you say she went straight into the water?'

'Yes sir, straight in.'

'She didn't hit her head on the side of the boat as she went over?'

It was again my turn to think. I screwed up my eyes trying to picture the scene, but got only a blank. But although I saw nothing I did seem to recall a sound. 'Well, sir, now that you mention it, there was kind of a loud crack before the splash. The sort of noise a human head might make against wood, if you know what I mean.'

'No, young lady, I don't know what you mean. I have never heard the sound of wood on bone.'

We sat there silencing another age or two. I twisted my sodden handkerchief around my fingers. He stared at me some more. I uncomfortabled but I wasn't about to be shaken by some young whippersnapper like him, so I carried on staring right back.

'She could have hit her head on the side, that could have been the sound. I don't rightly remember. Like I said, it was all so fast.'

'Very well,' he said. He peered at me over his fingertips again, as if they were a gunsight and

153

I the hapless prey. 'And when she went into the water, did you not try to rescue her?'

'Why yes, sir. Leastways, I wanted to but her falling seemed to make the boat skid away from her. I was much too far off to reach her.'

'Come now, it takes some time for a person to drown. You could have rowed the boat back to her.'

'Oh, no sir, I hadn't the oars. As I have told you, Miss Whitaker was in the act of taking them from me when she overbalanced and went into the water. The oars went with her, sir, and were as out of reach as she was.'

He said nothing.

'The oars were found floating on the lake afterward, if you remember, sir. I did try paddling the boat to her, with my hands, but I was then something like twenty feet away from her, the boat had so drifted. The problem I had was the boat was too wide for me to get both hands in the water at the same time, sir, and paddling with one hand at a time just made it turn a circle, sir.'

He nodded at this, recognising it as a detail that only one who had tried it could describe. 'Very well, that's all for now,' he said at last. 'You may go.'

I was near out the door when his voice caught up with me and hauled me back. 'Oh, just one more thing.'

I turned. 'Yes . . .?'

'That noise, that head on wood noise, or should

we say wood on head? Couldn't have been an oar, by any chance?'

I stared him out again, aware of the blood draining from my face.

'That I couldn't tell you, sir,' I said, 'for it's a sound I have never heard.'

We had two or three more encounters after that and it everytimed the same, he'd hark back to the business of the sound and again-and-again me about the oars, but I had nothing to add. I felt he unsatistfied the whole thing in some way but put that down to the man's nature and the exigencies of his job. In the coroner's court I would often catch him looking at me as if I were some puzzle he couldn't quite figure, an object of fascination to him. I had plenty more of the same questions from the coroner, who was a kindly old man who told me to sit down when I gave my evidence and made his clerk fetch me a glass of water. Answering him and upglancing and seeing Hadleigh with his eyes upon me then, I couldn't help wondering if this had been all along the point of his interrogations, to rehearse me for when the proper questions came. I felt that if we had met under different circumstances, a ball perhaps – not that I had ever been to one – or on a skating rink, Hadleigh would have liked me, but because of the Whitaker affair, I confounded him quite.

So why now did I think Hadleigh would want

to help me? Why would he believe my story, even suppose I could get to tell it to him? It was a big thing to expect a grown man, a sceptical police officer, to swallow – more like a fairy tale than a proper mystery – that my brother and I had a wicked governess who was plotting to steal him. Moreover, that she might not be human, but some manifestation from another world, even our previous and now dead governess, scorning the next world for this.

Then again, for all that he had not friendlied me, but continued to examine me with those sharp blue eyes of his, Hadleigh had proved my saviour in all the business of Miss Whitaker's brother, specially in that awful scene in the courtroom when the man stood up and shouted, such terrible things that I had to cover my ears, that it was all a whitewash, that his sister's death had not been properly investigated, that her employer was to blame for letting her on the lake with no one but a child to save her, that there was 'something fishy about the whole thing'.

I felt near to have died from the shame of it all, with everyone's eyes feeding off me, like crows on a dead rabbit, but it seemed no sooner had the disturbance started than Hadleigh and his men were upon Whitaker and had his arms pinned behind his back and him marched out of the room and not let back in again for the rest of the proceedings. It was the same when I outed the courthouse and again when I returned next day. Whitaker lay in wait for me but just as we pulled up in the horse and trap Hadleigh had his men upon him and him whisked away and no more harm done. I suspicion that he scared the man off too, for I never eyeclapped him again.

So the situation with Hadleigh was like a finely tuned balance, with not much required to tip it one way or the other. On the one hand, he had knight-in-armoured me, saving me pain and humiliation at the hands, or rather from the mouth, of Miss Whitaker's brother. On the other, he looked at me as if I were his special study, an enigma only he could solve, and his protection of me from Whitaker no more friendly to me than that. Still, I nothing-elsed, I had no other to turn to. It was Hadleigh or no one.

Deciding that I had nothing to lose by seeking his help was not the same, though, as getting it. The police station was in our little town. It was eleven miles away and I had no way of getting there except for carriaging by John. But I could not just say, 'I want to go into town,' it would not be allowed by Miss Taylor, indeed had never been allowed before she came, even by Mrs Grouse. Giles and I hardly evered to town, for all our needs were met at Blithe, where we were fed and watered and measured for our clothes and doctored when we illed.

This last made me think. We were doctored but we were not dentisted. Once, when I was smaller and had an aching baby tooth, they took me into town to see Mr Field, the dentist, an ornery old man who evidently hated his job and even more so when it involved children. Now it obvioused me that a dentist could not call upon me at Blithe, for he would need his equipment, the heavy leather and brass chair, which he could pump up with a pedal to bring you to his height, and the looming flamingo threat of his drill, which I had never seen in action but only heard from the waiting room, although that was enough to shiver me quite.

I thought at first of complaining of toothache so I would have to be taken to Mr Field, but that would not do, for if Miss Taylor came too, as well she might, then it would not opportunity me to visit the police station to see the captain. Only one solution suggested itself to me. Giles would have to be the one who visited the dentist. I would accompany him and, when the moment opportunitied, slip away to the police station.

It was a couple of days before I aloned with Giles, long enough to put my plan to him. His reaction was no more than I expected. 'The dentist? *Ask* to see the dentist? No fear! I'm not being drilled and filled or having my teeth pulled out one by one. The Spanish Inquisition used that as a form of torture, you know.'

'But, Giles, you wouldn't have to have your teeth drilled or taken out. There's nothing wrong with them.'

Giles inserted a finger into his mouth and ran it over his teeth, checking. 'How can you be so sure?

What if I get there and old Field spots something and gets that drill of his going?'

'But he won't, Giles, because there's nothing wrong with your teeth.'

'Oh, yes, so you're a dentist now, are you? And anyway, what if he says there's something wrong with one of 'em even though there's not, just so as he can pull it out and collect a fat fee?'

'He wouldn't do that. It's not allowed. It's . . . it's . . . it's against the Hippocratic oath.' I uncertained the truth of this, but when I explained what the oath was to Giles he didn't question it, which just goes to show that if pulling out good teeth isn't against it then it should be.

Giles suspicioned me one, weighing up his options. 'You're sure he won't do anything to me?'

'Cross my heart and hope to die.'

'Well, OK then, I'll do it. When do you want me to go down with the toothache?'

'Tomorrow morning would be good. We don't want to leave it too late in the day to get to Mr Field.'

At this point Miss Taylor reappeared and Giles started to back to his books.

'Oh, and Giles,' I hissed after him.

He turned and whispered, 'What?'

'Don't overact.'

Well, I might have saved my breath on this last because it seemed to serve only as an encouragement to Giles, who threw himself into the part of a boy with raging toothache with an enthusiasm so great as to put our whole scheme in jeopardy. We had three-quartersed through breakfast and I alarmed that he had either forgotten our plan or changed his mind, so I sharped him a kick on the shin under the table.

'Ow!' he let out. Miss Taylor suspicioned him one and then me, but said nothing and went back to buttering a piece of bread with the same intense concentration with which, I'd noticed, she'd been buttering it ever since we sat down to eat.

'Toothache!' I mouthed at Giles. 'Do it now.'

'No,' he mimed back and indicated the pile of bread and marmalade on his plate. 'I haven't finished yet.'

I exasperated a sigh, shot him a meaningful one and when he stubborned me one back, decided to take matters into my own hands, or rather feet, and sharped him another one on the shin.

'Ow!' It was much louder this time and could not be ignored.

'Why, Giles,' said Miss Taylor, finally giving her butter knife a rest and laying it and the bread down on her plate, 'I thought I heard you cry out before. Whatever is it?'

Giles glanced at me but I blacklooked him back and luckily he caught on that this was the perfect cue to go into his act. 'It's my teeth, Miss Taylor, one of 'em's aching real bad. Ow! Ow! Ow!'

She got up from her seat and straightwayed to him. Her arm snaked around him and she hugged him to her. 'There, there, don't take on so, my dear.'

'Oh, but Miss Taylor, it aches something terrible,' said Giles, breaking free of her with a push. He leapt from his chair. 'Oh, God in heaven, I think I'm going to die!' At this he collapsed to the floor and commenced wriggling around, as a mouse does if you skewer it with an ice pick, except that Giles held a hand to his forehead in that way you see actors do in photographs of them practising their craft.

Miss Taylor knelt beside him and stroked him to calm him. 'Hush Giles, hush, you must show me which one is hurting.'

Giles was prevailed upon to sit up while she cradled him with an arm. He stuck a finger in the side of his mouth. 'Gis gun heayah.'

Our new governess peered into his mouth. 'I don't see anything wrong with it.'

Giles shifted his finger. 'Or gaybe gis gun, I just gon't know. It's goo gard oo gell.'

Miss Taylor got him to his feet and helped him into the drawing room, where she laid him out on a couch, it apparenting now to all that the toothache had rendered Giles incapable of standing. The noise had attracted pretty much the whole household. Mrs Grouse fetched laudanum and I watched, heart overbeating, as she administered a few drops to my brother, fearing that if it drowsied him he might forget himself and give away our plan, which was so far working perfectly as John went out to ready the horse and trap.

It was at this point, though, that my scheme

began to awry. 'I'll be but a moment, Giles,' said Miss Taylor. 'I just need to fetch my coat and hat, and your own coat, of course.'

'But I —' I began. I had been hoping that Mrs Grouse and I would take Giles into town, as we had always done in the past. I knew that if Miss Taylor accompanied us it would be so much the harder for me to slip away. Now she seemed to be suggesting an even worse situation, namely that she would alone with Giles to town and I would be left behind. I panicked some, for what if I had just handed her the opportunity she wanted, to steal Giles away from Blithe and never return?

'But what?' Miss Taylor rounded on me, snaking me with her eyes.

'I thought I would go with Giles.'

'That will not be necessary,' she hissed before turning on her heel and leaving the room.

I deflated. The laudanum had not quieted Giles's pain at all; why would it, his agony being entirely theatrical? He now slid from the couch and lay on his back on the drawing-room rug kicking his legs and pounding his arms and screaming at the top of his voice. Mrs Grouse helplessed me a shrug. I knelt beside my brother and began to wipe his brow.

'Shh, Giles,' I alouded, then whispered under my breath, 'Giles, you must demand they take me.'

'Oh, sweet Jesus let me die! Please let me die!' he screamed, and then sottovoceed, 'Why, Flo, if Miss Taylor's coming, what need have I of you?'

I surreptioused a sharp tug of his hair, causing him to cry out with real feeling this time. 'You stupid little boy,' I hissed. 'That's the whole point, don't you remember, so I can get to town!'

'Oh yes,' he whispered back, as Miss Taylor returned to the room, coat on, hat in hand, with Mary in her wake holding Giles's coat. 'FLO!' he screamed. 'I WANT FLO!'

Miss Taylor pushed me aside and took my place. 'It's all right, Giles, I shall be with you. There's no need to trouble Florence.'

'It's no trouble,' I said starkly.

Giles began his kicking and pounding again. 'I WANT FLO! I WON'T GO WITHOUT HER! I CAN'T GO WITHOUT HER!'

'Oh, very well,' said Miss Taylor.

'I'll get my coat and hat,' I said and dashed from the room, still fearful they would set off without me if I did not haste.

CHAPTER 18

It was a strange party we made, carriaging toward town. John, usually unflappable, telling the horse to gee up and giving him some whip, which he never normally did; Miss Taylor, maintaining a frosty silence, still annoyed by my presence, or if not exactly by that, then that Giles's need seemed to be first and foremost for me, which of course would not at all suit her plans; and Giles moaning and whimpering like a stuck pig. Indeed, he so relentlessed the manifestations of his agony that I caught myself thinking that maybe, by some strange coincidence, he really did have toothache and that it was no longer an act. The boy had a talent for melodrama, I'll give him that, gasping out solemn imprecations that if he should die we should not mourn him but remember him only as he had been one summer's day in the garden a couple of years back, a day that seemed so very special to him, that the fact I had no recollection of it any more than any other day regretted me quite. Giles so tragicked I was quite sure he had forgot the whole thing was an act, which difficulted me in the extreme not to laugh out loud.

164

So spurred on by Giles's noises was John that we galloped into town. One thing struck me as strange as we entered the beginnings of Main Street, that Miss Taylor lowered her veil. Why should she do that, I wondered, why should she not want her face to be seen? Of course, Miss Whitaker had oftened to town, once-a-weeking there, and it wondered me now that if Miss Taylor were indeed one and the same as our first governess, whether there were not someone here whom she feared might recognise her, as though perhaps that hint of familiarity I had found in her expression might even more apparent to others. I had no time to dwell on the thought because we roared to a halt outside Mr Field's surgery and, after tying up the horse, John carried Giles inside, so maintaining the idea that the inflammation had spread from his mouth down to his legs and unabled him to walk.

Mr Field's timid little wife, who acted as his desk clerk and nurse, bade us be seated in his waiting room, a dingy collection of armchairs covered in scuffed red velvet (so as not to show the blood, Giles had insisted when we came before) that smelt of a potent brew of tobacco and chemicals and had the immediate effect of making me want to be sick. 'He won't keep you a moment,' said Mrs Field. 'He has a complicated piece of drill work to perform upon another patient and he is right in the middle of it.' In confirmation the whine of a drill started up, at which Giles immediately quieted, then began noising again but this time not in the tune of agony but in fear.

'You know what, Miss Taylor, my tooth seems much better,' he said, weaking her a smile. 'Yes, it truly is.'

'No, Giles.' She patronised him one back. 'It is but the laudanum starting to work. Once it wears off, you'll be in as much pain as before. Believe me, that tooth needs treatment.'

'No, miss, I promise you, I don't have toothache. I really don't. It was all a jape, honest it was. Wasn't it, Flo? Tell her, Flo, won't you?' He pleaded me a look, but at that moment there was a sudden groan from within the dentist's surgery which provided me the perfect opportunity to effect the next part of my plan. I put a hand to my brow and began to wobble. I sighed and made as if to fall from my chair.

'Oh, miss!' exclaimed Mrs Field, catching me, as she thought, just in time.

'What is it?' said Miss Taylor, who had all her attention on Giles and had not seen.

'The young lady, miss,' said Mrs Field. 'I thought she was going to faint.'

'It's so hot, so very hot in here,' I mumbled. It was easier to put in a more convincing perform-ance than my brother's, for truth to tell it was hot and the overpowering sickly smell made me genuinely feel ill.

'I fear she was alarmed by the sound of my husband's patient,' said Mrs Field. 'It takes some people that way, especially the young ladies.'

166

'I need air,' I said.

'But Flo,' screamed Giles, 'you can't go. Not now.' The stupid boy had forgotten that this was the very point of my being here.

'I'll see her outside, if you like, ma'am,' said Mrs Field, at which Miss Taylor, distracted totally by Giles, merely nodded. The dentist's wife helped me to my feet and outed me to the sidewalk. I relieved to see John sitting on the trap, having a smoke of his pipe and looking quite the other way. After a moment or two I assured Mrs Field that I was now well enough to stand unsupported and would be all right on my own.

'Well, if you're quite sure, miss . . .' she said. 'I do have things to do.' And she ducked back inside the dentist's office.

The moment the door closed behind her I gathered up my skirts and commenced to run. It fortuned that the police station was in the opposite direction from the way John was facing. Ours is a one-horse town, with only one main street, on which are situated all the shops and houses, saloons and hotels. I tore along the sidewalk and breathlessed a pause outside the police station to gather myself together. I knocked and opened the door and walked in. A young policeman at a desk half rose as I entered. Without giving him time to speak I said, 'I must see Captain Hadleigh immediately; is he in?'

'Why yes, miss, but I'll have to announce you first, for he's very busy just now and may not have

167

the time to see you on the hoof without an appointment.'

I could see that arguing would only use up more valuable time, so gave him my name. I ignored his offer of a seat, being too restlessed, and to-and-froed all the while he was gone into the inner office. There was a large clock on the wall and its hands seemed to be racing round, the pendulum tick-tocking like a demented woodpecker, pecking away at my remaining valuable time.

The desk clerk reappeared. 'The captain will see you now, miss.' He showed me into the room I remembered so well from all those months ago. Hadleigh upped from his chair behind his desk, walked around it and shook my hand. 'This is a surprise,' he said and indicated the customer chair on this side of the desk and then arounded it again and sat back down in his own.

He steepled his hands, like before. 'Well, and what brings you here? Have you something to tell me? Something perhaps that you forgot before?' There was a long silence. I could still hear the clock from the anteroom. Its ticking seemed now to have slowed to a melancholy heartbeat.

I swallowed. 'It's about our governess.'

'Miss Whitaker, yes of course, what else?'

'No, no, sir, you don't understand. Not Miss Whitaker. Our new governess. Miss Taylor.'

He raised an eyebrow. 'Nothing has happened to her, I trust? If so, I despair of your ever getting an education.'

I ignored his cynicism. 'No sir. It's nothing like that. It's that, well . . .' My voice died away like the sad cry of a whippoorwill fading on a winter wind. 'Yes?'

But what was I to tell him? Suddenly it all seemed so crazy. I sured he would think me mad. What exactly was there to say? That she had a snake inside her? That she could walk on water, that she had the night vision of a blind man? There was in truth nothing to tell.

'Well, sir, it is hard to explain. It's just that there is something about her that frightens me, that I feel sure she means to do us harm, or rather that she will do my brother harm, or if not that, then kidnap him and take him far away.'

He stared at me as he always had before, as if trying to make sense of me, to figure out what was really going on inside. 'Has she done anything harmful to you? Has she hurt Giles?'

'Well, no sir, not that you could say so.'

'Has she threatened to do anything? Has she said she will take him away?'

'No sir, but there is something so . . . so . . . well, peculiar about her. She has this strange look about her, sir, as if she has swallowed a snake and it sits inside her looking out through her eyes. And yet, at the same time, even though she looks nothing like her, I sometimes catch her face in an aspect that reminds me of, well, of Miss Whitaker, sir, and makes me think she is her.'

'But Miss Whitaker is dead, as you well know.'

I sniffed. I could feel tears brimming in my eyes. 'I – I meant . . .' My voice dropped to a whisper. 'I meant her ghost.'

I decided then and there not to tell him about the incident on the lake, that I had seen her walking on the water, for I knew it would serve only to incredible everything else. He stared at me the longest time. The clock outside wood-peckered slow as someone banging nails into a coffin.

'Have you seen a doctor lately?'

I sniffed and brushed away a tear. 'No sir, I –' I could say no more, for my throat choked up so.

He got up and walked around the desk and sat down on it. He reached out and put a hand upon my shoulder. 'Have you ever read *Macbeth*?'

I puzzled him a look.

'Do you remember the scene at the feast, when Banquo's ghost appears to Macbeth?'

'Yes.' It came out as but a squeak.

'There is no ghost. It is only Macbeth's guilt.'

I bit my lip and then pulled myself upright. 'I have nothing to feel guilty about, sir. Except perhaps that I was not able to save Miss Whitaker, that I could not think more clearly or act faster.'

'That is what I meant, of course.'

The clock outside began to strike the hour. It was noon. I returned to the present. 'Sir, I have to go. If she misses me it will suspicion her.'

'What?' he said.

I realised I had so upsetted I had forgot myself

and spoken in my private language. 'I mean, it will make her suspicious, sir.'

I got up and made for the door. He was round the desk and had his hand on the handle before I reached it. 'Listen, I can see you're upset,' he said. His face was close to mine. His breath smelt of milk and cinnamon, which somehow comforted me. 'I'll take a ride out your way when I have a spare moment and have a look at this woman. If there's anything wrong, you can depend on me to spot it.'

I wiped away an errant tear and gratefulled him a smile. 'Thank you, sir, thank you so very much.' And then the clock reached eleven and I was out the door – as though not to leave before the twelfth note would bring some awful doom down upon me – through the outer office, past the surprised clerk and flying down the street.

I reached the dentist's just in time. At the moment I breathlessed my way up, the door opened and Giles emerged supported on one side by Mrs Field and on the other by Miss Taylor. He was sobbing, his head bent and face buried in a handkerchief that I saw was covered in blood. When Miss Taylor looked up at me, I could not see her expression, because of the veil, and had no inkling of whether or no she had noticed my absence.

Seeing me, Mrs Field, in that deferential way she had, let go of Giles, relinquishing her hold on him to me. I put my arm around him. 'Why Giles,' I whispered, 'whatever happened?'

171

He bittered me a look. 'The dentist took out all my back teeth,' he spluttered, bubbles of red spittle on his lips. 'He couldn't find one that was rotten, so he took them all out just to be safe.'

CHAPTER 19

Have you ever thought what it will be like to be dead? Sometimes I think I know so well that I must have died already and be walking abroad, another ghost, to keep Miss Taylor née Whitaker company. Often at night I make my bed tight, and then slide in under the covers and lie with my arms stiff by my sides as though snug within my coffin. I hold my breath and imagine the blackness of my room is the dark inside my grave. I imagine the coffin lid over me. I think of my funeral, of everyone I know, Mrs Grouse, Giles, my uncle perhaps, although of course I can't really be said to know him, Meg and Mary and John, standing over this deep dark slot in the ground, watching me lowered into it, and then flinching at the sound of the first shovelful of earth hitting the coffin lid, and then that sound gradually dulling as my grave fills up and it is only soil upon soil. I think of the mourners returning home in the last of a winter day's sunlight and cosying themselves round the fire, where their talk gradually turns to other matters than me as the comfort of forgetting begins. I imagine that every so often one of them

173

will remember how earlier they left me alone in the cold earth, how the light is fading and I am starting my new existence there, in my new home, in my hole in the ground. And, my thoughts returning to my supposed dead body, I remember Poe's 'Premature Burial' and imagine myself alive still and screaming that I want to get out, clawing my nails away on the coffin lid, and that with six feet of earth above me no one can hear and I listen to myself screaming and screaming until first my voice dies to a whimper and then to nothing and I lie and listen to my own breathing until all the air is used up and then there is no more breathing or listening because there is no more anything at all.

I aloned much now, for Giles still angered with me for his lost molars, although they were only milk teeth and would have soon dropped out anyway. He protested because he was mainly able to eat only soup, which of course he suddened a great aversion to, and when he had finished blaming me, shunned me quite. I gratefulled him for the sacrifice of his teeth, for it had opportunitied me to see Hadleigh, however unsatisfactory that meeting was, and for not revealing my plan, although from the word or two I heard Miss Taylor let slip to Mrs Grouse I understood that when he was in the chair he had screamed 'all sorts of nonsense' about not having the toothache at all and how it had all been a big pretend.

'If that was pretending,' said Mrs Grouse, 'then

the child is a very great actor indeed.' Which made me suspect that, like me, the woman had never been inside a theatre in her life.

So, although I had alerted Hadleigh, it was at no little cost, for Giles now so avoided me that he clung instead to our new governess, regarding her as his protectress although, as I tried to point out, it had been she who had aquiesced with the dentist in the taking out of the teeth. I would often find Miss Taylor with Giles at her side, hugging him to her in a way I sured was unprofessional. Certainly Miss Whitaker never did such a thing and to me it didn't seem right. All this meant that while I had Hadleigh on my side, I had so thrown Giles into Miss Taylor's arms, quite literally, that I had unintentionally speeded the progress of what I believed to be her plan to make him her accomplice in his own kidnap.

It was the day after our trip to the dentist when another incident occurred that feared me quite. It was after luncheon and I had just left the dining room. I paused in the hall at a large mirror that hangs there and stood staring at myself. I saw a tall, gangling crane of a girl, all long limbs and extended neck, with a complexion so pale as to not look well. My eyes were marooned in great saucers of black, my white frock and apron hung from my bones as if I were getting smaller, not growing, and all in all I scarce recognised myself, I looked so ill. There suddened a movement behind me and Miss Taylor appeared in the mirror, staring over my shoulder at me.

'You are not pretty, Florence,' she informed me and inside me a white dove fluttered and dropped injured to the ground. 'But you have a certain attractiveness that is much more important than mere prettiness.' We both stood and stared at my reflection.

There was a rustle of silk and I turned and watched as, without another word, she awayed back down the hall. I turned again to the mirror and what I saw there made my blood run cold. For standing behind me, smiling in a triumphant, mocking way, stood Miss Taylor still. I instanted a glance over my shoulder but she herself was gone. I turned back to the mirror and there remained her reflection, laughing soundlessly, still gazing over the shoulders of my own image. I felt myself dizzy, I blinked, but when I opened my eyes, there she stayed. I shook my image free from her grasp and ran off down the corridor, after the real Miss Taylor, but could not help myself from stopping and looking back at the mirror one last time. And there it was still, her reflection trapped in the glass, head back, laughing a terrible, silent laugh.

That afternoon in the library I unconcentrated on 'The Tell-Tale Heart', wonderful tale though it is. I could think of nothing but that awful dupli-cate of my enemy, trapped like a lark in aspic, in that looking glass. I feared me to see it again, and yet at the same time I could not wait to return to it, to see if it were still there.

It so happened that as we were about to enter

the breakfast room for dinner Miss Taylor recollected something she had left in her room. She told Giles and me to sit down at table and not wait for her or else our food would go cold. This was something that had happened a time or two before and I had decided it was but an excuse to avoid eating, for in truth, although she had been here no more than a few of weeks, our new governess had grown thinner by the hour. Now it seemed to me the very skin of her face was stretched across the bones of her skull, and below her chin her neck, empty of flesh, hung down like a plucked chicken's.

Giles and I dutifulled toward the breakfast room, but the moment Miss Taylor rounded the turn of the stairs and out-of-sighted I grabbed Giles by the hand and tugged him down the hall the opposite way.

'Flo, what are you doing? This isn't the way to dinner! Let go, I'm hungry!'

'Shh, Giles, she'll hear you. Come, it will take but a moment. There's something I want you to look at.'

I near fainted when we got to the looking glass. I could not raise my eyes to look at it, so much I feared what I would see, but with Giles tugging at my hand, impatienting to be away, I slowly raised my eyes and saw my other self, that fearful lonely crane, before which stood my brother, puzzling his twin a half-hearted look and, dreadful thing, behind me, as I had always known it would be, stood the duplicate of my tormentor, looking straight out into my eyes, smugging me a smile.

Giles looked away and tried to pull me back toward the breakfast room. 'Come on, Flo, old girl, I'm starving!'

'Giles, wait, just a second, please!' I dragged him back and, seizing his shoulders from behind, steered him to look into the mirror. 'Look! Tell me, what do you see?'

He stood staring into the mirror, this time not at himself but up, at me, and surely at the woman behind me. A heartbeat or two. I held my breath.

'What do you see?' I said again.

'A witch,' he said at last. 'An ugly fright of a witch.'

I turned him around and hugged him to me, unable to contain my relief. 'So you see her too! You really see her!'

He pushed me away and askanced me a look. 'I see you, Flo, that's who I see. Only you aren't really ugly or a witch, I was just teasing when I said that.'

I shook his shoulders. 'No, Giles, don't go back on it now. Don't fearful and pretend you didn't see. You saw her, didn't you? Didn't you?'

Giles stranged me one. 'Who, Flo, who are you talking about?'

'Why, Giles, you know who. You know very well. Miss Taylor, of course.'

He turned again to the mirror and looked at it and then looked back at me. 'Don't be silly, Flo, how could I see her when she's upstairs? You saw her go yourself.'

I turned him back to the mirror once more and stabbed my finger at the accursed image which even now grinned out at me. 'She is upstairs, yes, but her double is here, trapped in the glass, do you not see? Do you not see!'

Giles stared at the glass a moment or two, and the expression on his image staring back at us was blank. I released my hold on him and he shrugged. 'I don't want to play this game, Flo,' he said. 'I don't like it. Anyway, we'll be late for supper.' And he turned and set off toward the breakfast room, leaving me looking after him, wondering if he had seen what I had seen, and if so, why he should pretend he had not.

I troubled all through supper. At first I doubtlessed that Giles had seen the hideous reflection trapped in the glass, for it had been as plain as his own face there. I asked myself why he should insist he had not and the only answer I could provide was that he was scared. He did not want to admit the truth. It even possibled that he genuinely believed he had seen nothing, because the alternative was too terrible to accept. But if that were indeed the case then why was Giles so calm now, laughing and joking with Miss Taylor throughout our meal, and only occasionally anxious when he happened to glance across the table at me? Miss Taylor herself ignored me, apart from one knowing look when she entered the room and sat herself down. But in that look I knew that everything of our delay in coming to supper was known to her, that she had seen us with the eyes of her image in the mirror, that she had left her reflection there as a spy. I felt as though I had swallowed a flock of restless starlings; I pushed my food about my plate, unable to manage more than a morsel or two.

'Why, Florence,' pleasanted Miss Taylor as if nothing had happened, when Mary came in to collect the plates after our main course, 'you've eaten next to nothing. Come now, surely you can manage a little bit more?'

'I'm sorry, miss, I don't think I can.'

'Come now, not even to please me?'

At this I gave a little laugh, for after what had happened earlier it was a rich piece of irony. But if she could keep up the pretence, then so could I.

'No, miss, not even for that.'

'Very well, then. Mary, you may remove the plates.'

After Mary had gone I bolded. I am not one to take things lying down and had made up my mind to fight this fiend, no matter what supernatural powers she might have at her beck and call. 'You know, miss, I have noticed that you yourself scarce eat enough to keep a sparrow alive.'

Her gaunt face flushed. 'I am not a growing girl who needs all her nourishment.'

'Yes, miss, but surely any body, any *living* body, has need of some sustenance.'

She picked up her napkin and wiped her mouth,

180

a gesture that pleased me, for I saw she was taken aback by my forthrightness and needed the pause to think. 'There are many reasons why a person may be off her food. Grief and loss – for example, you understand – can curtail the appetite.'

At this point Mary returned with our dessert, a rice pudding, and began to dole it out. When she reached Miss Taylor, our new governess motioned it away, defianting me one, as though to say she was what she was and would do what she wished and no questions of mine would ever alter that.

CHAPTER 20

That night I restlessed once more and at last false-nightwalked, and had the same result as before. I pushed open the door of Giles's room and found my brother fast asleep and Miss Taylor vulturing over him, almost licking her lips. So intent upon her prey was she, she neither looked up nor gave any other sense of awaring of my presence, so that in the end I left her to it and stole back to my own bed, where I shivered me until dawn, when I finally fell into something resembling sleep.

I nervoused all morning in the schoolroom, which, given what later occurred, made me think afterward that I had premonitioned the shock to come. Unable to settle, I asked permission of Miss Taylor to go down to the library to search out another book. Poe, whom I had always loved more perhaps than any other author save, of course, Shakespeare, was having a depressing effect upon my spirits. There was too much horror in my own life to want to read of more. I downstairsed and was in the main corridor of the western wing when I suddenly afraided for what I could see ahead.

There, in the dim light, for there are no windows in that section of the passage and you have only the light from either end, I saw I was approaching a looking glass, one that I had never taken notice of before, for why would I have glanced in it when the light was too poor to see much of my reflection? As soon as I awared of the mirror, my heart commenced to racing, its wings franticking in my breast, because even before I looked into it, I certained what I would see. I stopped and thought to turn back, but then curiosity, as it always will with me, overcame fear, so that I began to edge my way toward it. It was almost like a dream. For the first time I took in the pictures on the wall, dingy oils of long-dead ancestors of my uncle's, no doubt, doughty matrons and stern-looking men of business in tight collars and ties. And then I was at the looking glass, which was but a small one, a heavy gilt frame binding a square of dusty glass. And of course, when I lifted my head and looked directly into the glass, there she was, her face beside mine, not laughing exactly, but still triumphant. Her eyes sparkled as she looked out at me. She deep-breathed as though inhaling my scent and then her tongue snaked out and licked her lips, quick as a lizard's, so fast you might have missed seeing it at all.

Well, I turned and ran. I ran and ran, which even as my feet skittered along the polished wood floor I knew was stupid, for she could not follow, she was trapped in the glass, her own little world.

Eventually this knowledge drew me to a halt. I leaned against a door frame, panting, and gave myself a good talking to. The woman was in the mirror. She could not escape it, nor could she directly do me harm. Somehow I knew that, somehow I certained it was true.

Gingerly I turned and made my way back along the passage. As I approached the mirror I lowered my head to avoid any conjunction of our eyes, but as I passed it I could not resist; my gaze was updrawn and met hers and in her eyes that insouciant smile. I fasted past, and found myself in the library, where I flung myself into my favourite armchair, exhausted quite by the terror of it all. And then, as I slumped there, more lying than sitting, my eye caught it, upon the wall above the mantel. Why, of course, in my half-life in this room, I had looked at it a thousand times, possibly the biggest and grandest looking glass in the house, which I had at some level, I realised now, always loved, because it contained another room identical to this one that I so adored and, at a single glance, doubled the number of books in the room.

This time it so predictabled I did not recoil in fear. I rose from my chair and, as one who night-walks, dreamily made my way across the room and stood before her. 'You foul fiend, you witch,' I said through gritted teeth, although for some reason I uncertained whether I actually spoke the words out loud or whether they remained as bridewelled inside me as she was in the glass.

Alouded or not, she heard them or read them in my thoughts, for her lips broke into her by now familiar cruel smile and seemed, as I watched, to mouth back at me a word. 'Giles,' they pantomimed. 'Giles.'

I turned my back on her, for I would not give her the satisfaction of seeing my discomfort, the absolute terror that tiptoed my spine and threatened to burst my heart from my breast. I calmed over to the bookshelves and began taking out books as if selecting which to read, although in truth the faded gold leaf of the titles on their spines danced and jigged before my eyes and made as little sense as if the words had been writ in Sanskrit. I randomed three or four and left the room, because it too uncomfortabled me to sit and read them there.

It was only as I made my way back to the staircase, past her little outpost on the corridor wall, that the true state of things hit me. For now I thought upon it, I realised the terrible fact: there were mirrors all over Blithe. Almost every room contained at least one, they were in nearly every passage, and, without having to look, I understood that she had peopled them all, every last one, and that wherever I went in the house, she would be watching me, for she had sentinelled the whole place, and from now on there was nowhere indoors where I could go unobserved.

No one who has not known it (and who else but me can ever have known such a thing in this world?)

can imagine what it feels like to conduct your whole life under the eyes of another. As I walked the corridors I felt her watching me; when I ate my meals there was a mirror behind me, so that Miss Taylor, who opposited me, could view me from front and back; she really did have eyes on the back of my head. She was even in the small mirror on the dressing table in my room, which in protest I turned to the wall, for I would not give her the satisfaction of watching me undress or of making me undress in the dark.

I puzzled why Giles could not see these spies she had left behind in the mirrors; the only answer could be because she did not want him to. The last thing she would wish was to frighten him, for she needed to gain his confidence to seduce him away from Blithe. Moreover, my questioning him about them, which I did a time or two more before giving up, only served to reinforce the idea that my behaviour was strangeing, leading him further away from me and into her hungry arms. At the same time, she had made these mirror selves, these glass spies, visible to me because she wanted not only to watch me to detect any errant behaviour toward her, but for me to know I was watched and thereby deter any such rebellion at all.

I found myself walking stiffly; my shoulders would no longer relax, my arms and legs auto-matonned, my face masked itself, as my body adjusted to life under this new regime, for it knew not to betray my thoughts and feelings to her through a movement, a reckless expression or a careless gesture. I was now still more circum-scribed in my contact with Giles, because even when Miss Taylor was not present, it was hard to avoid one of her glass spies – one of her *spyglasses* – and being overlooked or overheard.

After a couple of days, though, it apparented to me there was one place free from our new governess's gaze. If, when I exited the library, I turned left, it took me back along the main corridor, with its glass halfway along, to the centre of the house, the hall, the drawing room, the kitchen. If, on the other hand I turned right, I would find myself at the foot of the west tower, my tower. There was no spyglass along the corridor here! Moreover, the staircase up to my tower room was devoid of pictures or mirrors, all presumably having been stripped off – for there were squares of lighter plaster where pictures had at some time hung – when the tower was abandoned from use. My tower room was unmirrored too, of course, for there was no wall space, it was windowed on every side. Not only that, but because Miss Taylor had never been there, even had there been a mirror, it would not have been peopled by her. Quite simply, all I had to do was walk to the western end of the corridor and sneak up to my tower and I was off her map.

The moment I realised this I once again made an excuse about needing a book from the library and made my way to the tower, climbed up the outside of the banisters and up the rickety stairs to my tower. I captain's-chaired me and spent a few moments wistfulling the drive, remembering the deliciousness of those carefree days, both pre-Whitaker and inter-governesses, when I had sat here reading, three-or-four-paging looks up the drive for any sign of Theo. What an age ago it all seemed now!

But when I had nostalgiaed for a bit, I realised something else. Although I had vanished from Miss Taylor's map, there were not many places I could have gone. The few rooms between the library and the tower might all contain mirrors, in which case my trail would end at the bottom of the tower. Now, the staircase looked unclimbable and so my disappearance might puzzle Miss Taylor for a while, but she was by no means stupid and it surely wouldn't take long for her to figure out that there was but one place I could be, and so my last refuge would be revealed.

It obvioused to me that the time might come when I would need such a bolthole, that at some point I might be pitched in a desperate struggle against this fiend who had come to haunt Blithe and would need a place to hide. It was important I should not fritter away the time in my tower now in mere princessing, but save it for the moment when this dire need might arise.

With this in mind, I was about to leave the tower when I caught a movement at the end of the drive which proved to be a man upon a horse trotting toward the house. Of course, it was too far to see the visitor's face but his stiff unyielding posture familiared to me from the early summer. Hadleigh! He had kept his promise, and sooner than I had expected. He had come! And how appropriately! As I princessed in the tower, he knight-in-shining-armoured up the drive.

I tore down the stairs and along the corridor, bolding so much at this sudden blessing that on the way I stuck out my tongue at the spyglass there as I passed, a temptation I had been careful to unyield to hitherto. I arrived in the hall just as the captain was being admitted by Mrs Grouse.

'Ah, Florence,' he said, removing his hat and coat and handing them to Mrs Grouse, who of course knew him from the Whitaker affair. He mischiefed an eyebrow at me. 'I happened to be passing this way and thought I would drop in on you all and see how you were getting along.' His thespian abilities were considerably greater than my brother's.

'We do very well, thank you, sir,' I said. 'We have a new governess.'

'Indeed? Then I should very much like to pay her my respects, if I'm not intruding.'

Mrs Grouse dispatched Mary up to the schoolroom to fetch Giles and Miss Taylor. They were some minutes coming down, which suspicioned me she did not want to see him, for she would have spotted him through the mirror in the hall the moment he entered the house.

'Are you working on any interesting cases, sir?'

189

I asked Hadleigh, by way of conversation while we waited.

'Oh, the usual, you know. Murder, arson, armed robbery and the like. Such things never stop in a bustling place like this.'

Mrs Grouse, deaf to irony, poor simple soul, tut-tutted. 'Is that so, sir? Well now, who'd have thought it? I always look upon this part of the country as somewhat quiet and lacking in excitement.'

Hadleigh meaningfulled a look at me. 'Ah well, so it is, on the surface, ma'am, but scratch away at it a little and you find that nothing is as it seems.'

Miss Taylor and Giles arrived. My brother hid behind her skirts, having found his several inter-rogations by Hadleigh in the past not to his liking. Our new governess shook hands with the captain and looked him straight in the eye, which I gladded at, for surely he must see the snake or whatever it was that lurked inside her.

It being that time of day, she suggested he take tea with us on the lawn and we duly went out and sat there while Meg summoned up bread and butter and cakes.

Hadleigh was, I realised, which I never had before, a clever interrogator, for he managed to ask her probing questions in the form of small talk. 'Have you been in this employment long?' he began, studying the distant lake as if the question were merely for politeness's sake and he could

190

not care less what her answer might be, indeed, might not even bother to listen to it at all.

'But five weeks,' she replied.

He laughed. 'You mistake me, ma'am.' He reached for another cake, all his attention seemingly on choosing the right one. 'I meant, have you been governessing for long?'

'For longer than I care to remember,' she said, tinkling him a polite laugh.

He was not to be so easily rebuffed. 'Come, come, it can't be so bad, not with charges as delightful as Florence and Giles. Where were you before that has so jaundiced you of your profession?'

'I did not mean that I do not like the work, Captain. I merely referred to not liking to think about the passage of years since I first began. No woman likes to be reminded that she is growing older.'

'And you know the children's uncle, I suppose?'

She took a sip of her tea. 'No, I'm afraid I've not yet had that pleasure. I was not employed directly by him.'

'An agency, then?'

She smiled and inclined her head slightly, as though acknowledging something shameful, which to persons of a certain class it might be, being hawked around like a labourer for hire.

Hadleigh smacked his hand down upon his knee. 'Then you're the very person who can help me!'

She doubtfulled him a look.

'You see, ma'am, I have these friends in much

the same station of life as the children's uncle who are in need of a governess and could use the name of a good agency.'

'Well, I don't know if the one I came through is any good,' she replied. It was like watching two fencers at work, except that Hadleigh showed less finesse when it came to the kill. He was more like a dog shaking a rat to death.

'Oh, but it found you, didn't it, ma'am?'

She tinkled him another one. 'That's exactly what I mean.'

'Ma'am, stop being so blamed modest.' He straighted her in the eye. 'Just tell me the name of the agency. My friend is a man of business, he'll soon determine whether or not they're any good.'

She stared at him a long minute and then told him the name of the place and its address in New York. Hadleigh thanked her with no more warmth than if she'd simply proffered him another slice of cake, but his lips pursed in a smug of satisfaction, as much, I suspected, that he had bested her as for the thing itself.

Shortly after, Hadleigh rose and said he had to go, and asked me to walk him and his horse to the end of the drive. Soon as we aloned I asked him, 'Well?'

'If you mean, do I think she resembles the late Miss Whitaker, I wouldn't rightly be able to say. I've only seen photographs of the other woman and most of them after they fished her out of the lake.'

I could not reply. My eyes teared at the thought of such a sight, although I had not been allowed to witness it. It was he who broke the silence. 'When I mentioned before about grief doing strange things to people . . .'

'It is more than that, sir.'

He stopped and we stared at one another. I tried to plead him a look, for I had not words to change his mind if he had decided I was imagining it all. He put his foot in the stirrup and lifted his other leg over his horse and climbed into the saddle. 'Listen, I have the name of the people your uncle used to employ her. I'll send to New York and have some inquiries made and see what we can find out, all right?'

'All right,' I said. And with that, he spurred his horse and left me standing at the top of the drive, thinking suddenly that here at least, outside, I was unmirrored and unobserved and that no one could see me cry.

CHAPTER 21

Although Hadleigh had not as yet actually done anything for me, that is, anything concrete in the way of assistance, the mere knowledge that he was, in this, at least, on my side, and that I unaloned in my quest to save Giles, was enough to buoy my spirits. Before his visit, my anxiety, the constant surveillance and the solitariness of my plight combined to freeze me quite, so that I completely helplessed and could not even think what little I might be able to do to stop the witch. Now, after I had lonelied and cried while I watched Hadleigh turn out of the drive onto the main road, I steely-resolved. I would do all I could in the way of battling this dead creature – for such I certained our new governess was, or how else could she waterwalk or inhabit mirrors? I more-or-lessed she was Whitaker returned, too, for what other revenant would want to haunt me so? Who else did I know who had died, and in my presence? Did she in some way blame me for not having saved her as I blamed myself? Was it enough to make her want to punish me by the harming or taking of the only thing

194

I truly loved, that best part of myself, my help-less little brother? It all possibled, at least.

But what to do? Ay, that was the question. I bethought me hour after hour with little to show for my effort. How does one battle a ghost? You cannot simply drown her, for Miss Whitaker had already shown that water cannot hold a dead spirit. And every day while I Hamleted about, paralysed by my fears, I had to watch Giles more and more insinuated into her arms. Ever since the trip to the dentist and the incident with the mirror he had waried of me, and any expression of hostility from me toward the governess drew an equal hostitlity from him to me; it was as if the boy did not want to be saved.

But do something I must. I thought of Hadleigh's inquiries in New York; he would not take what I said at face value, that was not the plodding police-man's way, which sees but one key to the unlocking of any case: information. This began to make sense to me, for to defeat your enemy, first you must know her. If I was to stop Miss Taylor, then I needed to find out exactly what she intentioned.

Well, having made this leap, there was but one place such evidence about our governess might be, and that was in her room. But how was I to access it? I could not simply pretend to be librarying when she and Giles were in the schoolroom and sneak in there, for I well knew from the Whitaker days, when I had had occasional peeps through the open door from Giles's room, that there was a large mirror on the governess's dressing table, so that the moment I entered I would be found out. Searching the room impossibled while the mirror remained.

I puzzled me over this for some days. I tried to devise plans to remove the mirror. I considered asking Giles to fake some accident and break it, which once he would have done, no questions asked, just for the sheer hell of it, but I knew such was no longer the case. Besides, with the mirror broken Miss Taylor would be unable to complete her toilette and so, logically, would simply replace it straightway. No, breaking it would not do.

At last I hit upon the possibility of covering it with a cloth. I could then about my business without her seeing anything of it at all. Except that even if I were unobserved by her from the mirror in the act of covering it, a thing impossible to contrive in itself, she would nevertheless know from the sudden obscuring of her view of the room that it had been covered and that there could be but one culprit, namely me.

Unless . . . unless it were done at night! If I entered her room when it was dark, and put a black cloth over the mirror I could then light a candle in order that I might see to search her belongings and when my task was completed, blow out the candle and remove the cover. The image in the mirror would observe only one thing, that the room appeared to be in darkness, and would not know the difference between night and my cloth.

No sooner had this idea proposed itself to me than its shortcoming apparented too. It would require Miss Taylor to absent the room at some point during the night and for long enough for me to do what I had to. With most people that would impossible, of course, for they rarely leave their rooms once they have retired for the night. But Miss Taylor did leave her room after dark! And so far as I knew, every night. For whenever I had restlessed or awoken in the night and gone to Giles's room, there she was, watching him, crooning to him in her monstrous way.

So sickened by these visits of hers to my brother's room had I been that on each occasion I had had no wish to linger; fear, too, of detection, of those cruel snake eyes looking up and seeing me, or her scenting me, drove me fast away. The upshot of my squeamishness and cowardice was I no-ideaed how long these visits of hers to Giles lasted. I suspected they were lengthy. Her demeanour on each occasion was of one almost in a trance; so enchanted did she seem to be with her prey, so distracted from all else, it unlikelied she would aware a slight noise perhaps from the adjoining room. Of course, if this assumption of mine was wrong, and her visits were brief, then I would have no time for a proper search of her bedroom and indeed would probably be caught in the act.

The sensible thing, I knew, would be to watch her for a night or two to learn the duration of her visits to my brother. But this I reluctanted; first, because every time I watched her there was the chance I would be caught, which would put her on her guard and scupper my plan of searching her room altogether; second, I had no way of knowing how many nights I had left before she put her plan into action. What if tonight I simply watched her and tomorrow she ran off with Giles?

There was nothing else for it. I had to move tonight. I carefulled preparations. The part of the corridor outside our bedrooms was unmirrored, so after Miss Taylor had sent me off to get ready for bed, while she was busy bedtime storying Giles, I practised walking the route from my bedroom to hers. I did it first with a candle and my eyes open, stepping it out so I would be able to do it by night. At one point when I put down my foot there was a groan from the floorboard beneath and I noted its position so that I would be able to step over it in the dark. I recorded the position of a couple of pictures on the walls so as not to accidentally brush against them in case it noised. Finally, when I had the route fixed in my mind, I blew out my candle and did it again with my eyes closed and then again twice more, until satisfied that I could navigate my way from my room to the governess's as silently as . . . well, as silently as a ghost.

Then I went to my room and outed from my closet an old black cloak. My plan was to over my white nightdress it to invisible me in the dark corridor, in case anyone should happen to be there, though who that someone might be other than Miss Taylor I could not have told you. Once in her room I would off the cloak, throw it over the mirror, light my candle and begin my search. When I had finished, I would extinguish the candle, retrieve the cloak, put it back on and slip from the room, the cloak thus having served two purposes. I thought this was a plan that would do very well and smugged myself for it as a way of concealing from myself my own gnawing doubts.

I slipped on the cloak and climbed into bed, pulling the covers right up over me so that if Miss Taylor happened to open the door to goodnight me (though really to spy on me) she would not see my strange attire. I had precautioned of blowing out my nightlight in case I fell asleep and disturbed the covers revealing my black cloak. If Miss Taylor looked in she would only have the light of her candle, which, from the doorway, I figured would be sufficient to show me seemingly asleep in bed but not to reveal the cloak.

Half an hour later I heard the door handle creak and sensed her standing in the doorway, watching me. I made my breathing heavy, letting out a faint half-whistle half-snore through my nostrils, and a second or two later heard the door gently close.

I need not have feared dropping off to sleep; nothing more unlikelied. I lay there, eyes barely above the top of the blankets, fearfulling the task ahead. I knew I had a long wait until my enemy made her way to my brother's room. From some-where in the house I could hear a clock tick-tocking and tinkling at the quarter hours. Outside, an owl hooted and I could not help thinking that this melancholy sound was heard in all the best ghost stories and that I myself was in one now.

At last I heard a faint noise from the other side of the schoolroom, which I guessed was Miss Taylor entering my brother's room, and I knew it was time to make my move. I threw off the bedcovers and slid my feet to the floor. I stood up and felt for my candle and matches, and slipped them into the pocket of my cloak. The room was utterly black, but I knew my route to the door. Once there I put my ear to it and held my breath, listening for any noise of movement without; once again the owl hooted, but all else quieted, save for the old house creaking and groaning as it was always wont to do as it settled itself down before retiring for the night. I turned the door handle, silently cursing the noise it made, normally unnoticed but now seeming like an alarm. I opened the door a crack and slipped through it, sliding my bare feet over the floor, which made me inappropriately think of Theo, now far away, an ocean between us, and of all the good times we had had on the ice. Skating the wooden floor like this risked splinters, but I judged that was better than any sound of a footstep, although I carefulled still to count each step. My heart upped into my mouth. I awared of a cold sweat upon my brow, my breath sounded to me so like thunder I wondered it didn't wake the whole house, and my spine shivered with ice. I so feared that I quite forgot to count and the first remembrance I had of the noisy floorboard was when I set my foot upon it and it let out a louder-than-before groan, as if reproaching me for having forgot. I stood still and held my breath, waiting, and sure enough I heard a sound. Only it wasn't in response to my clumsiness but seemed the faint whisper of a distant wind that then turned into the soft crooning I had heard that first time I caught our governess at her nocturnal tricks. So far, so good; she was with Giles. I alonged the corridor, past the door to my brother's room and reached Miss Taylor's. Of course, I could not quite certain where she was. I could not even sure that the connecting door between her room and my brother's was not wide open, except that my memory of it was that it had not been either time I had observed her before.

I felt the cold brass of her door handle in my hand and prayed it would not protest too noisily when turned. I gave it a slow and careful twist and there was no sound. I deep-breathed and pushed open the door.

The room was pitch-black save for a faint glow under the connecting door to my brother's room. In an eyeblink I had insided and gentled the door shut behind me; should she for any reason – not that I could think of one, but I wasn't taking any chances – venture out into the corridor from Giles's room, I did not want her spotting the door to her own room open. I was immediately problemed by something I had given no thought to in my planning: the room was so dark I could see nothing at all. Of course, this was exactly what I would have wished, for it meant that neither could the mirror see me. But I was not especially familiar with the room. I had not seen inside it since the Whitaker days. Although I could reasonably certain that Miss Taylor would have left the furniture – the bed, the dressing table, a closet, an armchair and a couple of smaller chairs, a nightstand and a small occasional table – where it had been during her predecessor's time, I had but a hazy memory of the position of everything then. I had had no chance to step out distances and I had no way of knowing if Miss Taylor had left anything else on the floor – her valises, say – where I might trip over them.

I had to hurry a plan. I knew the dressing table was along the wall opposite the door to my brother's room, so I set off sliding across the polished floor in that direction. Almost immediately I was obstacled as my foot caught in a rug which rucked and near tripped me up. It so suddened I all but cried out, which would have game-upped me quite, but luckily I stopped myself and managed to get a hold of myself before continuing. My heart was military-tattooing in my breast, so that I could scarce believe it inaudibled to the woman next door. I shook my foot free from the rug and placed it on top of it. Then I moved my other foot next to it and so proceeded into the room, limiting myself with small steps so as not to overstretch myself and unbalance me should I obstacle again. Each time I lifted a foot I felt cautiously in front for any obstruction, moved but half a foot and slowly carefulled it down again. In this snailing, ponderous manner I crossed the room. It seemed to take hours, although it was but one hoot of the owl, and he was at it, I knew, every minute or so. At one point I banged my knee upon something hard and guessed it to be the edge of the bed, which I knew was before the dressing table. I rounded it, made for the wall and, reaching out with my hands, felt . . . the wall – and nothing else. The dressing table was not where it should have been!

Of a sudden, the crooning next door stopped and it pin-dropped. I certained that at any second the connecting door would be thrown open and I would be redhanded, and fear froze me quite, the very blood in my veins turning to ice. Then I heard her voice, soft and low, 'Ah, my dear, I could eat you!' and I thought of that fiend but a few feet away, bending over my brother, saliva dripping from its lips. I had no time for such disgust, though. What should I do? If I made for the door into the corridor there was still a chance I could reach it before she opened the connecting door, although it was but a slim hope at best. No, I decided, it pointlessed even thinking of that. Whatever happened now, I would be caught, and so I might as well continue with my mission. At that moment, as if to reward me for my bravery, or recklessness

203

– call it what you will – the crooning resumed and I sickened at the thought of that thing stroking my helpless little brother's brow.

I told myself again that this was no time for such thoughts; I had to turn my brain to the problem in hand. She had had the dressing table moved. What I must think now was why and where to? I considered where it had been before and what might be wrong with such a place. How might the position of a dressing table important? I asked myself. And immediately responded, the light. It had been in the corner, the side of it against the wall opposite Giles's room, the back of it against the outside wall, the one which held the window, and so, well away from the light. It would make much more sense to place the table against the wall dividing the room from Giles's, but close to the window, so as to take advantage of the light when looking into the mirror. I gingerlied my way back across the room until I came to the wall, felt my way along it toward the window and there it was! I had Dupinned it right! But this was no moment to smug. I took the candle and matches from the pocket of my cloak and set them down on the dressing table, then whipped off the cloak. Such was my eagerness it struck something upon the table, some ornament or other, but quick as lightning my hand reflexed out and caught it before it could fall, a small glass bottle, her dead-lily perfume, no doubt.

Setting it down, I held my breath, thinking I should have alarmed her, but no, the crooning unabated. Carefulling, so as not to disturb any more of her knicknackery, I stretched out the cloak and draped it over the mirror. Then I picked up the matches and struck one, the sound of which noised to me like the rasp of John's great iron shovel when he is scraping ice off the walkways, so after I had lit the candle, I waited a few moments, until once more I certained all was well. There still being no interruption of the crooning, I began my search. On the table itself there was nothing other than the usual accoutrements of womanhood, brushes, and bottles of lotion and scent, a tablet of some sweet-smelling soap. The dressing table had two drawers, one on either side of the keyhole where you put your legs when you sat at it. I drew open the right-hand one first. It contained some dollar bills which, although I had no time to count them, seemed to me quite a hoard for a mere governess. Beside them I found a newspaper clipping that I recognised immediately, for it was a report I had myself seen before of the Whitaker inquest.

At this moment there was a cough from next door, which I recognised as Giles's, and I heard Miss Taylor's voice, 'Shh, shh, sleep, my love, there is nothing here to fear.'

I closed the drawer and opened its fellow on the other side. It contained nothing but some smelling salts and a bottle of liquid with a label bearing the name of a New York drug store. I had no time to study it now, for I anxioused I had already been too long in the room, so reluctanted it back into the drawer and closed it.

I went to the bed and felt beneath the pillows. I underedged the mattress all round with my hand, nothing. I looked under the bed and saw Miss Taylor's two valises. I crawled under and opened their clasps, but they were completely empty.

I opened her closet and searched the pockets of her coat and her dresses. Empty! I gentled the door of the closet shut and stood and looked around and puzzled me some more. There was nowhere else to look. The top of the nightstand was bare and its cupboard contained nothing more than a spare candle and an empty glass. Then my eye caught sight of the occasional table I remembered from the Whitaker days, over by the door to the corridor through which I'd come. I picked up my candle from the dressing table and tiptoed swiftly across to it. I slid open the table drawer but disappointed when I saw it contained nothing but a Bible. I was about to close the drawer when I noticed something, a corner of paper, poking from between the covers of the book. I set my candle down on the tabletop and took the book out. I opened it and two pieces of card fell out. I picked them up and saw straightway what they were. Tickets! My heart near stopped as I read the print on one. *SS Europa. New York to Le Havre. November 14th. First Class. Cabin Port D14. Sailing at midnight.* The other was exactly the same.

My brain overwhelmed. I dizzied and could

scarce keep upright, indeed had to stretch out a hand to the table to steady myself. November 14th. It was but two weeks hence. Two weeks! Two tickets! And that was when she meant to take Giles away. And not just away from Blithe but out of the country, to Europe, to France no less, where I would have no chance to follow her or ever get him back.

There suddened a difference in the room and it took me a split-second to realise what it was. Silence! The crooning next door had stopped dead. There was no time to lose. Keeping the tickets in one hand, with the other I hurried the Bible back into the drawer and closed it. Footsteps sounded from Giles's room, approaching the communicating door. It fortuned I was right next to the door into the corridor. In one movement I reached out and grabbed the handle, blew out my candle, opened the door, swifted through it and closed it behind me at the self-same moment as the door from my brother's room opened, the sound of the latter I hope masking that of the first. I stood in the corridor, leaning my back against the wall for support, near to fainting from what I had learned and from my narrow escape. I statued like that a whole minute or so, until the hoot of the owl broke my reverie, and it was then that I realised I had left behind my cloak.

CHAPTER 22

Next morning I lated after having so much awaked during the night, first in the long wait to begin my nocturnal adventure, then in the thing itself, and afterward when I tossed and turned, anxiousing about what I had taken, the steamship tickets, and about what I had left behind, my cloak. It obvioused Miss Taylor would by now have found the cloak, for she could not have brushed her hair without doing so, but I guessed she had not yet missed the tickets, for if so I certained she would have broken in upon me long before now. Even so, I also awared that when she thought about me having been in her room it would not be so very long before she thought to check the tickets. I therefore dressed quickly, took the tickets from beneath my pillow, where I had slept upon them for safety's sake, slipped them into the pocket of my frock and made my way, not to breakfast, but to the west wing. In the corridor I stopped at the mirror just before the library and looked into it, ignoring as best I could Miss Taylor's livid face angering out at me, and made to adjust my hair, using both hands so that she should see they were empty. Then I proceeded past the library, off our governess's map and upstairsed it to my tower. I felt underneath the seat of the captain's chair and, with my penknife, which I had brought with me for this purpose, slit open the leather. I slipped the tickets into the slit, pushing them into the stuffing and making sure they could not fall out.

Then I downstairsed to the library, where I picked up the book I had been reading there the day before, *Tales of Mystery and Imagination*, for I was back on Poe, even though he melancholied and frightened me, because somehow these days he suited my mood. Leaving the library, I made sure to slow past the mirror outside holding the book open before me and pretending to read from it. Seeing the book where before I had had none would, I hope, convince the watching fiend that I had merely libraried and not anywhere-else, so that she would not be driven to explore the tower.

As soon as I out-of-sighted the mirror, I hurried to the breakfast room. When I entered, Miss Taylor and Giles were already there, although from outside you might have thought not, for there was none of the usual chit-chat from Giles and none of Miss Taylor's simpering replies. The sight which greeted me when I opened the door near made my knees give way. For opposite Miss Taylor, on the back of the chair that was always mine, was my cloak, stretched out like a big black crow, its wings resting on the neighbouring chairs on either side. It near breath stopped me, I was so shocked.

Giles looked up at me and opened his mouth, about to say something, but before he could speak, Miss Taylor laid a restraining hand upon his and he closed his lips and silenced. She challenged me a look, her snake eyes piercing mine. I lowered my eyes and meeked my way to my place, heart acrobatting about in its shell. Reaching my chair, I took hold of that impious bird of ill omen, my cloak, and lifted it off the backs of the chairs and then folded it and, sitting myself down in my seat, placed it on one of those next to me.

I looked up and defianted one straight at Miss Taylor, all but catching her unawares. She was quick to recover. 'You left it in my room,' she said, triumphing as one does who has caught someone out in a lie or some other despicable act.

I merely nodded. 'Thank you,' I said and picked up my knife and fork.

She continued to stare at me for the rest of the meal, the food being nothing to her, who ate not even enough to notice. I didn't hunger at all, my stomach so churned with apprehension for what might be to come, but I determined to give her no satisfaction, so munched my way through everything in front of me, although every mouthful only served to sicken me more.

It was not long before Giles commenced to restlessing, he and the governess having, of course, been breakfasting for some considerable time before my arrival, and eventually he said, 'Please, miss, may we go now? I'm sure I've eaten enough to last me all day and you never eat so much as would keep a bird alive anyway . . .'

She unfastened her stare from me and looked at him as though she'd quite forgot he was there. 'Of course, my dear,' she murmured, and pushed back her chair. Giles stood up and rushed to the door and she followed him, in that stately silent way she had of moving, gliding across the floor as though walking on air. Only when she was halfway out the door did she pause, turn back and throw me a threatening one. 'I will speak to you later, girl,' she hissed, and for once it was not the manner in which she spoke, but the insolence of that word, 'girl', to one who, after all, she was employed to serve, that dreaded me quite, for it seemed to signal that we had moved beyond the boundaries of social propriety, that the gloves were off and that she was ready for an almighty battle.

As soon as their footsteps faded, I rushed me to the WC and regurgitated all I had just consumed, though even after my stomach was quite, quite empty, so that I was only retching air, I could not stop my convulsions. It was as if my body desired to purge itself of everything that had polluted it for so long, all my guilt, all my fear of losing Giles, who was the one person I had to cling to in this cold hard world, all the poison the Whitaker witch both living and dead had put into my heart. I weaked and scarce abled to walk and began to cry, for I did not see how I could ever manage to go on.

Afterward I near cowarded and fled outside, where I should be safe from the dozens of pairs of eyes with which she followed my every movement and monitored my every expression and gesture from every wall of the house, so that it seemed as if at all times she could at will peer into my very soul, a thought that shuddered me quite.

But, as I neared the front door, meaning to make my exit, I caught sight of her in the mirror there, the one where I had first seen her, and the smirking arrogance of the simulacrum she had left there, which seemed to mock my very helplessness, altered my course. I had not let Whitaker drive me to despair when she'd been alive, when she did that dreadful thing, the thing that would hurt me most after losing Giles, that is, deprived me of books, and I would not crumple and give in to her now. If she wanted a fight she should have one, no matter what dark powers she had at her beck and call. I would wasp her picnic. I would spoil her plan. I would not give in. I am not made that way.

I turned and made my way back along the hall and upstairsed to the schoolroom, where I found Giles sitting beside her at her desk. 'Seven sevens, come on, Giles,' she said, not unkindly, 'it's not that hard.'

'Thirty-nine?' hopefulled Giles. Math was not

his strongest subject; then again, it would be hard to say what was.

She shook her head.

'Well, then, thirty-seven? Or thirty-five. It's some number or other, I know.'

She began to chuckle, and then you could see her face change when it was half the way to a smile, and turn serious, and she looked up, stared a long moment at me, then abruptly stood, so suddenly that her chair tipped backward and fell over. She made no move to right it again. Giles looked up in surprise. 'What's the matter, miss? I don't mean to be so slow-witted. I am trying, honest I am.'

'It's not that, Giles,' she muttered, unconvincing him a smile. Before he could say any more she glared me a look, then turned and rushed from the room.

Giles puzzled me one. 'What's going on, Flo? What was all that business with your cloak at breakfast? What have you been up to now? I sometimes think –'

He got no further, for at that moment the door crashed open and the governess burst into the room and ran straight at us, eyes wild, hair unkempt and flowing as though she'd pulled all the pins out in a rage, her mouth contorted in a mad grimace. She was on me in a trice and had hold of my hair. I thought she would scratch out my eyes with her nails, for she was waving them like talons in my face.

'Where are they?' she screamed. 'What have you done with them, you little bitch?'

I could not help screaming too, for my hair hurt so. I tugged my head away and felt my scalp tear and saw I was free, while she stood there with a clump of my hair in her hand. We faced one another, two beasts in a mortal combat, she one side of the desk, I the other. She made to go one way around it; I retreated the other. I sought then to escape back the way I had come; she blocked me off. It was like some wild dance of death as we each parried and thrust, but even as we were locked in this duel I knew that if nothing changed it was I who must be the loser, for as things were, I was trapped behind the desk and must eventually give in and be caught.

There was but one thing for it. The desk was only a light deal thing, no more than a table, really, with no drawers full of books to weigh it down. I set my fingers under the lips of the upper edge and with a mighty roar pushed it at her and tipped it at the same time, so that I overturned it and all but knocked her over too. Before she had chance to recover I acrossed the room and outed the open door.

I tore down the corridor with the ring of her boots on the floorboards behind me in hot pursuit. I took the back stairs three or four at a time and jumped the last six or seven in one go, near coming to grief as I stumbled at the bottom, but managing to steady myself at the last. All the while I could hear her screaming after me, 'Where are they? Where are they, you little hussy?'

I came to a side door and wrenched it open and was out at last in the garden. I slammed the door shut and looked around hard. I considered the lake but then remembered her facility with water and that she would be able to shortcut across it, leaving me at a definite disadvantage. Then I thought of the other direction and the woods, which I had often walked through to meet Theo when he came through them to visit me, and we had same routed when I sometimes accompanied him partway home. I knew them well and their hiding places too, for Giles and I had often hide-and-seeked there and, saving any special powers she might have of which I might yet be ignorant, I certained I would be her superior amongst the trees. At least she would have no spies watching me and I sured I could conceal me quite. I hitched up my skirts and started to run even as I heard the door open behind me. I didn't, of course, think beyond getting away. I didn't consider what would happen after all this, or how life could ever be normal again.

I had a good start on her and out in the open I moved faster, for my legs were younger. I heart-in-mouthed, though, even as I gained distance upon her, for I never forgot she was a spirit, not of this world, which made me fear all manner of things, especially that one of her witchy ways might be the ability to fly. Still, when I over-my-shouldered she was a good couple of hundred yards behind and I plunged into the woods. At first I kept to the trail, heading into the heart of the forest, but when the path forked I took the lesser of the two, and the same another hundred yards or so further on when it forked again. Now I was on something scarce recognisable as a path but that was in fact the route Theo and I had determined to be the shortest between his side of the woods and my own. It was not the quickest, though, for it went through thickets of dense bushes and shrubs, and places where the trees had dropped saplings, so that a body had to sideways to squeeze through the narrow gaps between them.

As the undergrowth thickened and the going became harder I began to tire and my progress slowed. At one point I disturbed some rooks and they took off from their tree with a great noise of cawing and flapping of wings, which made me curse to myself for I knew it must have alerted my pursuer as to my general location. In a panic I bad decisioned and went off the route I knew into some bushes and soon found myself amongst brambles which reached out cruelly, as though perhaps my pursuer had some control over them, tearing at my frock with their thorny tendrils. Soon I was quite caught, and had to stop, give myself a quiet talking-to to calm me, for struggling only made the situation worse, and patiently and carefully unpick the barbs that held me, as if they were some of my many bad stitches when Whitaker had made me sew.

At last I got myself free and staggered into a small clearing, but scarce had time to celebrate this when there was another sudden flight of rooks, the cause almost immediately apparenting in a great commotion in the direction whence I had come. It so louded I convinced it must be a deer crashing through the undergrowth, for I could hear branches snapping as whatever it was forced its way through. I stared at the trail it was making, for I could not see the thing itself, only the shaking of the saplings and shrubs it disturbed, and at first I did not afraid, for I knew it was not the time of year for deer to attack. But then, as I waited for the beast to arrive and pass, I caught a glimpse of something black amongst the shaking leaves and knew I was undone, for there are no black deer and it could be but one thing, the governess's dress. I transfixed with fear, unable to think for a moment which way to turn and flee. There seemed to be no passage out of the clearing any better than the route that had brought me there, but as I prevaricated the bushes before me broke apart and there stood Miss Taylor, face livid, practically snorting with rage. She made to rush me but staggered back and I realised she was still held by the brambles, as I had been. I turned and, without thought, plunged into the bushes in front of me.

I crashed my way through them. When thorns grasped my dress, I snatched it from them, heedless of any rips or tears. No matter what the obstacle, I forced my way through. I could hear

217

my pursuer close behind me and expected any moment to feel her hot breath on my neck. But then, at last, I burst out of the thicket and onto a footpath. I was free! Not only that but I had chanced upon the path I had first been on, the one that led to the Van Hoosier side of the woods, not that I could hope for any help there, for the house was all shut up with the family away. Not thinking beyond immediate escape, I took to my heels and ran for all I was worth and certained I was at last leaving my pursuer behind. Thinking I had put some distance between us, without breaking my stride I over-my-shouldered to check. She was nowhere in sight and I was just congratulating myself, laughing wildly as I ran, when my foot struck something hard – a tree root – and over I went, unable to stifle a cry of pain as my ankle turned and I went down on it with my full weight. I lay there, my face in the dust, knowing full well my ankle was quite useless. I could hear her panting breath behind me, coming ever closer. And then I heard a noise in front of me that sounded something like a human cough. I lifted my eyes and saw before me, no more than a few inches away, a pair of black brogues. I lifted my head to see further and found myself looking at a pair of long heron legs I knew well and had never thought to see again.

CHAPTER 23

'Theo,' I gasped, 'what in the name of tarnation are you doing here?'

'Asthma,' said Theo. In confirmation of this he commenced to coughing and drew from his pocket his flask with the rubber bulb that Dr Bradley had devised for him, opened his mouth and gave himself a good squirt. There was a noise behind me and I rolled over on my side to find Miss Taylor standing there, looking much as I imagined I myself must look, dress dusty and torn and covered in burrs, hair unkempt and betwigged, face sweating and flowering with tiny petals of red, courtesy of the thorns.

I sat up and waved a hand at Theo. 'May I present Mr Van Hoosier, ma'am. Mr Van Hoosier, Miss Taylor, our new governess.'

She did not know how to react. After all, Theo was not only my friend but also her social superior. She smoothed down her dress and summoned up something like a smile.

'What were you doing?' said Theo. His expression was even more mystified than his general look.

'Playing hide-and-seek,' I replied.

He looked from one to the other of us. 'Well then, ladies, I think you're taking it a mite too seriously. It's only a game.'

He bent to help me up, indicating with a shrug of his eyebrows that Miss Taylor should take my other side. 'Florence was doing the hiding and I was doing the seeking,' she said, digging her talons into my arm. 'And I think I have won.'

'Ow!' I cried, and then added, 'My ankle!' for I did not want to give her the satisfaction of having made me cry out. 'I think I have turned it.'

With one arm under my shoulder to support me, Theo bent down to examine it. 'Well, it certainly does seem to be swelling up something grand. We shall have to help you back to the house.'

So they supported me, one either side, while I hopped along as best I could in the middle. No sooner had we set off than Theo began coughing and we had to stop while he gave himself another squirt of medicine.

'It's how come I'm here,' he said as we set off again. 'I went down with a bad attack of asthma the day before we were due to sail. My folks had to go off without me. I was in the hospital and then under the care of my aunt. Now they've sent me out here to recuperate in the better air.'

'You don't mind?' I said.

'Not at all. I'm master of the house. I have ice cream with every meal.'

'I didn't mean that, silly. I meant, not going to Europe.'

'I guess not. After all, it was only to see a load of old ruins and paintings and such and I reckon I can go another time and they'll still be there.'

As we neared the house Meg and John came running toward us, for Giles had alerted Mrs Grouse to my fleeing the house chased by Miss Taylor and they had all been looking for us. John took charge and lifted me into his arms as if I were no more than a feather, leaving Theo free to enjoy a good cough. Miss Taylor hurried off to change her dress while I was laid on a chaise in the drawing room.

Mrs Grouse mother-henned over me, wringing her hands. 'Oh dear, whatever has happened? Why did you run off like that?'

I had no answer. My first thought was to tell her all that had occurred and to trust to her good sense that she would see Miss Taylor for what she was and inform my uncle. The trouble was, I anxioused about being believed. What if I told her about the steamship tickets but our new governess came up with some story to explain them away? I should then have to hand them back and thereby return to her the power to take Giles away. But keeping them and staying silent might not avail me anything either. I knew nothing about the way steamship companies conducted themselves. For all I knew, it might be but a simple matter for Miss Taylor to say she had lost the tickets and get them replaced. I looked up and saw her in the mirror over the fireplace, thoughtfulling down at me, as if trying to guess my next move.

I resolved not to tell Mrs Grouse about the tickets, at least not yet. The best plan I could hit upon was to show them to Hadleigh, for they represented the evidence that he would want before being able to act. The weakness with this plan was the difficulty in contacting the captain. Time was running out. I had already used one of my fourteen days. If I could not get to Hadleigh then there would be nothing for it but to throw myself upon the mercy of Mrs Grouse. But, whichever I did, first I would need to have the tickets in my possession. Even were I to tell Mrs Grouse about the tickets, I could not let her know about the tower room because I did not wish to surrender it as a possible bolthole, a storage place for secret things and a base. And yet because of my ankle, there was no way I would be able to make the difficult ascent there.

'I will explain later,' I told the puzzled house-keeper. 'If you don't mind, I would like some time now to chat with Mr Van Hoosier.'

Mrs Grouse doubtfulled a nod and said she would fetch us a pot of tea.

As soon as she was gone I motioned Theo to come closer. He bent his head over mine and ambushed me a kiss plumb on the lips. 'Not now, Theo, there isn't time!' I said, my cheeks hotting up, for it shamed me to be kissed with the governess watching from her mirror. 'As soon as Giles hears that you're here he'll be along like a shot. Now put your ear to my lips and listen, for I have no idea if the mirrors can hear.'

He puzzled me one at this. 'The mirrors . . . can hear?' He upped his eyebrows, but when I took hold of his lapels and pulled him close he raised no objection, figuring no doubt it would put him in the way of another kiss. I soon disillusioned him that, twisting his head so that it was his ear lined up with my mouth, not his lips. I whispered to him about the mirrors and how Miss Taylor had practically the whole house watched. At this Theo let out a mighty guffaw and broke away from me. He stood over me, staring down.

'Florence, are you sure it's only your ankle that took a knock? You didn't by any chance get a bang on the head too?'

'Theo, it's true,' I hissed. 'I swear by anything you care to name.'

He condescended me a smile, put his hands in his pants pockets and took a casual turn about the room, stopping at the mirror and peering into it for a while, making adjustments to his necktie as he did. Satisfied he looked quite the beau, he came and sat on the end of the chaise.

'Florence,' he whispered, a smile playing about his lips, 'I have to tell you, she ain't there.'

'She's there, all right,' I hissed back, bridling at his mockery, 'but I'm the only one can see her.'

'Oh, I see – or rather I don't!' He patronised me such a nod I would have hit him were I not desperate for his help.

'Anyhow, never mind about the mirror now, humour me about it if you like, but just listen.'

223

I had decided to entrust him with one of my greatest secrets. After I had expounded to him my belief that Miss Taylor was planning to take Giles away and the confirmation of it I had received in finding the steamship tickets, I whispered him how to get to the tower room and where to find them. 'But not yet, Theo, not yet. You won't have time to do it before Giles gets here and she reappears. We must bide our time. I will tell you when.'

As if this were a cue the door opened and Miss Taylor, now in another dress, black like the other, glided in. She had put her hair up again and cleaned up the thorn cuts on her face and powdered over them so you would scarce have noticed anything different about her at all, if indeed there was. I thought that maybe it was not face paint that had restored her features; perhaps a ghost may renew itself whenever it fancies.

'Ah, Mr Van Hoosier.' She beamed a charmer at Theo. 'You are still here.' Theo awkwarded upright as if caught doing something he should not, as indeed he had been, listening to my seditious talk. 'It was so kind of you to take care of Florence, but I think that now I must ask you to cease your ministrations, for the poor girl' – here she sarcasticked me one – 'needs rest.'

Theo stood his ground. 'But ma'am, her ankle . . .'

'I have sent John for the doctor. He will be here directly. Now I think if you'll just step outside . . .'

Theo was left with no choice. He gave my hand a squeeze. 'You take care, Florence. I'll be back tomorrow.' She ushered him out as if he were a docile cow and I was left alone, listening to the drone of their voices in the hall. The door to the drawing room opened and Giles stood there, holding the handle, not coming into the room but warying me from the threshold.

'Giles,' I said, 'what's the matter?'

'Gee, Flo, what was that all about? You must have done something real bad to make her so mad.'

'Come in, Giles, and close the door,' I loud whispered him. 'Come on, hurry!'

He hesitated a moment but then did as I asked. He slowed over to me but still stood a couple of feet off, just out of reach. 'What's going on, Flo? Why did she chase you like that? Was it because you went into her room? You left your cloak there, didn't you? Why did you do that?'

'Never mind that now, Giles, you must listen to me.' I dropped my voice to a whisper because of the mirror. 'I have proof that she means to take you away. I found the steamship tickets.'

His face brightened. 'Steamship tickets? I'm going on a boat?'

'Yes, if she isn't stopped. To Europe.'

'Europe?' He thought a moment then said, 'Why has Theo come back from Europe so soon? Didn't he like it there?'

'He never went. He had an asthma attack.'

'Oh.'

'Didn't you speak to him?'

'Only to say hello. Miss Taylor told me he was just leaving.'

Right on cue I heard the front door close and through the window I saw Theo, walking backwards away from the house, looking at it with an expression that mixed puzzlement with concern. I feebled a wave, which was difficult, laid out as I was on the couch, but it obvioused he could not see and he turned and walked away down the drive.

The door opened again and Miss Taylor came in. She was all smiles with Giles, although I saw that he waried her as he had me. He had, after all, seen her wilding at me earlier, which must have somewhat shaken his impression of her as all sweetness and light. I bethought me that this was something I might work on, that it might opportunity me to drive a wedge between them.

'Giles,' she said, 'please go up to the schoolroom, there's a good fellow, and fetch Florence's book for her, will you? Oh, and her embroidery, of course.' She meaningfulled me one. 'After all, we mustn't give away her secret, must we?'

As soon as he was gone she strode over to me. 'Now listen to me, young lady, and listen well.' She practically spat the words out. I, of course had no choice but to listen, for I was as a prisoner shackled here by my useless ankle. 'I want what is mine. You will hand them over now or suffer the consequences.'

'I cannot do that.'

She sat on the edge of the couch, stretched out her hand and applied it to my ankle, squeezing hard the swelling so that it was all I could do not to cry out. 'Give them to me!'

'I cannot, for I do not have them about me.'

She released her grip and suspicioned me a long look, her eyes travelling up and down my body as though she might be contemplating searching me, or else was considering where about my person the tickets might be hid.

'Go ahead, look,' I said. 'You won't find them.'

'Very well. But you will tell me where they are.'

'That's what you think, you fiend.'

She stood. 'I can make life very difficult for you, little girl, if you persist in crossing me.'

'I will not stand by and let you take my brother away.'

'Your half-brother, you mean. And you are right, you will not stand by, for you will not be standing at all for some days. You will be lying helpless as you are now.'

'You will only take Giles over my dead body.'

'Let us hope it doesn't come to that.' She was annoyed, I could see it, frustrated that I intransigenced so. 'Come now,' she said, in a more conciliatory tone, 'you may as well give me what's mine, for they can in no way serve you and the loss of them is but an inconvenience to me. I have only to write a letter to get them replaced. Why not make things easy for us both by telling me where they are?'

'They are where you will never find them. And you are quite wrong, they are not useless to me. They are proof of your devilish plans.'

She long-silenced me one and then turned and glided from the room, leaving behind her a trail of anger and frustration.

CHAPTER 24

That afternoon the doctor visited and pronounced my ankle sprained and prescribed complete rest and keeping all weight off it for a week. So I lay in the drawing room pretending to sew but really reading my book, which I covered whenever Mrs Grouse or any of the servants came in. And this was my pattern for the next few days. Every morning John would carry me down from my room and set me up for the day on the couch. At mealtimes a small table was brought to me and my food laid out on it. In the evening John carried me back to my room. I had no idea what Miss Taylor had told Mrs Grouse concerning our chase through the woods but, whatever it was, it obvioused she had convinced her that it had been but a game, for it was clear the good housekeeper suspected nothing. At times when I aloned with her I bethought me to tell her all, but held back, for I still doubted being believed. No, my best plan had to be for Theo to get the tickets and then somehow convey them to Hadleigh and thereby prove our new governess's intentions.

The immediate problem I had with this was how Theo was to gain possession of the tickets, for Miss Taylor, taking the doctor at what I considered to be more than his word, had deemed 'complete rest' to mean no visitors. She even kept Giles's trips to see me to the minimum. Giles himself seemed to have gotten over his brief fear of her, which I suppose was only to be expected now that he aloned with her for most of every day. On his visits to me he parried any attempt of mine to renew talk of his impending trip with his usual childish prattle.

'Giles,' I whispered, when we aloned for an instant one morning, 'has she said anything to you about going away with her?'

'Flo,' he stonewalled, 'now that you've tried being without the use of one of your legs for a while, which would you rather have, a leg chopped off or one of your eyes gouged out?'

How was I to answer that?

It difficulted me greatly that I could think of no way to get Theo into the house to put my plan into action; the whole thing hopelessed, for she had banned him quite. So I was surprised on the third morning of my indisposition to look out the drawing room window and up the drive and see a familiar figure heroning its way toward the house. A moment later Mrs Grouse showed him into me.

'Theo,' I gasped, the moment we were alone, 'how did you get around her prohibition?'

'By appealing to a greater authority,' he whispered,

for I put a finger to my lips to shh him and indicated the mirror with a nod of my head. He pumped out his chest like a cock pigeon when it is courting the hen. 'I faked an asthma attack, so my people fetched the doctor and in passing I happened to mention it was a pity you weren't allowed visitors. Naturally he said that was a load of nonsense and that nothing would do you more good. So here I am.'

'How clever of you.'

'Yes.' He sheepished a little. 'Mind you, he did say it wasn't a good idea for me to go out at all, given the state, as he thought, of my asthma, but that's another matter.'

At this moment Miss Taylor brusqued into the room, evidently having seen Theo through one of her mirrors, followed by Giles, who bounded up to him and regaled him with questions and entreaties to play this and that. Miss Taylor patiented until the first flush of Giles's enthusiasm for our old friend had abated somewhat, then said, 'I believe I mentioned to you, Mr Van Hoosier, that the doctor has ordered complete rest for Florence. We don't want her getting over excited, now do we?'

Theo smiled. 'I have to say, ma'am, I don't rightly see how getting excited would have an effect upon a person's ankle, but in any case I have it on good medical authority that it will do her good to have company,' and he explained what the doctor had said, omitting the precaution about himself.

Miss Taylor stood chewing her lip and then said, 'Very well, come along now, Giles, this is lesson time. You can see Mr Van Hoosier later.'

When Theo and I aloned we chatted some more, whispering as I explained what he must do with the tickets, should he secure them, and what he must tell Hadleigh, and then he stood up and said in kind of a stagey way, 'Tell me, is there any book you require from the library?' He had his back to the mirror and was making his eyebrows dance about to show he was not in earnest. I straight-wayed what he was up to. Under cover of going to the library for me he could get to the tower and recover the tickets. I asked him for *Macbeth*.

So Theo set off. He went first to the library, found *Macbeth* where I had told him it would be and then made his way to the tower. He intentioned if he should encounter Miss Taylor en route there or on his way back to say he had taken a wrong turn when he left the library and gotten lost. With luck, Theo being so vague and stupid-seeming and all, he would be believed. As it fortuned, he met no one on his brief diversion, although Miss Taylor took it upon herself to look in on me while he was gone.

'Where is Mr Van Hoosier?' she demanded.

I could tell she suspicioned something. It obvi-oused she had seen him leave in her spyglass and had lost track of him when he left the library and turned right and went off her map.

'He went to the library to fetch me a book.'

This much was true and accorded with what she would have seen.

Just then Theo returned. He handed me the book and, as he did so, with his back to her and her mirror, patted his breast pocket. 'Well, Florence, I'm afraid I must be off,' he said, adding with studied significance, 'I have things to do.'

That is the worst about involving such as Theo and Giles in one's plots: they have not my gift for it. Miss Taylor immediately ear-pricked. 'Oh yes, Mr Van Hoosier, and what might those things be?'

Theo coloured and began to stammer, the which turned into a cough, and that in turn led to the necessity of a spray. When he had recovered himself he said, 'Oh, this and that, Miss Taylor. Some mathematics and Greek. My tutor keeps me hard at it and I must be up to the mark with my studies for when I am well enough to return to school.'

This recovery was good by Theo's standards but I inwarded a curse that he had all but ruined things by trying to be too smart. Now it obvioused that the governess knew he had the tickets. She would not know what he had them for, but it would have been better had she remained in the dark as to where they were.

CHAPTER 25

The next few days were an agony to me, laid up helpless as I was, not only unable to do anything to halt the progress of Miss Taylor's plans but also in the most terrible ignorance as to the furtherance of my own. I had no way of knowing what Theo was up to. It occurred to me that the answer might simply be nothing, nothing at all. Suppose he considered what he had seen, a half-crazed girl in a state of unseemly disarray pursued through the woods by her governess, together with what I had told him, that this same governess was a ghost, the spirit of a previous governess come back to haunt us and steal away my brother, although for what motive it was unclear; moreover, that this spirit could see like an owl in the dark, without recourse to candles, walk on water and watch people through all the mirrors in the house? What if he considered all that and decided I was plainly not in my right mind? It was a great deal to expect even someone so naïve as Theo to believe.

But then again, the boy besotted with me . . .

About the only entertainment I had during my

recuperation was in dodging my book out of the sight of Mrs Grouse and Meg, who both so mother-henned me that I was not often left with a whole hour to myself. I would no sooner settle myself down to read than one or other of them would be in to make up the fire or bring me a drink or some little delicacy, a cake or cookie which Meg had prepared especially (and no doubt consumed half a dozen of herself), so that I constanted grabbing my embroidery and holding it over my book. Thus I found myself reading in stops and starts and it was almost like the old three-or-four-paging days in the tower when I had to look up to see if Theo was upping the drive. I wondered that Mrs Grouse didn't in turn wonder how my embroidery made no progress, or if she secretly thought me another Penelope, unravelling by night what I stitched by day.

The other thing I anxioused about was what that witch our new governess might be up to with Giles. For apart from a few minutes here or there, such as after a meal, she kept him from me, away up in the schoolroom, my absence opportunitying her perfectly to poison his mind against me and seduce him to her plans. Although I had little chance to alone with Giles, when I did manage to whisper a question to him he reticented, hanging his head and avoiding my eyes, and then quickly changed the subject. Giles will not give up a secret easily, but he is not good at concealing the fact that he has one. It obvioused that now he was part of her plan, his secrets were with her, not me.

There was no way in which I could alter this for now; all I could do was Lady of Shalott my way through the days, waiting for Hadleigh to shining-armour up the drive. But on the fourth day it was not Hadleigh who came, but Theo.

I could tell there was something wrong the moment he walked through the door. He so anxioused that he almost rushed into the room and blurted it right out, but I held up a finger and nodded toward the mirror to caution him to hold his fire. He came and nexted me on the couch.

'Did you see Hadleigh?' I whispered. 'What did he say?'

Theo shook his head miserably. 'It took me until yesterday to get into town. I had another asthma attack, a real one this time – it's very bad at the moment – and was laid up, so my tutor wouldn't countenance letting me go. Not that I was capable of it anyhow.'

I impatiented through all this, for Theo's asthma did not hold the interest for me that it did for him. When does the illness of anyone other than one's self? But I said nothing, for I did not want to impression him I did not care. Theo was now my only ally until Hadleigh should come.

'So what happened?' I hissed, but before he could answer Theo plunged into a fit of coughing, the worst I had ever witnessed him have, so that between coughs his intake of breath was a rasp, like someone sawing wood, or scraping nails on a slate. It teeth-edged me quite.

Theo took out his spray and gave himself a good puff and the fit eventually quieted. 'Well, yesterday I was much better and asked if I might go out in the carriage for a drive. My tutor didn't want to accompany me – he never does, he prefers to swot his life away at his books – and so, once in the carriage, I ordered the man to drive me into town. There I said I wanted to visit the stationer's to see if they had in any new books and so was able to sneak off to the police station.'

'But you didn't manage to see Hadleigh?' I difficulted to keep my voice from exasperating. I so wished it could have been me and not Theo walking those sidewalks; I felt I should not have failed, although in this I was soon proved wrong.

'No, that's what I'm coming to.'

'But why ever not?' I knew I was sounding angry but I could not help myself. My brother's very existence might depend upon this and to be so let down hopedashed me quite.

'Because he wasn't there!' Theo snapped that one back at me in the same tone, wormturning at my annoyance with him. Mollified, I held up a finger, for he louded enough for the mirror to hear.

He lowered his voice. 'His clerk said he was away working on an important case. He's in New York. He'll be gone for a month.'

A tear stole from my eye and down my cheek,

I felt so the frustration of being balked at every turn. 'Then there is no hope. No hope at all.'

'Wait, Florence, you haven't heard it all yet. The clerk asked me my business and I mentioned that I was not there on my own behalf but from you, at which the clerk said in that case he had something for you, a letter.'

'Keep your voice down!' I hissed again. 'A letter, where is it?'

'Why, inside my jacket. Do you reckon it's safe to pass it over here?'

'Wait a moment, let me think.' I looked up at the mirror. If Theo came any closer either my modesty would be compromised or it would obvious he was passing something to me. 'Listen, where is it in your jacket?'

'In the inner breast pocket on my right-hand side. The tickets are there too.'

'All right, I'm going to speak normally now. When I do, you do just as I ask and I'll slip my hand inside your jacket and take the letter, OK?'

Theo wide-eyed at the pleasurable impropriety of this. 'OK!'

'Theo,' I alouded, 'I have slid down on the couch somewhat. I wonder if you would be so kind as to lift me up a little?'

'Why of course, Miss Florence, I shall be delighted to assist you.' He really did hopeless any kind of subterfuge! Nevertheless, he stood up and, bending over me, got his hands under my elbows and made to lift me up. I slid my right hand inside his jacket, felt instantly the letter and tickets and extracted them, and, as he released me, slipped my booty under my embroidery, it being the last thing anyone in the house had ever evinced any interest in. With Theo between me and the mirror, I managed from there to transfer the contraband inside the bodice of my frock.

The strange thing was that although all this must have suspicioned Miss Taylor in the mirror, she did not put in an appearance in person. I wondered at this, for she knew Theo had the tickets, and here he was, behaving strangely before her very eyes. It puzzled me quite. It was almost as if she did not care any more about the tickets and made me think that, as she had threatened, she had simply written for and obtained replacements. If this were the case, it suited me, for holding on to the tickets had never been a guarantee of preventing her plan, but rather only to have the proof of its existence. What it also meant was that Miss Taylor had no fear of me, which could only be because she had no knowledge of my visit to Hadleigh or that his visit here had been anything but what it surfaced to be. On the other hand, perhaps now she had no need to fear any aid to me from that quarter, for Hadleigh was apparently out of the picture and would be so until long after she had implemented her plan and awayed my hapless brother.

Theo stayed with me a couple of hours, during which time, of course, Meg came in, so that we were soon feasting on bread and honey and cakes.

No one had sent to fetch Miss Taylor and she chose not to come of her own accord. Were it not for the impending danger and the letter – which of course I could not yet read – burning a hole through my bodice, we might have pleasant after-nooned. As it was, it was all too easy to slip from superficialling a remark about this or that, a book or some such, back to the matter which now pre-occupied us both, and each of us had at times to stop the other mid-speech, for at some moments we often forgot to quiet before the mirror. It even occurred to me that this might be Miss Taylor's scheme, to alone us and give us rope enough to hang ourselves by our forgetting we were watched.

Although we tried to recapture our old jollity, and I think that Theo almost did – because for him, perhaps, all the business with our new governess was but a bit of a game, something he did not truly believe in – there was something strained in our relationship. The fault was mine; I was using him, for I wanted him not so much as a friend that afternoon but as a means of making slow hours pass more quick.

It eventuated that he had to leave and I aloned my dinner off a little table, not even being able to read as I ate for fear of discovery by one of the servants. Afterward Giles came in and bantered with me for a while, but in truth I did not want his company either but longed for him to be called up to his bed and for John to come to fetch me to mine.

In the end time passed, as it always will, and John deposited me in my bed. As usual, Mary brought me my nightgown and made to help me change into it, as she had every night of my indisposition, but I told her I did not need her and sent her away. It feared me the letter from Hadleigh might be revealed as she took off my dress. When I quite sured she was gone, I slid the letter and tickets under my mattress, changed into my nightgown, blew out my candle and slipped between the sheets. I had a long wait now until Miss Taylor looked in and then retired for the night – that is, as much as she ever slept the whole night, what with her nocturnal visit to Giles and all.

After her brief inspection, with no timepiece visible in the dark I counted the long watches of the night by the hoots of my old friend the owl, surely the most inaccurate clock any person ever had, but when I certained it was well past midnight, the witching hour as they say in books, I decided it safe to light my candle and take out the letter. I had been thinking of nothing else these long hours, as well you might imagine, for I had no idea what it might contain. Why should Hadleigh write to me? What could he possibly have to say? I unoptimised about it, for I feared it would be but a lecture on grief and remorse, that I should read and dwell in my imagination less and get out into the world more.

Dear Florence,

I am leaving this letter for you because a special assignment takes me away from my post for a few weeks. I wanted to reassure you that I have not forgotten the business we discussed, although at the time we spoke I had severe doubts for your reason and, had I been a medical man, might have diagnosed a serious case of hysteria in you. For that I now owe you an apology, because although I have to say your feelings about your governess are too fantastical for a sensible body to credit your suspicions, they may not be entirely without foundation. After my visit to you I made immediate contact with the agency that arranged Miss Taylor's employment as your governess. The first thing that was somewhat strange was that she did not answer an advertisement for the post because they did not place one, relying instead upon the teachers they had already on their books, although Miss Taylor was not one of those. Not only that, but when she contacted them, she was not looking for general employment, but asked specifically about the post at Blithe. The lady I spoke to formed the impression that Miss Taylor had contacted several other agencies as well,to see if the post was one they had been asked to fill. Unfortunately the agency was none too diligent in checking Miss Taylor out. They were so delighted to have someone who was ready to take the post without any haggling as to salary (your uncle, it seems is none too generous in that respect) or other conditions such as wishing to interview the children first and so on, and who moreover knew of the unfortunate circumstances under which the post had become vacant and who did not mind – it seems such accidents not uncommonly discourage many applicants – that they simply offered it to her.

This in itself would not matter, a bird in the hand and all that, except that, when pressed, they admitted that they were in such a hurry to appoint her, having no other suitable candidate, they took the two letters of reference they had from her at face value and made no further checks. I am now in New York and yesterday attempted to visit the two referees, only to find that the addresses in the letters do not exist. Now for that to happen with one address might be put down to a simple mistake, but two? Something is not right here.

I suggest you show this letter to Mrs Grouse, who I expect will confront Miss Taylor or may wish to write your uncle about it. He will no doubt want to investigate the matter further and should it prove

Miss Taylor has indeed fabricated her history then I am sure she will be dismissed and any bother to you and Giles removed. I hope this clears the matter up for you.

With all good wishes
Your friend
Frank Hadleigh

I clenched the letter in triumph. I had it! At last I had it, the proof, the ocular proof that I was not some crazy child, but that our new governess was not who she purported to be, but a fraud, a fake. Along with the steamship tickets, it would surely be convincing evidence she was up to no good and enough to persuade Mrs Grouse to order her from the house without waiting to hear from my uncle. I wanted to dance. I wanted to remove the cloth I threw over the mirror every night and pirouette before the evil witch's very eyes. I no longer cared if she knew what I was thinking, for I had all but won. Giles was safe!

CHAPTER 26

I could not wait for it to morning. At the very earliest intimation of light seeping in around the edges of the drapes, I hauled myself up so I was sitting on the edge of my bed and, with some difficulty because of my ankle, which, although much stronger now, would still not bear my full weight, managed to pull off my nightgown and replace it with my frock. By the time I had finished this the first lark had sung and it was now light enough for me to reckon it the time when Mrs Grouse would be up and about, which was always before we children and Miss Taylor.

I concealed Hadleigh's letter and the steamship tickets inside the bodice of my dress, then hopped across the room to my wardrobe, took a spare chemise from it and hopped to the door. Because I could not walk normally, short of laying me down and dragging myself inch by inch, hopping was my only means of locomotion. It anxioused me that it was so noisy Miss Taylor must hear me bumping around, but it fortuned she did not. There was no mirror in the upper corridor between my room and the staircase, so I did not fear being observed.

When I reached the staircase I sat me down on the top step and shuffled my way onto the next and so on and in this fashion I soon downstairsed. With the aid of the newel post at the bottom, I hauled myself upright again and hopped my way to the kitchen, where I found the housekeeper at breakfast with the servants. When I entered they were all laughing heartily at some joke or other, but the laughter stopped as soon as they saw me, for no one expected me to be able to move around on my own, and certainly not to come hopping in upon their meal. Seeing me, Mrs Grouse blushed and hurriedly took her napkin to her mouth, wiping away the smile. It obviosed she was embarrassed; it was bad enough having to eat with the servants, without being caught fraternising with them too.

'Why, Miss Florence,' she said, 'what on earth are you thinking of? You know very well you're not supposed to be on your feet.' Then, seeing my expression, she said, 'There's nothing wrong, I hope?'

'There is a great deal wrong, Mrs Grouse,' I bolded. 'And I must speak with you privately right away.'

Extremely agitated by my tone, the good woman abandoned her breakfast forthwith and had John carry me into her sitting room. He was about to put me down on the couch there but I cried out, 'No, wait!', pointed to the mirror on the wall and bade him carry me over to it. He exchanged a baffled look with the housekeeper but nevertheless complied. Once at the mirror, I draped the chemise over it, for this is why I had brought it, which occasioned another puzzled look from John to Mrs Grouse, which she returned with a shrug.

'I do not want her watching us,' I said to Mrs Grouse as John laid me down on the couch, at which the honest man's eyebrow began to twitch in a most uncontrolled way.

Mrs Grouse signalled him to leave us and, soon as he was gone, said, 'And who might "her" be? Is it someone who lives in the mirror, perhaps?' Her tone was patronising, pretending she thought my action might be reasonable, which of course, for anyone who did not know what was going on in the house, it was not.

'Miss Taylor,' I said.

Mrs Grouse merely stared at me.

'I have some things to show you,' I said and reached into my bodice and produced Hadleigh's letter and the steamship tickets. She overed to me and I handed her the latter.

'What are these?' she said, after studying them a moment or two.

'They're steamship tickets for a voyage from New York to France,' I told her.

'Well, I see that. But what's the meaning of it?'

'I took them from Miss Taylor's room.'

She stared at me, both puzzled and alarmed. 'I don't think you should have done that, my dear. That's not at all right. You shouldn't even have been in her room, let alone have taken things from her.'

'But don't you see, they're her tickets.'

Mrs Grouse frowned. 'But how do you know what they are, miss, when you can't read?'

'Never mind that now. The point is, they mean she is planning a trip. A trip for two.'

'A trip . . .?'

Really, Mrs Grouse was uncommon slow. 'Yes, for her and someone else. And look at the date.'

Mrs Grouse studied the tickets some more. 'Why, that's the end of next week. But I don't understand. She has said nothing to me about leaving. And she could not go next week, for she would have to work out her notice period, which is three months.'

'Ah, but you see she cares nothing for such things. She simply wants to take Giles.'

'Giles?' Mrs Grouse looked mystified beyond belief, her poor face crying out that this was all too much for her. 'But why should she want to do that? It doesn't make sense.'

At this I stumbled somewhat. For I could not tell her the real reason. I carefulled not to mention my theory that Miss Taylor and Whitaker were one and the same. My action with the mirror had already strained her credulity, although it had necessaried if we were to have privacy away from the governess's prying eyes.

'I – I don't know, but I am sure as anything that's what she intends. Anyway, that's not all. Look at this.' And I handed her Hadleigh's letter.

It took her some considerable time to read it.

When she reached the end, she said, 'Frank Hadleigh. Isn't that the police captain?'

'Yes. I – I met him when we went to town to take Giles to the dentist and confided in him my suspicions about this evil woman. As you can see, they were entirely justified, for she has obviously tricked her way into her post. And why should she do that unless it were for some wicked purpose?'

Mrs Grouse scrutinised Hadleigh's letter some more and I saw understanding spread across her face, and then a smile. 'I knew it! I knew from the start there was something not right about that woman. Making me eat with the servants, indeed!'

She rose from her seat, her face a mask of determination. 'We'll see about this. Oh yes, we will, we'll soon see about this.'

She brusqued from the room, leaving me stranded on the couch, and I heard her march to the breakfast room and thrust open the door. Miss Taylor and Giles were evidently not yet there, for I heard her footsteps straightway march back out again and start up the stairs. I desperated to know what was going on and began to struggle to pull myself into a sitting position. It fortuned that Mrs Grouse had left the door open, for as I finally managed to sit up and swung myself round so that I could put my feet to the ground, I heard voices upstairs, from which I deduced that Mrs Grouse had met Miss Taylor and Giles on their way down to breakfast. I could hear Mrs Grouse's angry tone, but frustratingly could not make out one word of what she was saying. A moment later Giles burst into the room.

'Flo!' he panted, obviously having run all the way downstairs, his eyes aglow with excitement. 'You have to come quick. Miss Taylor and Mrs Grouse are having an almighty row!'

Then he stopped and remembered my ankle. 'Oh,' he said. He dashed across the room and offered me his shoulder to lean on, which was so like the old Giles and not at all like the new, uncaring one he had become under our new governess that it eye-watered me quite. I pointed out to him that he was offering me the wrong shoulder, for it was on my good side, and he hurried around me and I leaned on the other one.

From above we could hear both women's voices now, the two of them shouting, but at the same time not distinct enough to possible us to understand anything. Giles and I had just outed the door into the hall when there was an almighty crash from above, followed by a thunderous bumping noise, and we were just in time to see the housekeeper come tumbling down the stairs, nearly all the way to the bottom, where her body came to rest while her head seemed to carry on and whiplash onto the cold hard tiles of the hall floor with an almighty crack. She lay there completely still.

Giles hopped me over to her. We reached her just as Miss Taylor came running down the stairs, her expression all alarmed. At that moment John and Meg, having heard Mrs Grouse crashing down the stairs, burst into the hallway.

Miss Taylor looked around at us all. 'She was all excited about something,' she said, her eyes flicking from one to the other of us as though seeking acceptance for her words. 'She was waving her hands about and, well, she was on the top step, with her back to the stairs and she must have overbalanced, for she went tumbling backwards. I – I tried to grab her, but it all happened so fast and . . . and, well, she was too far away.' I noticed that in her hand she clutched Hadleigh's letter and the steamship tickets.

Meg was on her knees by the housekeeper. She laid her head upon the other woman's breast. Straightening up, she took charge. 'She's still breathing and I don't see any blood, so there's hope. John, get out the horse and ride to Dr Bradley. Tell him to get here with all possible speed. Miss Taylor, this isn't a sight for children. You must get them right away.'

'Yes. Yes, of course,' Miss Taylor murmured. I saw her slip the papers into her pocket. 'Come along, children!' She made to walk around the stricken housekeeper, obviously intending for us to go up to the schoolroom, but then, realising we were not following, she turned and, seeing Giles struggling, his shoulder under my arm, remembered my ankle. She walked back to us. With John gone for the doctor there was no one to carry me upstairs. She motioned Giles aside and put her arm beneath mine. 'Come, we will go to the library.'

She helped me along the long corridor. Neither of us spoke. I too upsetted about Mrs Grouse to think of anything else. I had known the woman all my life, or at least as long as I had memory for. She was often a silly old fool, but she had a kind heart and always meant well.

In the library Miss Taylor deposited me in a large armchair and began pacing up and down, her face, which I had only seen masked or false-smiling or angry, now contorted in an agony of anxiety. It pleasured me to twist the knife.

'You have murdered her!' I bolded.

She stopped in her ambulation and faced me. 'No! Don't say such a thing. It was an accident. The poor woman got excited about something and overbalanced and fell. That is all.'

'You pushed her, you fiend!'

Giles alarmed a look from her to me. 'Flo, you mustn't talk like that. Why would Miss Taylor want to do that?'

'Because she isn't Miss Taylor,' I said, glaring her one.

She took a step backward, as if I had prodded her, like one schoolboy goading another to fight.

'Not Miss Taylor?' Giles puzzled, then started to laugh. 'Why, sis, of course she's Miss Taylor. Who else would she be?'

'Miss Whitaker!' I said.

Our new governess stared at me a long moment, as I imagine a pugilist might stare at an opponent, weighing him up. At last she smiled and shook her head. 'You mustn't mind your sister, Giles. She has these strange fantasies.' She walked over to the fire, pulled something from her pocket, which I knew must be Hadleigh's letter, and thrust it into the flames. There was nothing I could do but watch it vanish into smoke, first flaring up and then the edges curling, so that it folded in upon itself and then turned black and crumpled to ash and disappeared as if it had never been. I totally unevidenced now.

Giles looked from one to the other of us and then shrugged. 'That was my idea, a long time ago, miss,' he said. 'I don't think that now. Miss Whitaker was a real meanie. She wouldn't let Flo come in here at all, or look at books. You're not like her.'

Miss Taylor beamed him a kindly one. 'Thank you, Giles.'

'And, miss, you want to know something else?'

'What, my dear?'

'We haven't had our breakfast.'

We walked and hopped back to the breakfast room. Mrs Grouse still lay at the foot of the stairs, the servants having been afraid to move her. Meg had comfortabled her by placing a pillow beneath her head and throwing a blanket over her. For a woman who often could appear angry or anxious

253

when animated, the housekeeper looked strangely peaceful in repose. I could see the rhythmic rise and fall of her breast but she gave no other sign of life and certainly none of any awareness of what transpired around her.

We had just finished breakfast, or rather Giles had, for I ate as little as the governess, which is to say nothing at all, when we heard the doctor arrive. Shortly after, Miss Taylor was sent for, and from the way Dr Bradley behaved toward her (for Giles and I watched and listened by cracking open the dining-room door) it seemed that, at least in his own mind, he had appointed her head of the household. He told her that Mrs Grouse had suffered a concussion and was presently unconscious. When Miss Taylor asked what exactly that might mean, Bradley shook his head and muttered, 'I'm afraid I cannot rightly answer that. It may be like an after dinner's sleep, as it were, from which she will awake unharmed and refreshed in the morning, or it could be that she will lapse into a coma, from which position the outcome could be more serious, much more serious. What I propose is that John and I carry her to her bed and make her comfortable there. I will visit again in the morning and, in two or three days, if there is no improvement, then I suggest we move her to the county hospital, where she can be kept under proper observation, just to be on the safe side.'

All this was duly done, and once everything had settled down again, we repaired once more to the library. I found the constant hopping tiring, but the one ray of light in my shattered universe was that having put my ankle to the ground a few times now, I could tell the pain was lessened and felt to myself that by the morning I would be well enough to walk upon it once more, although I decided I would quiet this fact, for which I had my reasons.

So there we were, the three of us in the library, me sullening a book, Giles at his lessons with Miss Taylor and billing and cooing with her as though nothing of any great moment had happened, as though his sister had never called her a murderess, as though none of us had ever heard of steamship tickets. There was but one big difference from the way things had been before, and that was that we were constantly broke in upon, for now, taking their cue from the doctor, all the servants deferred to Miss Taylor and constanted in and out to consult her on matters concerning the running of the house.

The next morning Dr Bradley drove up in his carriage and brought someone with him. 'I passed this young reprobate walking up the drive,' he said.

'Theo!' I exclaimed. I couldn't help myself, for never had I so happied to see my clumsy heron. With Hadleigh absent, Mrs Grouse here in body but definitely not in spirit, and Giles suborned from my side by the witch's evil spells, he was all I could look to for assistance.

Miss Taylor could hardly refuse Theo's visit, not

with the doctor standing there; although the medical man clucked about the boy ignoring his advice and coming out when he should have been resting up at home, he did it in such a kindly fashion you could tell he did not mean it too seriously. Theo hobbled me to the drawing room, where I instanted over to the mirror with his manly pocket handkerchief and covered the glass.

I described to him what had occurred between Miss Taylor and Mrs Grouse, for he had had only the official version from the doctor.

'It is a big thing to accuse a person of such a deliberate piece of violence as pushing someone downstairs,' said Theo, looking down at his great hands. He stole me a sideways one without lifting his head, and I could tell that he was trying to weigh me up. I knew he wanted to see me as this pretty young girl he could be in love with, and yet in his mind that impression was fighting with one much darker, of a strange girl who made things up or had gothic fantasies induced in her by too much reading. 'With Hadleigh's letter gone, you have nothing in the way of motive to suggest.'

'There's the steamship tickets, I have those.'

'Actually you don't. She has them now.'

'You have seen them.'

'Yes, but –'

'But what, Theo? Would you not support me in this?'

'Of course, you know I'd do anything to help you,

256

Florence. But be realistic. A couple of kids. Who would take our word against hers? Besides, who would we be appealing to? Hadleigh's away, my folks are the other side of the Atlantic, my tutor is so unwordly he wouldn't dream of challenging a woman such as that, or know where to take the information, and Mrs Grouse is completely out of this world.'

'Let's hope she recovers soon,' I muttered. 'For she was finally on my side and she's our best hope.'

'Your only hope,' murmured Theo, which cruelled me quite, his putting it like that.

CHAPTER 27

It was now but little more than a week until Miss Taylor's evil plan would come to fruition and she and Giles would be gone. I brain-racked for some plan of my own with which to counter hers, but was problemed in this by igno-ranting exactly what her plan was. Oh, I knew its ultimate intention, but I did not know the mechan-ical details of how that aim was to be achieved.

My most immediate fear was that if I did not do something soon, I would be too late, that any hour might be the one in which she whisked my brother away. But then I realised that she could not do this for one simple reason, namely me. For I knew about the steamship tickets and the date and time of the ship's sailing, which was at midnight on the Friday at the end of the next week. Suppose she stole Giles away tomorrow, then? The servants would soon aware of this. I would tell John about the tickets and he would ride to town with this information and hand it to the police. They would telegraph to New York, where their colleagues would arrest Miss Taylor when she attempted to board the vessel.

In fact, this situation would apply not just tomorrow, but right until the very final day, and even if she left it until the last possible moment to flee Blithe, by the time she and Giles offed the train in New York, the police would already be at the dockside.

Indeed, I could not devise any plan for her that would work, but at least one thing obvioused me now. I quite safed until that last day. Unless, of course, she meant to somehow get me out of the way before then, as she had done Mrs Grouse, in which case she could steal Giles away and no one would know anything about the ship at all.

Mrs Grouse was my one great hope; if she recovered consciousness then the game would be up for Miss Taylor. I tried to visit the housekeeper's bedroom but our governess had appointed herself as her nurse. Each morning she set Giles some tasks to get on with in the schoolroom and then repaired to the housekeeper's room. She guarded it from the servants, so that no one else entered, and had Mary bring her blankets so that at night she could bed herself down in an armchair beside the other woman's bed.

After two nights of Miss Taylor sleeping in Mrs Grouse's bedroom, which was on the floor above where Giles and I slept, I felt safe enough to enter again the governess's room. I cloaked her mirror, as I had on my first visit, lit my candle and set about making a more thorough search than I had before. I took the two valises from under her bed and found one empty as before but discovered the other was now heavier. I undid the clasps, looked within and found myself letting out a loud cry, a shriek that would frighten an owl. Inside was a complete set of my brother's clothes, a smart jacket and pants, a clean shirt and enough linen for several days. It sured me quite of her intentions, the first real proof that she was going to kidnap Giles. My legs turned to water and I had to steady myself against the bedstead to keep from falling.

It must have been some minutes until I came to my senses and remembered where I was. I remembered too the cry that had escaped me and immediately anxioused the fiend might have heard. I hurried the valise closed and slipped it back under the bed. After I had waited several minutes and no sound of discovery coming, I commenced a thorough search of the rest of room, and found . . . nothing. I had hoped to find the steamship tickets in the desk drawer still, so that I could take them and perhaps, even at this late hour, prevent her using them, but they were no longer there. She had once-bitten-twice-shyed and hidden them elsewhere.

As I no-traced of them in the room I surmised she had wisely precautioned and was keeping them about her person. I looked again in the other drawer of the desk and found nothing save what had been there before, namely the bottle of medicine. I closed the drawer and was about to take my cloak and leave the room when I suddenly bethought me to open the drawer again. Perhaps the medicine had some significance after all, some part, although I could not imagine what, in her plot. I outed it and looked more closely at the label, which bore the single word: CHLOROFORM. I stood staring at it, not knowing at all what that meant, but then the owl hooted, which jarred me into sudden action. Without thinking, I slipped the bottle into my pocket, closed the drawer, blew out my candle and grabbed my cloak.

My heart was pounding as I corridored it back to my room. I had no idea whether or not the bottle of medicine mattered, but I guessed that even if it did, she would not think to check for it, for I had not disturbed it last time I entered her room when I had taken the tickets. Those being safe, I pretty sured she would think everything else so too. Next morning, before anyone else abouted, I made my way up to my tower and left the bottle there.

Three days after Mrs Grouse downstairsed, Theo called and I explained that there was no change in the housekeeper's condition. We sat in the drawing room, having covered the mirror.

First I told Theo about my significant find, of the set of Giles's clothes in the governess's suitcase. 'There you have the definite proof that I have guessed her plans correct,' I said.

'By jiminy, yes!' he said, leaping from his chair with a great smile of triumph, but then the smile faded and he sank back down again. 'Florence, did you look closely at the clothes?'

'Why yes, well, closely enough to know they were my brother's. Why?'

'Well – and I'm just playing devil's advocate here, you understand, trying to see things the way a sceptical adult would if you told them – the clothes might be old ones, things Giles has outgrown. She might have taken them for a relative, perhaps. There could be an innocent explanation.'

'Oh Theo!' I exasperated. 'Whose side are you on? What about all the other evidence?'

'OK, OK! I was just saying what they'll say.' But his face still doubtfulled. I awared how he would agree anything to please me.

After a moment or two's uncomfortable silence I told him what I had deduced about Miss Taylor's plans.

'Then you have nothing to fear,' he said, 'for she hasn't thought things through properly. No matter how she arranges things, you will be able to sound the alarm in time to prevent her. It's as simple as that.'

'Unless something happens to me before then,' I said.

We again sank back into silence and ruminated on this dread thought for some while. 'Theo,' I said, remembering the medicine bottle, 'what is chloroform?' For I had been able to find nothing on it in the library.

'Why, it's an anaesthetic. It's used by dentists

and surgeons to render patients unconscious so they won't feel any pain during an operation. But Florence, what a strange thing to ask.'

I told him I had found it in Miss Taylor's room.

'That's a very peculiar thing for a governess to have,' he said.

'But Theo, don't you see? Isn't it obvious? She means to use it on me! That's how she intends her plan to work. She will put me to sleep with it and steal away with Giles. By the time I wake up and give the alarm she will already be on the high seas.'

'By God, I think you've got it!' Leaping from his chair again, Theo began pacing the room. 'That is how she means to do it.'

'Then it's easy,' I said. 'All I have to do is be careful about what I eat and drink and especially not to accept anything that may have been contaminated by her.'

Theo stared at me, wide-eyed. 'Why, don't you know, Florence, you don't give a person chloroform to eat or drink!'

'You don't? Then how . . .?'

'You soak a cloth with it and hold it over the person's mouth and nose so they breathe in the fumes. They go out like a light. The beauty of it is that if they start to come to, you can just give them another dose the same way. Of course, you mustn't give them too much or they could die.'

I shuddered at this. 'Theo, do you think she means to kill me?'

Theo didn't answer but resumed his pacing. His eye caught the mirror, covered with his handkerchief, and he gazed at it for a moment or two and then looked from it to me. 'I don't know.'

'You don't know whether she means to kill me?'

'No, I mean, I don't know about this whole thing. When you say things like that, about your governess killing you, it all seems, well, a bit fantastical, if you think about it.' He laughed and waved a hand at the mirror. 'I mean, a woman who can watch you through mirrors? After all, when I look into the mirrors here, all I see is myself. You know, Florence, maybe . . . maybe . . .'

'Theo, she has steamship tickets.'

'She could be planning a trip with someone else, not necessarily Giles. She may have a gentleman friend.'

'Then why come and work here? And why sneak off without her pay? Besides, she asked especially for the post here and her references don't exist.'

'Well, maybe she thought the job would suit her and she'd get in before anyone else. And maybe she fabricated the references because she was down on her luck and desperate for a job and hadn't worked as a governess before.'

'She's down on her luck and desperate but can afford to sail to Europe?'

'Maybe the tickets aren't for her. Maybe she bought them on behalf of someone else. Maybe an old flame sent them to her. There could be a hundred explanations.'

'Maybe, maybe, maybe! As if any of those things were likely.'

'Are they any more unlikely than a dead governess coming back in a different body and walking on water and living in mirrors?' He was practically shouting now and this led to a coughing fit which lasted several minutes. He had trouble getting his spray out of the pocket of his jacket but finally managed it and gave himself a good dose, whereupon the coughing subsumed and he sank into a chair, sweating and exhausted, his breath coming once more in those sawing rasps.

It fortuned for the good relations between us that at that moment we heard a carriage upping the drive and, looking out the window, saw Dr Bradley, come to make his daily visit to Mrs Grouse. We went and opened the front door for him. He took one look at Theo, who paled and whose skin was waxy as a plucked chicken's before it is put in the oven, and grunted.

'Hmmpf! I have come to see one patient and find I have to deal with two. You're in a bad way, my young friend, and if you keep on refusing my advice you'll end up in a worse. And I suspect you're not using your spray enough. I depend upon you, you know, to test its efficacy. Now go and sit down until I have seen Mrs Grouse and then I'll give you a ride home.'

He mounted the stairs and Theo and I returned to the drawing room, where he sheepished in a chair and I difficulted to not give him a piece of my mind, so distraught did I feel at his sudden lack of faith in me, but held off because it obvioused he so illed.

Eventually I heard the sound of downstairsing and went into the hall to find the doctor with Miss Taylor hovering at his side like a fallen angel. Seeing my inquiring face, the doctor said, 'There has been no improvement in Mrs Grouse's condition, I'm afraid. Fact is, if anything, she's worse, which surprises me somewhat. I'm going back to town and I'll have an ambulance sent out to take her to the hospital. She'll be better off there.'

Miss Taylor meeked him a bow of the head. 'I'm so sorry,' she insincered, 'I tried my best . . .'

'Oh, no, no, no, ma'am,' replied the doctor. 'I didn't mean that . . .' His voice died away as if to say he wasn't entirely sure what he did mean, while he looked at the governess as though something about her puzzled him. I remembered he had treated Miss Whitaker for migraine a couple of times and it struck me that perhaps some spark of memory of her had been kindled by Miss Taylor.

Theo left with the doctor and for the rest of the afternoon I towered it on my own, reasoning that our new governess was too preoccupied with her patient to concern herself over what I was up to. As far as she was concerned, she had me like a bird in a net, fluttering my wings helplessly. I had chosen the tower over the library a little for old times' sake, when the discovery of my reading was all I had to worry about, but mainly so that I could watch the drive. As soon as I saw the ambulance, a large wagon pulled by a team of four, up the drive, I downstairsed fast as I could and waited in the hall. I wanted to catch sight of Mrs Grouse and get some idea of the condition she was in. I feared me the fiend might have put a pillow over the poor woman's face to prevent her going out of her control, where she might yield up her secrets. The two ambulance men carried Mrs Grouse out on a stretcher. She was completely unconscious and looked like a waxwork or an oversized doll, lifelike but lifeless. Just before they slid the stretcher into the vehicle I made a dash for it, giving Miss Taylor no time to stop me, and planted a kiss on the housekeeper's lips. To my relief they were warm and although she showed no response I drew comfort from the knowledge that she was still alive.

CHAPTER 28

Although it seemed now that my heart beat faster and that flocks of birds were in my stomach, so that I could scarce eat or sleep, I found myself both dreading and wishing for Friday, for I sured that was when the witch would make her move. Mostly, though, I longed for the day to come, no matter how much the thought of what I must go through terrified me. I wanted it all to be over. I wanted the opportunity at last, after so much subterfuge on both our parts, to join battle with her and overcome.

And at those times when the fear grew so great that I wanted instead to run away, I could always comfort myself with the knowledge that nothing could happen until the last day, and that even then, when she found the chloroform gone, she would have to come up with a different plan.

So it was that I near fainted when I came down for lunch on Thursday and found John, Meg and Mary in the hall, all three in their Sunday best and surrounded by baskets and carpet bags. Meg was hugging Giles while Mary was doing her best to suffocate him by kissing.

'What's happening? Where are you going? You surely can't be leaving us here alone?' I stammered.

There was a rustle of silk behind me and our new governess was by my side. She smirked me one. 'I thought it would be nice if Mrs Grouse had some visitors. Dr Bradley says that in such cases the sound of familiar voices can help a patient recover her senses.'

Meg pinched my cheek. 'And we all want to see Mrs Grouse, too. We've known her and worked with her and lived with her all these years, and we can't bear to think of her alone. I've two baskets of goodies I've baked for her so she'll have some home comforts when she comes round.'

'But Giles and I –'

'Will be perfectly all right,' said Meg, beaming one at Miss Taylor. 'I've left a mountain of food for you and Miss Taylor knows all about it. It's only for two nights. We'll be back by noon on Saturday.'

My heart sank. By then it would be too late. By then it would all be over. I had not reckoned with this in my imaginings of the witch's scheme. She had outmanoeuvred me quite.

I followed the trio, who all gratefulled Miss Taylor with a mixture of smiles and curtseys and forelocking, out the front door. John had hitched a horse to the old wagon which he used to haul supplies from town and he helped the two women up into it, which occasioned much laughing, for Meg was so fat she could not manage the climb at all and he had to put his shoulder beneath her derrière to get her over the side. Then he climbed up onto the seat, threw me a wink and shook the reins. The three of us watched the wagon disappear up the drive.

Miss Taylor turned to me and triumphed me one. 'Well! So here we are.'

I defianted her one back, squaring up to her for the battle to come. For I would not let her see in my face the great panic I felt inside. It was lost! The game was up! I had no one to help me now. For all I knew, this might be the moment she made her attack. Who could guess what powers the fiend possessed? What evil tricks had she learned during her short stay in Hell?

Instead, she held out her hand to Giles. 'Come, Giles,' she said, and the two of them walked back into the house. I myself could scarce move. My legs and every other bone in my body shook. I cursed myself for meeking it while the servants were still here. I should have thrown myself upon them and screamed and told them all . . . except, I knew I would not have been believed. Theo was right. It too fantasti-called for anyone without an imagination.

Once in the house, I listened, trying to hear where the others might be. I looked here and there and frequently over-my-shouldered, for I did not want to be caught unawares. I sneaked upstairs and heard voices coming from the schoolroom. Miss Taylor fairytaling Giles.

I walked back along the corridor past the mirror there and then stopped. I went back, lifted the mirror from its hook and, holding it to my bosom, downstairsed as fast as I could. I outed the back door and ran to the lake. I put the mirror on the ground and jumped up and down upon it, until the glass was all in pieces, then hurled the frame into the water.

During the course of the afternoon I did the same with the mirror in the upper corridor. The one in the entrance hall was fastened on the wall with screws and would anyway have been too heavy for me to lift. So I took a cane from the umbrella stand and smashed the glass, and when it was all in pieces I went around the edges of the frame with the handle of the cane, making sure not a sliver remained in which she would be able to see where I was.

Afterward I took a broom from Mary's cupboard and swept up the shards of broken glass, for I did not want Giles to accident upon them. In all the time I was doing this, removing from her the advantage of her spyglasses, she did not appear. At first this surprised me quite, for I expected that when she saw through the mirrors what I was up to, she would descend upon me in a fury. But then it struck me. It was worse that she did not. It meant she considered me powerless; it simply did not matter to her where I was or what I did.

Now that she could not see me moving about the house, I needed to sit and think and make plans of my own. I went into the kitchen and took bread and cakes and cookies and filled a stone jar with water and tied it all up in a cloth and made my way along the long corridor and upstairsed it to my tower. It was the one place she would not easily find me; even Giles didn't know about it and I considered myself to be safe there, but there was another reason to be there too: I needed to be able to watch the drive, for if Theo should put in an appearance I could not afford to miss him. With everyone else gone, he was my last hope.

It was a long afternoon and although I Robinson Crusoed the drive, squinting to see a friendly sail, there was no sign of Theo. I had to face the grim possibility that after yesterday's attack his asthma now so serioused that he would not be paying me another visit before I Armageddoned with the governess. When the sun went down it began to cold, and distant dogs barked and the owl hooted. Of course, I could not light my candle for fear Miss Taylor might happen to step outside the house and see the light, but it fortuned I had no need of it, for it near full mooned, filling the tower with a pale, icy light, and I took this for a good sign that something, at least, was on my side.

That night I slept upon the trapdoor. I reasoned that it would be difficult, if not impossible, for a strong man, let alone a normal woman, to lift it from below with my weight upon it. Of course, Miss Taylor was not a normal woman and I had no way of knowing what powers a ghost such as she might have. I knew she could walk on water. I did not know though if ghosts really could walk through walls or if such tales were just so much foolishness. I would have to wait and see and above all hope she would not think of me being in the tower at all.

I feverished the night away. At some time I must have fallen asleep, for when I opened my eyes the harsh white light of the moon had given way to a grey dawn. A fierce wind howled about the tower and sent ragged clouds scudding across the sky like frightened birds fleeing the oncoming winter. When I moved, my every limb and muscle ached as if my body unwillinged to face the day.

I shook this silliness out of myself and got to my feet. I found my supplies and, even though my stomach churned, forced myself to chew my way through four or five of Meg's cookies. I took a good swig of water and used the rest to splash my face, its iciness fulling me awake and ready for the task. As I lay there last night, it had come to me, a way in which I might make all turn out right, a way to save Giles and perhaps banish our governess, new and old, for ever. But for my plan to succeed perfectly, I needed Theo Van Hoosier to show up. I looked out at the drive and saw there was no sign of him, but that was hardly surprising, for it yet earlied and it would be at least an hour or so before he abouted in the visiting kind of way. I walked to another corner of my tower and looked down at the rear of the house, at the outbuildings which I knew it more importanted me to watch, for it was here, if I guessed correctly, that the governess would make her first move.

I had a long wait. The sun got himself up and proceeded to climb the sky, although I only glimpsed him now and then through holes in the mournful day's canopy of grey. Meantime, I restlessed back and forth in the tower, now checking the drive, now pacing to the back to check the outbuildings. And at last I had my reward! There was a movement and I saw the governess, holding her cloak about her tight, her head bent against the force of the wind, slip from the back of the house toward the stable. I didn't waste a moment. I lifted the trapdoor and downstairsed and downbanistered in a trice. I flew along the corridor to the back door and outed. The wind gusted so hard it near knocked me off my feet, but I bent my head into it and ploughed on. The stable door was open and I carefulled an eye around the edge of the lintel and saw her as I had guessed she would be. She had lifted a harness from the wall and was walking toward Bluebird's stall. I didn't need to see any more but about-turned and, this time with the wind behind me, tore back into the house, upstairsed two at a time, flew along the corridor and flung open the door of the schoolroom. Giles was sitting looking at a picture book and at my wild entrance jerked his head up in alarm.

'Flo! Where have you been? You missed breakfast and supper and Miss Taylor told me you were ill.'

'Well, I'm not! Come quick, I have something to show you!'

He doubtfulled. 'Flo, I'm not sure. Miss Taylor told me to wait here. She – she's taking me on a little trip.'

'It won't take but a minute, Giles. It's something special. A secret place! A really secret place. The best hiding place in all of Blithe. No one will ever find you there.'

'Well, OK, but only for a minute, mind.' He got up. I noted that he was wearing his best apparel.

I led him to the end of the corridor and downstairs and then to the tower stairs. 'OK,' I said, 'up you go!'

He stared at the débris heaped across the bottom steps and then asked me, 'But how?'

'Ah, that's the beauty of it. It looks impossible, don't it? All right, follow me.'

As I began going up the outside of the banisters, putting my feet in the gaps between, I glanced back at my little brother and saw him wide-eyed with wonder. Without any further prompting he was up and after me, for no boy can resist a climb. I pulled myself over the banisters and then turned and hauled Giles after me. We sat on the stairs laughing, like the good old days. I had no worry, for I knew it would take Miss Taylor considerable time to harness Bluebird and hitch up the trap. There was no danger yet.

We got to our feet and Giles raced me up the stairs but at the top had not the strength to lift

275

the trapdoor into the tower. I pushed it open for him and a moment later we were in my secret kingdom, lords of all we surveyed.

'Look!' shouted Giles. 'There's Theo!' and sure enough, halfway up the drive was that familiar heron striding toward the house.

'Where?' I replied, slipping the bottle from the pocket of my dress.

'There! There! On the drive, can't you see, Flo?'

I unscrewed the bottle and tipped some of the liquid onto my handkerchief. 'Ugh, what's that smell?' said Giles, and he began to turn his head, but too late, for I had the cloth over his face and my arm around his head like a vice, gripping him to me, muffling his protests with the cloth until he ceased to struggle. I let him rag-doll slowly to the floor and bent over him to check he was still breathing.

That certain, I arranged him into a comfortable position, placing a cushion beneath his head, for I did not know how the chloroform worked and I figured that if he were comfortable he would be less likely to wake. Besides, I did not want my little brother awaking stiff or sore – as I had done – from lying in a bad way.

CHAPTER 29

O nce I had comfortabled Giles, I outed the trapdoor, closed it behind me, down-stairsed, downbanistered and corridored at breakneck pace. When I reached the front door and looked out the window, Theo was standing staring at the house, puzzling and scratching his head. It obvioused he had rung the bell several times and, having received no reply, was confused as to why. It didn't matter about him ringing the bell, because Miss Taylor could not have heard it from the stables. I just gratefulled I had got here before Theo walked away.

I opened the door and stepped through it and his expression relieved to see me. 'Florence, where is everybody? I thought perhaps you'd all died of the plague.'

'Theo,' I said, grabbing his hand, 'there's no time to waste. I need your help, come quick!' He stood still, dumbfounded. I tugged him. 'Come on!'

We ran along the front of the house and around the side, bringing us to the back of the house, but at the opposite end from the stables where Miss Taylor would be still at work hitching up the horse.

By now it well late-afternooned and the sun was already thinking about retiring for the night, not that he had been out much all day anyway. I led Theo past some old glasshouses that had long ago fallen into disrepair, there being no one to tend them, and brought him to the thing that was at the heart of my plan.

'I need your help to get all this stuff off,' I said, waving a hand at the old well. Theo stood staring at it, at its low walls and the planks laid across them and then the heavy slabs of stone in turn laid upon them.

'It's a well,' said Theo.

I impatiented. There was no time to lose. 'Yes, yes, of course it's a well; what else would it be!' Seeing his face, I relented. 'Theo, I'm sorry, but if I am to prevent that witch from taking Giles we need to do this now.'

'But why?'

I exasperated, hands on hips. I wondered whether I could tell him but deep inside I knew that doing so would result in an argument which I by no means certained of winning. Theo so often scrupled about the littlest thing and he also cowarded over anything that was against the rules. This was very much against the rules! Besides, I needed to hurry. The witch might be finished in the stables at any moment.

'I don't have time to explain now. Please, please, Theo, help me!'

He made no reply but just stood there, staring first at the well and then at me.

'Very well!' I snapped. I strode up to the well, grabbed the top paving stone and began trying to lift it. Puffing and panting, with the greatest effort, I managed to raise one side of it a couple of inches, but then my strength gave out and I had to let it drop. Without looking at Theo, I seized hold of the stone again and began once more grunting and groaning as I struggled with it. That was too much for any Yankee gentleman to stand. Theo rushed to me, seized the other side of the stone and began to lift too, and between us we managed to slide it off the one beneath and place it on the ground. As we let go of it, Theo commenced to coughing, which necessitated the use of his spray, but as soon as the fit subsided, he was ready again for the fray. In this manner, huffing and puffing, grunting and groaning, coughing and spraying, we managed to lift all five slabs and place them in a neat pile upon the ground.

Then we removed the four thick planks, one by one. These were not so heavy and when Theo began coughing after the third one, I slid the fourth off on my own. When we were done Theo looked down into the well and whistled. 'Phew! That's some hole. Does it even have a bottom?'

I didn't answer, for the less said about the well the better. I took his hand and carefulled him back around to the front of the house and in through the front door.

'Say, what happened to the mirror?' he said, seeing the empty frame.

'I smashed it.' I prouded. 'I had to make sure she couldn't see what I was up to.'

'And what are you up to?' He stood curiousing me one. 'What's all that business with the well for?'

I put a finger to his lips to quieten him. 'No talking now,' I whispered. 'I have no idea where she is. She was in the stables but she may have finished there by this time. Follow me and don't say another word.'

Checking carefully first at the corner at the end of the hall that we coast-cleared, I led him into the long corridor and down to the other end, where we outed and came to the bottom of the stairs to the tower and I started to banister up. When I was halfway I stopped and beckoned Theo, who stood looking up at me, evidently exhausted. 'Well, don't just stand there, come on!'

A moment later we were up in the tower. Giles still peacefulled on the floor, his breath rising and falling nice and steady, which relieved me quite. Theo looked from my brother to me. 'Chloroform,' I said. I showed him the bottle and the cloth. 'Stay here and keep watch over him. If he starts to wake, give him another dose.'

Theo took the cloth and sniffed it, dropped it and immediately began to cough. He slid to the floor deathly pale and gasping. Sitting with his back to the wall, he fumbled his spray bottle from his pocket and gave himself another blast, which seemed to quiet him. He set his spray down on the floor beside him.

'Theo, just rest for a while. I'll be back directly!' I said. I lifted the trapdoor and back downstairsed fast as I could. I long-corridored and outed the back door. I reached the stables just as Miss Taylor was coming out and I guessed that the trap was now all harnessed up.

'Miss Taylor! Miss Taylor!' I screamed. 'Come quick! It's Giles! He's had an accident!'

Her face went pale as the corpse I knew she had been. 'An accident, what do you mean?'

'Please!' I turned and began to run. 'Just come!'

I pulled up my skirts and took off and fairly flew along the back of the building, giving her no time to think. I swear I felt her breath hot on my neck, so close behind me was she, but I had the speed of the devil and she could only just keep up. I stopped, panting so hard I could not speak. I held out a shaky hand, pointing at the well.

'Giles . . . the well . . . I told him not to . . .'

She understood immediately, rushed to the wall around the well and bent over it. 'Giles!' she screamed. 'Giles! Are you all right?'

I pushed her aside and climbed up onto the wall, resting on my knees, and held on to the pole that had once held the bucket rope so that I could swing my head right over the centre of the opening. 'There he is!' I shouted. 'I can see him! I think he's moving!'

'Watch out, let me see!' she said, tugging at my leg. I climbed down from the wall and in an instant she had replaced me, clambering up onto her knees and, with one hand holding on to the pole, stretched out her neck and peered down. 'Where is he? I don't see anything. Giles! Giles!'

I cast around and saw a hefty branch lying by the well. I picked it up and swung it hard and struck the hand that was holding the pole. I swear I hit it so hard you could hear her metacarpals snap, but she hung on for dear life, her knuckles white as bone. I swung again and caught her another one even harder than the first. There was another crack and her fingers uncurled from around the pole. I dropped the wood and flung my full weight at her and with both hands gave her such a shove that over she went, into the well. She was gone with a single scream. I had Hansel and Gretelled her with one magnificent blow.

I peered over the edge of the well. There was nothing but blackness, a deep hole that might go to the very centre of the earth, for all I knew. My whole body, my torso, down to my fingers and toes, was shaking with the triumph of it all and also with the fear. For I knew not what powers the fiend had. I knew she could not be killed, for she was already dead. But it possibled she might know how to fly. I lifted the end of one of the wooden planks and dragged it over the edge of the wall. Resting it there, I went to the other end, lifted it and slid it across the chasm, so that it ended up resting on the wall on either side, as it had been before. I did the same with the remaining planks until the opening was covered quite. In this fashion I would know if she had escaped while I was gone. Then I betook me back to the house.

I made my way straight up to the governess's room. Her two valises were on her bed, both closed. I prayed they would not be locked and it fortuned so. I opened the one containing Giles's clothes, removed them and took them next door into his room, where I put them away. I opened the other valise. I looked around the room and found her hat, coat and purse, but everything else was packed. I opened her purse, found some money and took it all. Then I put the purse and the coat into the valise that had contained Giles's things. Making sure both valises were fastened tight again I took them downstairs and out the back door to the well. I relieved to see none of the planks had been moved. Unless she possessed the power to pass through solid objects, which I had seen no sign of, she must be still trapped. I took the end of one of the planks and manoeuvred it onto the one next to it, heart in mouth, for any moment I expected her to come shooting out like a genie released from a bottle, but nothing occurred. I took first one valise and then the other and dropped them through the gap I had made. Then I manipulated the plank back into position and headed back to the tower.

When I put my head through the trapdoor, Theo was where I had left him, his spray bottle by his side. He had that ready-for-the-oven-chickenskin look about him again and his breath rasped like a file. But something else stranged too, something in the way he looked at me, that somehow mixed fear with disdain.

'Theo, I know you're poorly,' I said, 'but I need your help again and I must have it now.'

'Very well.' He spoke like someone in a dream as if not really connecting with what I said. With a great effort, he dragged himself to his feet and followed me to the trapdoor. I quicked one at Giles, saw that he still peacefulled and then descended.

Theo stumbled twice on the stairs and had difficulty climbing over the banister rail, but I urged him on, for I could not have him quitting on me now. For the first thing anyone familiar with Blithe, such as John, would ask would be, who moved the stones?

I helped Theo around the house as if he were the one with the bad ankle now. We came at last to the well. I was relieved to see my four planks still in place, evidently undisturbed. 'Help me lift the stones,' I told Theo. Without a word, like a dead man with no expression or an automaton with no will of its own, he bent and took one side of the top slab of the pile we had made. I took the other and we began to lift. It was much, much harder than before, because then we had simply slid the stone from the pile and put it down. Now we were actually lifting it from the ground. I seemed to have the strength of a hundred men, which I put down to the excitement that was coursing through my veins. Theo, though, had only that of a pale and trembling boy. Nevertheless, he bent himself bravely to the task, his face a grimace of agony. In this fashion we lifted the first slab onto the planks. No sooner did we have it in place than Theo started coughing, as though he had been holding off all this time. He patted his pockets, but didn't take out his spray. He shrugged, got the fit under control and we commenced on the second stone. By the time we had that in place, Theo was coughing all the time, but I drove him on. It seemed to take an age, but at last we had three slabs in position and were nearly finished with the fourth, but just as we were levering it onto the one below, Theo staggered and let go where he was holding it, so that I had the whole weight on my own. I near dropped it on my foot, which surely would have broken every bone in it, so suddenly did Theo release it, but I pulled myself together just in time and, thrusting my body against the edge of the slab, with a loud cry from the very effort of it, slid it into position.

Theo was now coughing uncontrollably. 'Theo, use your spray!' I cried.

'I cannot.' He sucked in air with a terrible wheezing noise. 'I left it – I – I – I left it – up in the – in the tower.'

I put my shoulder under his and arounded him the side of the house. We went in through the back door and made our way to the foot of the tower. I lowered him gently to the ground, leaning him against the wall. 'Theo, wait here, I'll go fetch the spray.'

I upbanistered and hauled my tired body over it and onto the stairs, pausing to look back at Theo, who paled and lifelessed against the wall, no longer coughing, but panting like a runner after a long race, or the way that when you caught a fish and laid it on the ground beside the lake and watched it, it would gasp as if for air until it expired. I turned and ran up the stairs. In the tower room I made straight for the spray and on the way noted that Giles still peacefulled and breathed nice and steady. I was about to go down through the trapdoor when something suddenly anxioused me, some thought I could not at first identify.

Then there it was, that look Theo had given me when I returned to the tower room, that fear of me in his eyes, followed by the resigned way he had followed me and helped me with the planks and stones. What could it mean?

I suddened an instinct and walked across the room and looked out the back window. Below me I saw the well, perfectly in view. I knew then that not so long before, Theo had stood here. And I knew that he had seen. And I knew Theo. If there were any doubt about what he thought of my action he would have remonstrated with me, he would have refused to help me. It obvioused why he had not. It was that fear I'd seen in his eyes. He had gone along with what he considered my madness because it was the safest and easiest way. It meant one thing. As soon as he awayed from Blithe, he would tell.

I outed the trapdoor and downstairsed. From the top step of the last flight I looked down and saw Theo, all white and waxy, panting out his life. 'Florence, hurry!' he gasped. 'Please hurry!'

I did not move.

He repeated his plea. 'Florence, please! Why are you just standing there, please!'

I did not move and watched in horror. Seeing me statue like that, he began to push himself up. He fell forward, flat on his face, and I all but rushed down to help him, for I thought he was near done for, but then his body twitched and he pushed himself up onto his hands and knees, like a dog, head hanging loose between his arms. 'Florence . . .' His voice scratched the air and it was like someone cheesegrating my soul. 'Florence . . .'

He pushed with his hands and got himself upright. He managed to get one foot on the ground, so he was now only on one knee, like a suitor popping the question, only what he said was, 'Florence, don't do this! I didn't see a thing! I won't say a word.' The effort of talking was too much and he commenced to coughing so brutally it painfulled me quite too. Somehow, with what reserves of strength I do not know, he got himself onto his feet.

He staggered toward the stairs. I backed away and leaned against the wall behind me, watching in horror as he advanced. He reached the stairs and all but collapsed against them, sliding down, but at the last moment clutched the rail with his hands and then, after a dreadful pause, hauled himself upright again. 'Florence!' His voice sawed through my heart.

I made no reply and he lifted one foot and put it between two of the banisters. Pulling hard with his hands, he hauled himself up and got his other foot between another two banisters; resting the weight of his long body over them, he reached out a bony, plaintive hand. 'Florence, please, give it to me!'

I held fast against the wall, clutching the flask behind me. I watched in dread as he lifted one leg like a drunk trying to mount a horse and, after two or three futile efforts, threw it over the banisters. He pushed up with the other foot and got his body on top of the banisters. He lay there, one leg and one arm either side, resting on the rail. He tried to say something but the word or words just gargled and died in his throat. His breath gave one tremendous last rasp and then there was nothing but silence. Poor Theo, my poor heron boy, who used to graceful on the frozen lake; poor, poor Theo would skate no more.

CHAPTER 30

My first difficulty was to downstairs without disturbing Theo. His dying on me like this had not been part of my plan, but now that it had happened I recognised it had necessaried all along; for his straightforward nature would never have been equal to the task of maintaining my secret. I overed to him and put my ear to his side. There was no sound from those poor tired-out lungs. It mercifulled that after so much misery they were now at rest. I lifted his head a little and pressed my lips to his and gentled him the kiss he had always craved but never properly received. It took but a moment; I had no more time to lose. I slipped the spray bottle into the pocket of his jacket and went up a few steps. I overed the banisters. I could not use them to get down to the ground because Theo was in the way. I did not want to push his body off the banister because already a plan was forming in my mind which necessitated him remaining where he was. I was here some ten feet from the ground and there was nothing for it but to jump. I deep-breathed, closed my eyes and let go. I landed hard

289

and my right ankle, the one that had been injured before, so sored I thought I had broke it, so that for a moment I anxioused putting my weight on it, in which case I would be trapped and have some mighty difficult explaining to do. I got myself up and slowly let my weight onto my right foot and was relieved that although it pained me some, it did not prevent me walking.

It was now dark, but it fortuned the sky had all but cleared, with only a few rags of cloud remaining and the full moon gave me good light. I went to the barn and found John's wheelbarrow. I wheeled it in through the back door and along the corridor to the bottom of the tower. I set it down beside the staircase directly below Theo. Then I hauled myself up the bottom two banisters and tugged him off. He fell like a sack of potatoes straight into the barrow. I clambered back down and took the handles of the wheelbarrow, silent-praying that I would be able to lift them, for I did not know if I could manage Theo's weight.

I deep-breathed again and lifted and surprised me; he seemed to weigh no more than a sparrow, and as I pushed him back along the corridor and out the back door I thought how weak and frail his illness had made him. He was long but he was not broad, and that was my good luck. I took him into the barn and wheeled the barrow up the loading ramp that John used for horse and chicken feed and the like. It was a hard push, light as Theo was, up the incline, but I just put my head down and ran right at it and was up it in no more than a few seconds. I left the wheelbarrow and its contents there and next-doored to the stables, where Bluebird was waiting patiently, all harnessed up to the trap. I took his bridle and, stroking him and whispering kindly to him, led him into the barn, where I positioned him so the trap was below the loading bay. Still crooning to him softly, I climbed up onto the seat of the trap and put on the brake. Then I jumped down, went up onto the loading bay, took the handles of the wheelbarrow, turned it to face the trap and with one almighty shove tipped it up so that Theo tumbled down into the back of it.

I had to rest me a moment or two after that. I was sweating and panting. I went to the apple barrel, took one out and offered it to Bluebird. After he'd finished it and having certained that he was content, I went back up the ramp, got the wheelbarrow and took it back into the barn, leaving it as I had found it.

Then I went back into the house and made my way up into the tower. Giles was still sleeping, although now he restlessed a little and murmured to himself. I took the cloth with the chloroform on it and gave him another dose, but only a quick one this time, for I feared giving him too much. I waited a few minutes to certain he was breathing easily and normally and then slipped out of the tower and up to the governess's room to fetch the money and the other item I had taken from her bag. I went to my own room and put on my black cloak.

I returned to the barn, took Bluebird's bridle and led him outside. I mounted the driver's seat and gentled the reins so that he began to trot. The wind had dropped and the night was crisp and clear and the moonlight showed me the way almost as plain as day. Bluebird of course knew the road to town, it was almost the only place he ever took the trap, so I had little need to steer until we reached the drive to the Van Hoosier place. I turned into it and made my way about halfway up it. I dared not go any further lest Theo's tutor or the servants hear the noise of Bluebird's hooves.

I had Bluebird turn around, so the back of the trap was facing the edge of the woods, and then I put on the brake and climbed into the back. Somehow Theo seemed to have grown heavier in the hour or so since I had wheeled him up the ramp, or perhaps it happened that I had weakened from all my exertions, but it took me some considerable time to manhandle his body over the edge of the trap. All the while I heart-in-mouthed, fearing someone might come. It was now well into the evening and I reckoned it to be long past the time Theo should have been home for supper. The servants might be searching for him already and if they found me here, all would be up with me.

But at last it was done. I was so tired I would fain have laid me down there and then and slept, but I knew I could not. I mounted the box again, took off the brake and flicked the reins to gee up Bluebird. I greatly relieved to turn again onto the main road; the greater the distance between me and Theo, the better.

It colded now and even under my cloak I shivered. The frost had come down hard and the road was slippery, so that sometimes the wheels of the trap would slide across it in a most alarming way. I had so little experience of driving the trap, just a few minutes when John occasionally let me try for fun, that I nervoused to go too quickly, even though I knew those other horses, the horses of the night, were flying fast. I met only a farmer's cart upon the road and, soon as I saw it, drew the hood of my cloak over my face so that I would not be recognised. The driver of the cart did not hail me but simply raised his whip by way of greeting, which I repaid with a silent nod.

After that I aloned with the moon and the squeaking of the bats that darted here and there; fear rose up my gullet, like food too rich to digest, but not of the night, which I regarded as my friend, but of what I had to accomplish and of not being able to do it.

Eventually lights began to appear in the distance in front of me and to multiply the further I went, and in a few minutes I outskirted the town, passing the first scattered houses. I turned round and picked out of the trap the item I had taken from Miss Taylor's room, her hat. I lowered my hood and placed the hat firmly upon my head and drew the veil over my face, entering Main Street with my features shielded from view as Miss Taylor's had been when we visited the dentist. There were few people about, for it was a night to indoors and huddle around a fire, an idea that appealed me now. At the turn to the railroad station I made a mess of controlling the reins and could in no way get Bluebird to turn, so that before I knew it we were almost past the turn.

'Whoa, boy!' I called out, giving the reins a good jerk, for stopping him was one thing I could do. The good old horse duly halted. I hopped down from the box and, taking his bridle, turned him around and, when he was pointed in the right direction, got back up on the box and flicked the reins to start him up again. In a couple of minutes we were trotting up to the station.

Right away the silence was gone. There was a bustle of people walking to and from the station and many buggies and carts going in either direction too. I awared the clanking of metal and, as I approached the railroad station itself, the hiss of steam, for there, like a dragon lying in wait for me, sat the locomotive, its long tail of passenger cars stretching out behind it. Men were shouting, doors crashing shut, horses whinnying. At first I afraided at all this commotion, but when I saw that no one paid me any attention, for I was but another among many, I realised it was to my advantage. I stopped the trap by a hitching rail, climbed down and hitched Bluebird to it. I knew where I was going from the time we brought Giles here when he went off to school. Looking neither right nor left, I marched straight into the booking hall, past the people gathered there, many of them saying good-byes to loved ones, and up to the ticket window. There was no one behind it.

I looked around. A man and woman had come up behind me. The man was carrying a carpet bag and it evidented they were going for a train. I looked up and saw the station clock and near dropped dead from shock. It wanted only ten minutes before nine o'clock. If I didn't hurry I would be too late for the Flyer, which I knew departed upon the hour.

The man and woman were behind me now, waiting in line, and I sensed them impatienting. The woman bent her head over my shoulder. 'You have to tap the glass,' she said and gave the window a sharp rap with her knuckles. As if by magic a small bald head bobbed up behind the counter in front of me.

'Yes, ma'am?' he said.

'I'd like to buy a ticket on the Flyer for New York, please.'

'Would that be a return, ma'am?'

'No,' I loud-and-cleared. 'Just the one way. I shall not be coming back.'

He handed me a ticket and I paid him from the money I had taken from Miss Taylor's purse. The man behind straightway began purchasing tickets for him and his companion and didn't seem to give me another thought.

I walked out of the ticket hall to the track. As I approached the train a cloud of steam hissed from the locomotive and engulfed me, for which by instinct I gratefulled, for it hid me quite, until I reminded myself that this would not do, that I needed to be seen. I duly walked the whole length of the train and back to the front again, nervousing inside, for the locomotive was pawing the ground, anxious to be off, snorting louder and louder as it eagered. At the front car I found a group of some six or seven men mounting the stairs and bolded up to them. Spotting me, one of them pulled another man aside and, sweeping off his hat, indicated the steps. 'After you, ma'am.'

I nodded a thanks and upped the steps. The car was more than half full, for the train had made many more stops before this one. I walked along the aisle, looking this way and that as though searching for a seat. Near the end of the car a man in a loud check suit and a bowler hat glanced up as he saw me pass. He hastily moved a carpet bag from the seat next to him and said, 'Here, ma'am, this seat is free.'

I did not know what to do, for I could not take the seat, but nor did I feel I could rudely ignore him. My moment's hesitation near cost me dear, I can tell you. Collecting myself quickly, I nodded a thanks and waved a dismissive hand and proceeded to the end of the car and out the door, as if to go through to the next car in the hope of finding a better seat. My plan was to descend by the steps at the end of the car and make my getaway, but as I exited the first car into the second a couple of ladies were coming through from the opposite direction and I had to give way to them.

When they had gone I was about to descend the steps when I heard a voice behind me. 'You'll find it just as busy the whole length of the car, ma'am.'

I turned and found the loud check. He took off his hat and leered me one. I faltered, feeling trapped. There was a sudden great hiss of steam from the locomotive. The train gave an almighty jerk and I had to grab hold of the door frame so as not to stumble.

'I – I.'

'Come on, ma'am, I won't bite you, y'know.'

'Why, of course, thank you,' I said. 'But you see, I wasn't going to look for another seat. I was after my bag, which I left a couple of cars back.'

'Why, ma'am, I'd be happy to go fetch it for you. If'n you'll just describe it to me, that is.'

The train lurched again. 'You can't miss it, it – it's red. Bright red velveteen. I put it down on the last seat in the car before this one. I – I was waving goodbye to my sister and wouldn't you know I was so upset at leaving her that I went and forgot all about it. What a nincompoop I am! Would you really be so kind as to go fetch it for me?'

He put his hat back on and tipped the brim to me. 'It'll be my pleasure, ma'am. Now, you just go back there and sit where I was sitting – and be sure to take the seat by the window – and I'll be back directly with your bag.'

As he disappeared into the next car the train jolted again and this time there was another hiss, a loud grinding of metal upon metal and through the open doorway I saw the booking office begin to move. I looked right and left; there was no one in sight. I whipped off my hat and stuffed it under my cloak and downed the steps and stood on the bottom one. The train was moving at a brisk walking pace and gathering speed all the time; if I didn't jump now it would be too late. I jumped and managed not to stumble, which was just as well, for I no longer wanted to draw attention to myself.

The trackside was still busy with people waving their friends goodbye and porters hereing and thereing. I pulled my hood over my head and fast-awayed, not going through the booking hall this time but around it, and could not help smiling to myself at the thought of the loud check searching for a red velveteen bag he would never find. Of course, Miss Taylor would have had a bag if she had really caught the train, but if I had taken one I would have had to leave it on board, and it later being found abandoned might suspicion things more. I had to hope that any witnesses to the veiled woman at the station misremembered whether or not she was carrying baggage.

In the street outside I last-looked at Bluebird

and the trap. The good old horse stood waiting patiently as I had left him. He was in for a mighty long cold wait, which brought a tear to my eye, for I sorried to have caused him that. I thought of Theo, lying on the cold ground with the frost now stiffening his hair, and, I do confess, shed a tear or two more at that.

What had taken so little time in the trap, even though at the time I felt I slowed because of my inexperience at driving, now seemed to take an age on foot. It must have been a good twenty minutes before I cleared the outskirts of the town. I tireded not only because I would normally have long been in bed but from all that I had been through, the heavy work of lifting the wood and stones off the well and then putting them back, hauling poor Theo around, the running hither and thither, and also at the very thought that I now had ten miles to walk or else all so far would be for nought.

The road lonelied and now every noise spooked me. Each cry of the owl made me jump, each skimming bat made me duck. A couple of times I heard carriages coming and had to leave the road and hide behind a tree. More than once I stumbled and fell, hurting my knees and grazing my hands. The wind got up and for the last few miles blew directly into my face as if trying to hold me back.

What made the journey worse was my anxiousing. For it suddenly struck me that there was one part of my plan over which I had no control. When Theo did not return home his tutor and the Van Hoosier servants would begin to worry and eventually they would go out to look for him. If they didn't find him around the grounds of his own house then it would logical next to seek him at Blithe, where they knew he was a frequent visitor.

I desperated to search my mind. How exactly had I left Theo? It obvioused that his people would not be able to take the shortcut through the woods to Blithe because it would impossible in the dark, but would have to up their drive and go round by the main road. My hope was that they would come across Theo as they upped the drive. Now, I had dumped his body beside the drive, but how close to it did I leave him? If it was too far away, they might simply walk right past him in the dark and proceed to Blithe, where of course they would find the house in darkness and no reply to their knocking at the door, with the servants all gone and me not there. This in turn would surprise them, for they would not know about the servants being sent away. They might think something had happened at Blithe, something that perhaps involved Theo – for his absence and the absence of everyone from Blithe would too much co-incidence not to connect. If they should enter the house and find me gone, I would not be able to explain it away.

At one point I so wearied and the road ahead so endlessed that I all but decided I might as well give up and lay me down to sleep where I was and let them find me and do to me what they would, for I was almost past caring. Then I looked up and saw to my left, a few hundred yards away, the chimneys of a great house topping the trees. It was the Van Hoosier place! I was not more than half an hour from home.

The thought of Blithe and Giles and all at last again being as it had always been spurred me on. I quickened my pace, heart-in-mouthing it past the entrance to the Van Hoosier drive as I feared any moment the family's servants might come rushing out, hunting for Theo. But no one did. By now I was tripping and stumbling at every step, I so exhausted, and it seemed another age before our drive came in sight. At last there it was and I alonged it almost at a trot, finding new energy from being so close. Inside the house, I straighted to the kitchen, poured myself a big glass of milk and cut myself a hunk of bread and a piece of cheese and sat at the kitchen table and devoured them as if I hadn't eaten for days, which, when I thought about it, was the plain truth.

When I had sat there about half an hour I found my eyelids beginning to droop and knew it was time to move again or else I would be asleep until the servants came back and found me, and a great deal more besides. I opened the stove, took a poker and stirred up the fire. I took Miss Taylor's hat and thrust it into the flames and watched until it had turned to ash and could never again be seen for what it was. Then I long-corridored toward the foot of my tower. It shivered me quite, what had happened on the stairs there, and as I pushed open the door that led to them I half expected to see the shape of Theo stretched out on the banister rail. It looked strangely empty without him. I overed the banister and upstairsed. I had kept all thought of Giles from my mind or else I would have been able to do nothing, for at heart I feared I might have given him too large a dose of chloroform and anxioused that after all I had been through I might have done the very thing I feared most.

Indeed, I near screamed out when I lifted the trapdoor and saw him lying there; he so stilled and paled in the moonlight he looked like a corpse, and for a moment or two I could not go to him for fear of confirming my worst thoughts. But when I did I saw his breast rise and fall gently and finally let my own breath out.

It problemed me now how to get Giles back into his bed. I shook him and he stirred and muttered something I could not make out. I got behind him and put my arms under his shoulders and raised him up so he was sitting. I dragged him like this over to the open trapdoor and laid him down with his feet toward the hole. Leaving him there, I went down the first few steps and stood with my head and shoulders through the opening. Then I pulled Giles toward me. It fortuned he was so small and light. I pulled him down by his feet and eventually got him so he was lying on the steps, with his feet a couple of steps above mine.

At this moment I near let him go, for I sudden-frighted when I heard a cock crow. Sure enough, the first red of dawn was fingering the sky and I knew I must hurry, for I had not long before the servants would return. We made our way down a step at a time, me going first and then pulling Giles after me, until we footed the first flight of steps and reached the landing. Now it was all much easier. I gentled Giles to the floor and went back and closed the trapdoor. Back down with my brother I got my shoulder under his and carried him down the rest of the stairs as he had helped me when I hurt my ankle. What I dreaded now were the banisters, for I doubted I had strength even for the littlest exertion. When we reached the point where we had to overbanister I leaned Giles against them so that his head drooped over. Holding on to him so he did not fall, I bent and lifted one of his legs and hauled it up over the banisters, so that he ended up lying along the rail, an arm and a leg either side, as poor Theo had done. Then I overbanistered myself and stood on the other side, resting a moment, catching my breath. It was the last thing I had to do, I told myself, the very last thing. I gave Giles a tug but it was a might too hard and I felt myself fall backwards, so that we both landed in a heap on the floor with him on top of me. No matter, it was not a big fall and there was nothing broke. I rolled

Giles off me, got to my feet, pulled him to his and this time picked him up and carried him in my arms, gratefulling that I am tall and strong and he is but little and light.

I upstairsed him to his room, where I undressed him, pulled on his nightshirt and put him to bed. As I left the room, I paused in the doorway and looked back at him for a minute or so to observe the rise and fall of his breath and make sure all was well. I had already begun to turn away when I awared that something in the picture of my brother sleeping peacefully jarred, although I could not think what. I almost dismissed the feeling as a silly illusion such as extreme fatigue will cause, for staring at the scene I saw nothing untoward. And then there it was. A book, on the little cupboard by my brother's bed. Of course, as if Giles ever took a book to bed!

I walked over and picked it up and recognised at once Miss Taylor's Bible, the same in which I found the steamship tickets. At first I thought to leave it there. I was so tired and longed for sleep, and after all, it was not unthinkable that she had forgot it; her bags were all packed and in reality no doubt she had.

But then it might suspicion someone because she had not taken it and I did not want any hint of doubt that she had left. I tucked it under my arm and downstairsed, stumbling like a drunkard as I went, for I could scarce now stay awake. In the kitchen I opened up the stove, picked up the poker, gave the fire another stir and and was about to drop the book into the flames when something fluttered out and floated like a butterfly to the floor. I picked it up and found myself looking at a photograph. My eyes so ached for sleep they would hardly focus, and I stared at the image not able to make sense of what I saw.

Something familiared about the young woman I was looking at, something in the way she stood or her dress, as though I had seen the picture before. I reached out for the memory, but could not grasp it and I almost tore the wretched thing in two, the feeling frustrated me so.

I shook my head, screwed up my eyes and focused again on the woman's face and then I saw. Of course! It was Miss Taylor, only younger, without the lines time must since have etched upon her face, though with that same determined, all-knowing look, that same smug smile. I relieved a sigh. So that was it, that was what I had recognised; all was explained.

I picked up the Bible with my other hand and consigned it to the fire, then the picture after it, to let the witch burn as she would surely burn in Hell. I watched as tongues of flame eagerly licked its edges. The top of the picture caught fire first and the evil woman's face blackened and then disappeared. And then, there it was again, as I stared at what was left of her, the body without the mocking face, that feeling of some memory I could not touch, only strangely more powerful now, overwhelming me quite, so my legs went weak beneath me and I almost feared to faint. I reached out to snatch the picture from the fire, but too late; it burst into flames and I had to pull back or be burned, and then it was gone.

The lost memory nagged at me all the way back upstairs, and I almost wished I had not burned the photograph, for I sured if I had had chance to look at it properly I would have found what bothered me about it so. But it was too late now and I told myself to let it go, for it was only my fanciful mind, exhausted beyond endurance and seeing things that were not there.

When I reached my own room it was full daylight. Too tired to undress myself or even pull back the bedclothes, I collapsed onto the bed and fell into a deep sleep.

CHAPTER 31

Of a sudden I felt a hand around my neck from behind and another cover my mouth and nose with a cloth so that I near suffocated. The cloth smelt of something strong and strange, like the dentist's surgery and –

I awoke and found I aloned on my bed. I had but nightmared. I began to relax me again, meaning to go back to sleep, but then a dagger went through my heart. I bolt-uprighted. The chloroform! What an idiot I had been to make so simple a mistake! I leapt from the bed and ran to Giles's room. He still peacefulled asleep. I bent over him. He stank of the stuff. I dashed to Miss Taylor's room and by her washbowl found a tablet of soap. I sniffed it. It reeked of lilies, strong as if it were the flowers themselves I smelt. I poured some water into the bowl and carried it to Giles's room. Taking a cloth, I covered it in soap and scrubbed his face with it. He stirred and flung his head this way and that, as even in sleep a boy will have a natural aversion to water, but he did not wake. At the end he smelt of lilies, which might be strange for Giles but not so strange as chloroform.

I was just replacing the bowl and soap when another thought so sharped me I almost dropped them. What had I done with the chloroform bottle? I felt my pockets. It was not in any of them. What if I had dropped it in the trap? Or somewhere else, the stables, perhaps? How would I put that on Miss Taylor? Or would everyone just assume it was something to do with her?

It suddened to me that if I had not dropped it, then it must be still where I had used it, in the tower room. I relieved me a sigh, for no one would find it there. So, congratulating myself, I was on my way back to my own room when another thought struck. Suppose they searched for Miss Taylor? It was not beyond the realm of possibility that someone might suggest looking up in the old tower. Especially if the police were involved, for a man like Hadleigh would leave no stone unturned. I turned around and made for the tower.

Putting my head through the trapdoor, the first thing I saw was the bottle, and the cloth with it, lying where I had left them. I climbed up into the room and picked them up. I could not resist a little smile. That was it! Everything now taken care of. Nothing at all left to give me away. At that moment some movement must have caught my eye for I looked out at the drive and there, at the top of it, saw the wagon upping it. The servants were back!

I dithered a moment. I could leave the bottle here, but then it might fortune a search would take

308

place before I had chance to up here again. It was a risk I dare not take. On the other hand, I had to move fast, for it would be worse still to be caught bottle-handed. I outed the trapdoor and tore down the stairs. I outed the back door and downed to the lake. I ripped the label from the bottle, tore it to shreds and scattered them to the wind. I bent down to the water, filled the bottle, stoppered it and flung it as far as I could into the lake.

I walked back toward the house and at the well slid the cloth between the narrow gap between two of the planks of wood, poking it right through, so it fell into the chasm below. I could not help thinking that it would help Miss Taylor sleep.

I entered the back door as the servants came in the front. I could hear them chatting happily. I had turned the corner of the back stairs just as Meg and Mary alonged the corridor below. By the time they came to see why we did not downstairs to breakfast I would be sleeping peacefully in my bed.

CHAPTER 32

'So, it seems she is gone, then?' I took a sip of my tea for I needed to swallow to clear any doubt from my throat. 'Yes, she is gone.'

Hadleigh stared at me the longest time until I so uncomfortabled I had to speak again. 'She just took off one night. She didn't even say goodbye to Giles. Last anyone saw of her was boarding the train for New York. She left the horse and trap at the railroad station. Poor Bluebird was out in the cold all night.'

He stared at me another long minute then shook his head, and took a sip of his own tea. We were in the drawing room. He'd called soon after he'd gotten back. It was near a month since Miss Taylor . . . left.

'Funny she should just go off like that,' he said. He quizzed me one. 'Why do you think she would do that?'

'Well, maybe it was because of you. I showed her your letter. Maybe she figured she'd be dismissed anyhow, after lying about her references and all. She left right after that.'

'Without Giles.'

I chuckled, as though at myself. 'I guess I was wrong about that.'

He stood up and carried his cup and saucer over to the window and stood looking out. Everything was white outside. It was December now and we'd had a lot of snow. He took another sip of tea. 'And this business of Mrs Grouse's accident. She had nothing to do with that?'

'Oh, no sir, I was with Miss Taylor when that happened. It wasn't anything to do with her at all.' It felt queer defending my old enemy, especially of a charge I knew to be true, but the last thing I wanted was Miss Taylor getting blamed for that and Hadleigh going looking for her; who knew what stones he might overturn? 'I'm sure Mrs Grouse would tell you just the same.'

'If she could remember anything about it.'

I bowed my head. 'Well, yes sir, if she could remember.'

'I gather she makes good progress?'

'Yes sir. Apart from not recollecting the day of the accident, she is almost her old self. Dr Bradley expects her to be able to resume her duties in a few weeks.'

He turned and looked at me, that same penetrating stare. Then he shrugged and set his cup and saucer down on the tea tray. 'Well, I must be going. I'm glad it all worked out.'

I followed him to the door. 'Yes sir, thanks to you.'

311

'And you'll be getting a new governess, I presume?'

'Why, yes. When Mrs Grouse gets back and writes my uncle about what's happened.'

Suddenly Hadleigh looked me up and down. 'I've just noticed. You're all in black.'

'Young Mr Van Hoosier, sir.'

He looked shocked. 'Good God, he was so young.'

'Asthma, sir. A terrible affliction. We are all upset for him, especially Dr Bradley.'

'Well, yes, a doctor hates to lose a patient.'

'It's not just that, sir, it's the failure of his treatment that makes it so much the worse for him. Dr Bradley thought he had asthma cracked with that spray of his. Now he says his experiment has failed, for it did not save Theo, and the illness may have to wait many years for such a treatment as the one he thought to have found.'

'Ah, so the young man's death is a double tragedy, then.'

'At least poor Theo is clear of his suffering now.'

He fingered the brim of his hat. 'Yes, that's one way of looking at it, I suppose.' He turned and outed the door and I ran after him into the hall and held open the front door for him. He stopped in the doorway and put on his hat and coat. 'What happened to the mirror?'

I followed his gaze to the empty frame. 'Oh, it got broke.'

He shrugged and outed the door. I watched him

312

walk toward his horse, but at the last moment he turned and stalked off around the side of the house. I closed the door and took off down the long corridor and a few minutes later I was up in my tower. It was still my private place, for when Giles woke from his long sleep that day he didn't remember being there. He told me of this dream he'd had that he and Theo had been together in a castle. He said it had seemed so real he'd thought it must be true, but I pointed out that it impossibled, for Theo had not even been to see us that day, and later, Giles said he wished it had been true, for it turned out to be the day Theo died and he would dearly have liked to have seen him one last time.

I looked out the window and saw Hadleigh trudging along the side of the house. He made his way around to the back and then started down toward the lake. Of course, now it was frozen quite and on top of it there were a good few layers of snow, so many falls had we had of late, that if you didn't already know, you wouldn't even guess there was a lake there.

Hadleigh did know, of course, and he stood there a long time, staring out over the water, at the spot where Miss Whitaker had tragicked a whole governess ago. I wondered what our new governess would be like. I wondered whether it would be Whitaker again and felt it would not, for I somehow thought that this time I'd trapped her soul for good, but anyhow it didn't anxious me now, for I knew I had her measure quite. Besides, I had my tower and, until she came, I had Giles to myself. Things were how they were when they were best. With luck it would take some time to find another teacher and until then it would be as it should, Giles and I together. Nothing would ever upset that now.

Abruptly, Hadleigh turned and walked away from the lake. He passed the old well without even giving it a glance and disappeared somewhere below me. I crossed to the other side of the tower and saw him emerge at the front of the house. He trudged through the snow to his horse and mounted it. He took one last look at the house, then turned his horse away. I sat in my tower and watched them up the drive, horse and rider merging into one dark shape, a black rook upon the white snow.